COLD EVIDENCE

A Cass Leary Legal Thriller

ROBIN JAMES

Chapter 1

IF HE COULD HAVE KILLED a man with a spatula, Detective Eric Wray would be looking at life in prison.

"Eric," I said, trying to keep my voice calm and even. He knew what I was going to say. For a brief instant, he pointed the spatula at me.

"Your eggs are burning," came the Irish brogue-laced voice of Killian Thorne. He stood in my hallway, leaning against the wall, watching the two of us with an amused, infuriating half-smile.

The last time these two men were within ten feet of each other, one had come away with a fat lip, the other a black eye. Now, only I and my two yapping dogs stood between them. Marbury and Madison had quickly chosen sides in the pitched battle to come. Madison was far more vocal. She splayed her front legs out, arching her back. She growled at Killian. Marbury curled himself around Eric's feet, ready to serve in the rear guard if need be.

They hated each other. Plain and simple. In addition to being my most infamous former client, Killian Thorne had once been my fiancé. Now he was ... well, a complicated visitor, to say the least.

"You should have called," I said to Killian. "This isn't the best time."

"Is there somewhere we can talk in private?" Killian asked, nonplussed by Eric or either of the dogs.

"She said it's not a good time," Eric barked. "That means you should leave."

"This is between Cass and me," Killian said.

"I believe I told you what would happen the next time I saw you," Eric said.

"You what?" I said. "I'm sorry. What?"

Eric took a step forward. He at least put the spatula down. The dogs stayed at his feet, ready for action. Madison emitted a low, rumbling growl. At least I think it was the dog. Eric was turning damn near feral himself.

"All right," I said. "Killian, take a walk with me."

"Cass," Eric started. I turned back and glared at him. I jutted my chin out, grimacing to give him my best attempt at a "stand down" signal. I imagined I'd mostly pulled off some sort of lizard face.

I didn't wait for Eric's response. I grabbed Killian's arm and pulled him with me out the front door. Killian followed me all the way down the paving stones and out onto the dock.

Mid-November, but it was still warm out. My brothers were planning to pull the dock out later this morning. Which was great, except it would exponentially raise the testosterone level. If there was anyone who disliked Killian Thorne more than Eric, it was Joe and Matty.

"What's going on?" I asked Killian. He took his time walking to the end of the platform with me. The water was unnaturally calm. You could throw a single pebble and watch it ripple across almost the entire lake.

As if Killian could read my thoughts, he did just that. A small stone had wedged itself between the aluminum planks of the dock. He picked it up and skipped it with an expert flick of his wrist. We watched together as it bounced four times across the water.

"You should have called," I said.

"Things are going well with Detective Wray, I see," he said. There was sarcasm in Killian's tone. It made me want to shove him straight into the lake.

"Let's pretend for a second that it's any of your business," I said. "What are you doing here? And what's with the suitcase?"

Killian had graced my doorstep carrying what looked like a fully packed black bag. He'd made a show of dropping it in the hallway as Eric watched. It was then Eric had picked up the spatula and brandished it.

Killian didn't answer right away. He looked out at the water. A gaggle of geese landed maybe twenty yards in front of us. The lead goose rose up, flapping his wings, creating a ruckus, before settling back down.

"Your great-grandfather knew what he was about when he picked this land," Killian said. "It's the flattest point on the whole lake. Facing west like that. He never wanted to miss a sunset. I can close my eyes and be in Ireland." Then he did. Killian lifted his chin, drawing in a breath of fresh air.

"Why aren't you?" I asked.

He opened his eyes. "Why aren't I what?"

"In Ireland?" I asked. "In Chicago. Anywhere. Why are you here?"

He turned to me. "I've a favor to ask."

"You said that," I said. "And you told me it was one I couldn't refuse, if I recall. So clue me in. You're in trouble again, aren't you? I know that look. I'm not your lawyer anymore, remember?"

I'd spent over a decade as the person most responsible for getting Killian Thorne out of trouble. As the main litigator for the Thorne Law Group, I'd defended him countless times against criminal charges. Killian had taken over the family business. To the outside world, and to me until the very last case I defended, Killian ran an import/export business. To the FBI, Killian led one of the most lucrative branches of the Irish mob in North America.

His silence spoke volumes. He just kept staring at the geese, ignoring my increasing frustration. A common tactic of his.

From inside, I could hear Marbury and Madison still barking at the window. Eric could have put a stop to it, but didn't.

"Fine," I said. "Stand out here and brood. I still haven't had breakfast."

I also still hadn't gotten dressed. I was wearing a pair of old boxer shorts and a University of Michigan sweatshirt. When I turned to try to storm back up the dock, Killian caught my sleeve and held me back.

"I need a place to stay," he said. "Just for a few days. I've got business nearby."

"You want to stay here?" I asked.

"If it's not too much trouble." He smiled.

"Not too much ..."

He had me speechless. I took a breath, centering myself. "What's going on? You show up out of the blue. With a suitcase. On the morning after Eric and I ..."

I swallowed the last part of my sentence. There was no need for it. At the same time, an unsettling feeling crept up my spine. Eric and I had been through hell and back over the last couple of years. Now, finally, we were in a place to move forward with our relationship. And yet here Killian, my ex, was.

"Do you have someone watching my house?" I asked, my anger rising.

Killian met my eyes. "No. Of course not."

Was he lying? Had he ever told me the truth about anything?

"Are you in trouble?" I asked.

He smiled. "No more trouble than usual."

I looked skyward. "Great. As I recall, your usual is pretty awful. Is there a warrant this time? Who have you talked to?"

"Relax, Counselor." Killian laughed. "It's not that kind of trouble. Even if it was, it's not your job anymore, remember? You quit."

"I was fired," I said. "I was worse than fired. Maybe you've forgotten. Your brother Liam nearly sent me to the bottom of Lake Michigan with a cement briefcase tied to my waist."

Killian winced. "No one will ever put you in that position again," he said. "You're safe."

"But you're not," I said. "Is that it?"

"Don't be so dramatic, a rúnsearc," he said, using an old Gaelic term of endearment he had for me. "I just need a place to stay for a few days where no one knows me. I told you. I've got some business not far from here. And I wouldn't have asked if there was a better option."

"Any option would be a better option," I said. "Killian, I have a life here. You can't just come crashing into it. Complicating it again."

"I don't recall things being complicated between us," he said. "Now that one? That's a different story."

Killian pointed toward the house. Eric was apparently done waiting quietly inside. He stepped out onto the porch. He'd dressed in a tee shirt and jeans. His service weapon was clipped to his belt. It meant he was heading into work. Or that he was about to shoot Killian. At the moment, I wasn't sure which I wished least for. Eric and I had an unfinished conversation regarding his future plans.

"Just a few days," Killian said. His hand was on my arm. "That's a promise. There's never been a promise I made you I haven't kept. Can he say the same?"

"Don't start," I said through gritted teeth, hoping Eric couldn't hear him.

"You owe me," he said. "So does he."

His words stopped me cold because they were true.

"This is how you plan to collect?" I asked.

I walked back up to the house. If I couldn't move the mountain that was Killian Thorne, I'd have to try to move the one that was Eric Wray.

"What's he want?" Eric said, his voice low.

"I'm not fully clear on that yet," I said. "Can you just let me handle it though?"

"If he's here, I'm not leaving," Eric said.

"Eric ..."

"Not up for discussion," Eric said.

My phone rang from inside the house. I moved past Eric to get to it. It was Miranda, my office manager. I'd never been more glad to talk to her.

"What's up?" I answered.

"Hey, Cass," she said, her voice cheery, but with a mysterious lilt to it. It meant some other kind of trouble, I knew.

"There's a woman in your office who wants to talk to you. I tried to get her to make an appointment but she says she won't leave until she talks to you in person."

"Are you okay? Are you there by yourself?"

"No," Miranda said. "I mean, I'm okay. Jeanie and Tori are here. Actually, your brother Matty is too. He dropped Tori off."

"What does she want?" I asked. On the porch, Eric and Killian were having words. I just prayed it wouldn't come to blows in the few minutes I turned my back on them.

"I think she wants a lawyer," Miranda said.

"I'm on vacation," I said. Two weeks ago, I'd just wrapped up a major murder trial. This was supposed to be my time off.

"Yeah," Miranda said. "I figured you'd say that. Only, she showed up with a briefcase full of cash."

"What?"

"Ten thousand dollars, Cass," Miranda said. I could practically see the dollar signs floating behind her eyes. "She says you're the only one who can help her. How soon can you get here?"

Eric and Killian had resorted to shouting. They were both oblivious to my presence. I could have burst into flames and neither of them would have even noticed.

That's when I knew my answer to Miranda. "I'll be there in fifteen minutes," I said. I hung up the phone, threw on a pair of jeans, and headed out to my car. Eric and Killian were still arguing with each other as I drove away.

Chapter 2

"WHAT DO WE KNOW?" I said to Miranda in a hushed whisper. We stood in the office lobby at the foot of the stairs. In the conference room directly above us, I could hear a woman crying.

"She's been like that pretty much since the second she walked in," Miranda said. "Poor thing. At one point, I was afraid she was going to pass out. In her condition, I think that's a real possibility."

"Her condition? She's pregnant?" I asked.

"I'd bet my paycheck on it. Not showing yet but she's got that look. Hollow eyes. Pale skin. Exhausted. She probably threw up in a bag in the car on the way over."

"Hope it wasn't the bag with the cash in it," I said. It was a weak joke. Miranda smiled and nudged my shoulder.

"I was thinking the same thing! Anyway. Just talk to her. She wouldn't tell me much. But the woman needs help. She's your type. I can spot 'em a mile away."

"My type?" I asked as Miranda pulled me along upstairs. She put a blank legal pad in my right hand and a fresh cup of coffee in the other.

"Oh, you know. Damsels in distress. Fallen women. Lost causes. Your usual. Only this one's got the cash!"

"Shh," I cautioned her. "She'll hear you." Though with the sobbing coming from the other side of the door at the top of the stairs, my claim was dubious.

Miranda licked her finger, reached out in a motherly gesture, and smoothed an errant hair down on the side of my head.

"Go get 'em," she said, blinking.

Shaking my head, I took a sip of the steaming hot coffee and opened the door.

The woman sat facing the door. She was young. Maybe thirty, with a pale, freckled face, and a thick mass of auburn hair. She dabbed at her swollen eyes with a tissue and rose to meet me.

"Th-thank you for coming in," she sniffled. She extended a hand to shake mine, then quickly withdrew it, realizing she was still holding her used tissue.

"Have a seat, Ms ..."

"Chapman," she offered. "I'm Elizabeth Chapman. Call me Beth."

"Beth?" I said. I smoothed my jacket and took a seat opposite her at the table. I set my legal pad down and took another drink of coffee.

"Can I offer you something?" I asked. She looked like she could use something stronger than coffee. Beth's hands trembled as she tried to fold them in front of her on the table.

"Your secretary has been very kind and accommodating," Beth Chapman said. "I'm fine."

She hiccupped out the word fine, indicating she was anything but. She went mute after that. Silent tears spilled from her eyes. I gave her a moment to compose herself.

"Ms. Chapman," I said. "Um. Beth. Are you in trouble? How can I help you?"

She shook her head almost violently. "No. No. It's not me. It's Ty. Tyler. My husband. They're making a horrible mistake. This is a nightmare. He said everything would be okay but I knew it wouldn't be. Those men were so sure of themselves. The way they looked at him. At me!"

"Beth, why don't you start from the beginning? What's going on with your husband and why do you think I can help?"

"You have to help!" she shouted, her bloodshot eyes going wide. Then she checked herself. Her shoulders sank and she closed her eyes, letting out a slow, shaky breath. She grabbed another tissue out of the box in the center of the table and blew her nose.

Miranda came in with a carafe of coffee. She set a cup in front of Beth Chapman and refilled mine.

I kept my face as neutral as I could, but eyed Miranda with suspicion. She did not, nor was ever expected to, serve me coffee. It was evidently driving her crazy, sitting downstairs wondering what was going on. That, and I knew the promise of great sums of cash drew her like a bear to honey.

"Thank you," I said to Miranda through gritted teeth. She took the hint and hustled back down the stairs.

"Has Ty been arrested?" I asked.

Beth nodded her head. "Last night. They came to the house. I was in bed. Ty was downstairs watching television. They took him away in handcuffs, Ms. Leary. Like some common criminal. They wouldn't listen. I told them I had money to pay for his bail."

It was then she picked up a small canvas tote bag and laid it on the table. Just like Miranda had said, the thing contained several large stacks of twenty-dollar bills. "I went to the bank first thing this morning," she said. "I took everything we had out of savings. Will this be enough?"

"What's your husband been charged with?" I asked, though I already sensed what she'd say.

"Murder," she said, confirming my suspicions. "They're saying he killed that man behind the Harmon Arms. The one they found last week. But it can't be true. Ty's not a murderer. He's an HVAC technician!"

It didn't seem prudent to point out that those weren't mutually exclusive. But Beth Chapman stated it as though any fool should know they were.

I wasn't familiar with the case. In the aftermath of my latest trial, I hadn't really paid attention to the local news.

"Do you know why the police think your husband did this?" I asked.

"He won't talk to me," Beth cried. "I knew something was going on. A few days ago, this deputy showed up at the house.

Ty went out on the front porch to talk to him. I was up in my craft studio. I do these stained-glass pieces. I have an online store. Anyway, Ty told me to stay inside and not to worry. Only I could overhear some of what they were saying from the second-floor window. My studio faces the front of the house. That cop was asking Ty all sorts of questions about where he was the Friday night before. Whether anyone could vouch for his whereabouts. Ty was so calm about it. Acted like it was nothing for a policeman to just show up at the door, asking him for an alibi. When he came back in, he told me to forget about it. I know he was trying not to upset me. I'm ... we're ... I'm pregnant," she said.

"I see," I said.

"We've had trouble in the past. A couple of miscarriages. So I think that's why he's been downplaying all of this. But how can I not be upset?"

"Mrs. Chapman," I said. "If the police have arrested Ty and taken him into custody, it means they convinced a judge they have probable cause to believe he committed this murder. That doesn't mean he is guilty, of course. But it means they have some preliminary evidence that's pointing them in that direction. Do you know the man they think your husband killed?"

"No!" she shouted. "That's just it. I've never seen or heard of this guy before in my life. The police won't tell me anything. This detective gave me his card and told me he wants to ask me some questions."

She slid a Woodbridge County Sheriff's Department business card across the table. It had Detective Rodney Patel's name and number on it.

"I didn't want to talk to them until I talked to a lawyer. Not for me. But for Ty. I asked around. Everyone says if you're ever in this kind of trouble, Ty's kind of trouble, that you're the one to call. He needs the best, Ms. Leary. I'm telling you. On my life. On this baby's life. Ty's not a murderer."

Behind me, the door opened. Miranda stood there, not so subtly, clearing her throat. She had my tablet in her hands.

"I'm sorry," I said to Beth. "Will you excuse me for one second?"

My office adjoined the conference room. I gave Miranda a pointed stare and ushered her in, closing the door behind us.

"Tyler Chapman," she whispered, shoving the tablet in my hands. "Arrested last night for the murder of John Lansky, forty-two. A long-term resident of the Harmon Arms."

She had a local news article pulled up. "I thought you said she wouldn't tell you anything before I came in."

"Well, I overheard a little ..."

"Overheard," I said, shaking my head. I expected to see a circular indentation around Miranda's ear where she'd likely been holding a glass to the door. Nevertheless, I skimmed the article.

The victim, John Lansky, had been found bludgeoned to death in the woods behind one of Delphi's more seedy motels. The online details were sparse, but this was a brutal crime. Lansky's killer had broken every single bone in his face. They'd used what looked like a government ID photo in the article, probably Lansky's driver's license. Before the last few minutes of his life anyway, John Lansky had a broad nose, deep set blue eyes, and a large, square jaw. He had a scar running through his left eyebrow that split it in two.

"I know him," I said. "I've seen him somewhere."

The answer niggled the corners of my brain. I wanted to say I remembered him wearing work overalls.

"Maybe the gas station?" I said. "Does it say what he does? Did?"

"Local handyman," Miranda said, pointing to a paragraph further down in the article.

"Huh," I said. "It'll come to me."

"Are we going to help her?" Miranda asked.

"I have no idea," I said.

"But you'll talk to the guy," she said. "The husband. This Tyler Chapman. I already checked him out. He works at Bo Bonham's heating and cooling company. They've got the contract for all those new condos going in off of Wymer Road. One of my girls from Bunko is building there. She says Tyler's a great guy. Very knowledgeable."

Miranda, too, seemed to think HVAC expertise ruled out homicidal tendencies.

"You've been busy," I said, never ceasing to be amazed by Miranda's amateur detective skills. She'd figured all this out in the fifteen minutes I'd been talking to Beth Chapman.

"You like her," I said, pointing toward the closed door.

"She's a lost puppy," Miranda said. "Reminds me of my sister's girl. Sweet. I think maybe it's worth a visit to the county jail."

I raised a brow. "Let me guess. You've already set it up."

"Four o'clock," she said. "Deputy Patel's expecting you."

"Miranda ..."

"Just talk to the guy. Take a look at the file. Then decide."

From my window facing the parking lot, I saw a black SUV pull up.

"Eric's here!" Miranda sang out. "Oooh. He looks angry about something."

Miranda peered out the window. Sure enough, Eric slammed his door and strode toward the back door with purpose.

"Something else I should know about?" Miranda asked me, eyes wide.

I opened my mouth to answer, then realized there was no way to do it quickly. Between Beth Chapman, Miranda, and Eric Wray, I had my choice of frying pans and fires.

"See if you can stall Mrs. Chapman," I said.

"I'll try to get her to eat something," Miranda said, clasping her hands together. Her face lit up with her new purpose.

"Cass!" Eric called up.

I found my bravest smile, and headed into the fire.

Chapter 3

"I don't see any visible signs of injury," I said to Eric as he stood in the lobby, jaw clenched and glaring at me.

"Come on," I said. "We can talk in Jeanie's office. She's in court in another county all day."

Eric made a positively feral noise as he followed me into my law partner's office and shut the door behind him.

"Thought you could make a clean getaway?" he said.

"That was the idea," I said. "I'm glad you're still breathing. Can we say the same for Killian?"

"For the moment," Eric said through gritted teeth.

"Good. And I'm sorry. I didn't know he was going to show up like that. I swear."

Eric sat on one of Jeanie's leather couches. Above us, I heard the conference room door open and shut, also the faint sounds of a woman sobbing.

Eric looked at the ceiling, hearing it too.

"Everything okay up there?"

"I'm not sure yet," I said. "Potential new client. One I wouldn't mind picking your brain about."

Eric's face fell. "Nice try changing the subject. Our immediate problem is your ex."

I let out a sigh and joined him on the couch. "What's he telling you?"

"Not much," Eric said. "Other than he's got business nearby and needs a place to stay where no one can find him. I'm telling you right now, and I told him. He's not staying at your place."

"How'd that go over?" I said, eyeing him.

"He said that's your call, not mine. Then I got reinforcements. Your brothers showed up."

I buried my face in my hands, picturing how well that must have gone.

"Seriously," I said. "Is Killian still in one piece?"

"More or less," Eric said.

"Where is he now?"

"In retreat," Eric answered. "Killian told them the same thing about needing somewhere to lay low for a while. Matty pulled out his phone, snapped a picture of Killian, and threatened to post it on social media."

"Lord," I said.

"You kind of have to hand it to your little brother, though. Pretty ingenious. Joe and I were just planning to smash his face in if he didn't take off."

"Eric," I said.

"So anyway, he's gone. For now. But I suspect he'll show up here any minute."

"So what? You're going to lie in wait?"

"No," he said. "Believe it or not, I may actually be in the mood to help the guy. If he can't be persuaded to leave town, he can stay with me."

"Oh great," I said. "That has the makings of a buddy comedy right there. Why, pray tell, would you be willing to do that?"

"Because I owe him," Eric said.

There it was. I'd gone to Killian in my last time of need. While Eric was jailed for a crime he didn't commit, Killian had made sure he was protected on the inside. It was a debt I knew he'd come to collect. I just hadn't figured on it being this soon.

"Because I asked him to help you," I said. "Eric, I can handle Killian. You don't have to ..."

"No," he said. "Believe it or not, I'm grateful to the guy. At least for one thing. When I'm not thinking about smashing his face in, that is. I don't like the way he still looks at you, Cass."

I reached out and touched Eric's face. "You don't think ..."

He took my hand. "I said I don't like the way he looks at you. That's not your problem. And though I really wish you hated the guy as much as I do, the reason you don't is one of the things I love most about you. Twisted as that sounds."

"Which is?"

Eric smiled. "You're stubbornly loyal. Or royally stubborn. Both."

"You're not mad at me?"

"No," he said. "You had a life before we got together. A big and messy life. So did I. I can't hold yours against you any more than you can hold mine against me. But ... whenever Killian Thorne shows up, it's dangerous for you. You know that, right?"

"Eric ..." I was going to argue with him. Say all the things I usually say. I wasn't part of that side of Killian's life anymore. I knew how to handle him. Those things were true. But so was this.

"Yes," I said simply.

Eric looked as surprised at my honest answer as I was at saying it. He kissed my palm.

"Okay then," he said. It was enough.

I heard the door above us open and close again. Beth Chapman still waited on me up there.

"Do you have to deal with that?" Eric asked.

"I do," I said, rising. "Let me ask you. Have you heard anything about a murder victim they found in the woods behind the Harmon Arms?"

"That's a county case," Eric said.

"Yes. Detective Patel's," I answered.

"Just what I read on the news," Eric said. "I'm still officially on leave. If the sheriff's department has reached out to Delphi P.D. for help, I'm out of the loop on that."

"Are you planning on rejoining the loop?" I asked. "Because if you aren't, there's the matter of that job offer I made you. It's going to depend on how the rest of my day goes, but I might be in need of a private investigator again sooner rather than later."

Eric scowled. "You're getting involved in this thing?"

"Not sure yet," I said.

Eric rose. "You and your affinity for murder cases."

"Touché," I said. This got me my first smile out of Eric since Killian showed up. It sent the usual thrill through me.

"If I do get involved," I said. "I could be in a position to sweeten the pot for you." There was the matter of the ten thousand dollars of cash sitting up in my conference room.

Eric pursed his lips. "I'll steal your line. It depends on how the rest of my day goes. I've got a meeting with the chief in about an hour. You free for dinner later?"

"I'm not sure," I said. Miranda had set me up for that jailhouse meeting with Tyler Chapman at four.

There was a knock on the door. Miranda poked her head in.

"Cass," she said. "I'm sorry. But you might wanna ..." She pointed upward toward the conference room.

"Right," I said. "Eric, we'll circle back."

"Yeah."

Miranda shut the door again, leaving us alone.

"Just remember what I said about Killian," Eric said. "I know I can't tell you what to do in your own house. Or ... ever. But I've got a bad feeling about what's going on with him. I don't know him like you do, but he seemed rattled. Like something's scared him."

"Like what?" I asked. The news surprised me. I hadn't gotten that sense from Killian at all in the few minutes we spoke this morning.

"I don't know," Eric said. "But I believe him that he doesn't want to be found. This wasn't just some smarmy way to worm himself back into your life. I mean, it's that too probably. But something's got him spooked. That can't be a good thing. Just be careful. And I'd really prefer it if you didn't meet with him alone."

"Killian isn't going to hurt me," I said.

"Maybe not," Eric said. "But maybe it's more someone's trying to hurt him. You can't be close to that."

"Thank you," I said, taking Eric's hand. "For trusting me. And I'll be careful. That's a promise."

I went up on my tiptoes and kissed him on the cheek. Eric slid his hand to the small of my back and drew me closer. It felt good. It felt right. Then he left.

I headed back upstairs to deal with Beth Chapman. She'd been crying in my absence. A lot. She blew her nose into a tissue and rose to her feet as I walked back in the room.

"I'm sorry to keep you waiting so long," I said.

"It's okay. Anything you need," she said. "Just so long as you'll help me. You'll help Ty?"

I took a breath. "I'll meet with him. That's all I can promise for now."

She nodded vigorously. "Thank you. That's all it'll take. When you see him. When you meet him. I know you'll understand. He didn't do this, Ms. Leary. He's innocent. You'll see."

I nodded and handed her another tissue. I stopped myself from saying what I really thought. Odds were, Beth Chapman didn't really know her husband at all.

Chapter 4

Tyler Chapman was already waiting for me in one of
the jailhouse interview rooms when I got there. He did
something that surprised me from the outset. When I walked
into the room, he stood up in a gentlemanly gesture. As I
walked to the table to set down my bag, he pulled my chair
out for me.

"Thank you," I said, extending my hand to shake his. "I'm
Cass Leary."

"Thanks for coming," he said.

He towered over me, at nearly a foot taller. He had a trim,
athletic build but was wide through the shoulders. He stood
rod straight with military precision. His haircut, too, was
close-cropped. A little longer than military-style, but not by
much. He was blond, handsome, with keen gray eyes that
searched my face. With his tiny, beautiful, titian-haired wife,
the two of them could double for Ken and Barbie.

"Sit," I said. "Are you doing okay in here?"

Chapman sat. He kept his back straight though, his hands folded in his lap.

"I'm fine," he answered. "I'm sorry my wife bothered you to come all the way down here."

"Your wife's pretty worried about you," I said. "I have to admit. I'm a little at a loss. I don't usually meet with potential clients this early in the game. I haven't had a chance to review the arrest warrant, the charging document, or anything about your case beyond what's been published online."

He said nothing. Just stared straight ahead. If Tyler Chapman was upset, he showed no outward sign of it.

"Mr. Chapman," I said.

"Ty," he interjected. "Just call me Ty. Please."

"All right, Ty. Have you said anything to the police?"

He blinked. "No."

"Nothing at all. You didn't profess your innocence even? Confess your guilt?"

He stared straight ahead. I got not even a flicker of a reaction in those cold, gray eyes.

"The news has it that the victim was beaten to death behind the Harmon Arms. They're saying there were witnesses who saw you go back there with him. Is that true?"

"I can't answer for what other people say they saw," Ty answered.

"Fair point. And good answer," I said. "Do you understand what's going to happen next?"

"I'll be arraigned," he said. "The prosecutor thinks he's got probable cause to charge me with first-degree murder."

"Well ... yes," I said. His lack of emotion puzzled me. There was no fear in his eyes. He was reacting about as well as one would when the dentist explains how they'll fill a cavity.

"That means they have to prove that you premeditated the killing of this man. Um ..."

I pulled my notes out, looking for the victim's name.

"John Lansky," Chapman offered. Still not a shred of inflection in his voice.

It got hard to separate my defense lawyer brain from my regular brain. Dammit if I wasn't curious. If I didn't want to ask all the questions, everyone else would have. Did he do it? Did he know the guy? What happened out there at the Harmon Arms?

"John Lansky," I repeated. "Listen. Are you aware your wife brought ten thousand dollars' cash to my office to get me to agree to help you?"

"I never asked her to do that," Chapman said.

"Right. So I guess I should have started all this by asking you the only real question that matters. Do you want my help?"

There. It was subtle. Just a slight jerking of his chin, but Ty Chapman finally gave me a reaction. I waited a moment. When he didn't respond, I started to get angry.

"Mr. Chapman. Ty. Do you want my help?"

He looked at me. "I don't want to spend the rest of my life in prison."

"Well," I said. "I guess that's a start."

"You can help me by telling my wife not to worry."

I smiled. "I don't think that's realistic, do you? She's pregnant. Her husband is sitting in a jail cell charged with murder."

"You asked me if I'm all right in here," he said. "I can take care of myself. Beth knows that too."

"I have to ask you," I said. "How is it that Beth has so much cash lying around?"

"She makes these stained-glass ornaments," he said. "And window art. They're very good. She's talented. I make good money installing air conditioners, but I'm not talented like she is. People pay a lot of money for what she creates. We've been lucky."

"So who is John Lansky to you?" I asked, unable to help myself.

Chapman's expression went cold again.

"Ty," I said. "It's good that you haven't said anything to the police. But at a certain point, if your goal is to stay out of prison for the rest of your life, you're going to have to talk to someone. You don't have to hire me. To be honest, I'm not even sure I want to be involved. I don't know yet."

"But you're leaning that way," he said. I couldn't tell if he meant it as a statement or a question.

"I'm interested," I said. "Your wife can be pretty persuasive."

"Is she all right?" he asked, fixing his eyes on mine.

"I'm not sure," I answered as honestly as I could.

"She's fragile," he said. "She tries to be strong, but isn't always. Beth's been through so much. We've lost a few babies. Did she tell you that?"

"She mentioned something. She was pretty adamant that I do whatever I could to convince you to hire me to defend you."

He dropped his gaze again.

"I'll ask you again. Do you want me to?"

His nostrils flared. "And I'll answer again. I don't want to spend the rest of my life in prison."

"Did you kill that man?"

No answer. I half regretted asking.

"What would you do for me?" he asked. "If you decided to take my case?"

"Well, first I'd take a look at what they have on you. But it would help *me a* lot if you leveled with me about what that is."

"I told you. I can't speak to what other people say they saw."

"Did you know John Lansky?" I asked.

No answer.

"Did you go out there? To that motel?"

No answer.

"Do you have any explanation for whatever physical evidence the cops say they have tying you to the case? Because I don't have to see their file to know it's there. Detective Patel isn't going to write an arrest warrant off witnesses who only say they saw you with the victim. Not unless they actually saw you kill him."

Still nothing.

"All right," I said. "I'm interested enough to have a look at the case file. And maybe it's better that you don't say anything else to me until I do. I'm going to have questions. A lot of them. I think this is more about whether I want to help you than convincing you to accept that help. We need to be clear on that."

Ty Chapman narrowed his eyes. "Are you good at this?" he asked.

I folded my hands on the table. "Yes," I said. "I am, in fact, very good at this."

"That's what I've heard," he said. "That's what Beth has heard too."

"And you know I can't make you any promises. Except for one."

I let my words hang there for a moment. I had his attention.

"You don't have to tell me everything," I said. "But whatever you do tell me better be the truth. Always. I don't care who else you've lied to. I don't care if it's Beth you've lied to. To me, the truth."

He tightened his jaw but didn't break my stare.

"I haven't lied to you yet," he said.

"Good."

"How much?"

"What?"

"How much will it cost Beth if you take my case?"

"For a murder charge? If this goes to trial? More than the cash she brought in the bag, Mr. Chapman."

"Ty," he said.

"Ty. Your wife will need to fill a few more bags."

"She knows," he said.

"Okay," I said. "So do you want me to be there when you're arraigned next week?"

"If it helps keep me out of prison for the rest of my life."

It was such an odd thing to say under the circumstances. Ty Chapman was like talking to a stone wall. On the other hand, if he was that way for me, he'd been that way for the police. Half of criminal defense work was keeping defendants from shooting themselves in the foot.

"Fine," I said. "Then I think I'll tell your wife I'll take her retainer."

"But you would work for me," he said. "Not Beth."

"That's correct," I said. "I don't care if it's the Queen of England paying your legal bills. You and you alone would be my client."

"And you couldn't tell anyone what we talk about?" he asked. "Ever?"

"Right."

He nodded. Then, he abruptly rose.

"I think I'm ready."

"You're what? We haven't …"

"You know everything you need to know," he said. "You can tell Beth we talked. Tell her not to worry so much. Tell her she needs to pick up those prenatal vitamins at the pharmacy. I didn't get a chance to."

He knocked on the door. The guard opened it. He cast a glance my way. I shrugged. Ty Chapman held his wrists out, waiting patiently for the guard to cuff him again. Then he left me sitting there.

I knew I probably should have just washed my hands of both Chapmans. The money gave me pause, sure. But I also couldn't walk away until I read exactly what was in that charging document. I pulled out my cell phone and punched in the prosecutor's office phone number. They put me directly through to Rafe Johnson when I told them which case I was calling about.

"Hey, Cass," he said. "I figured I'd be hearing from you. We can meet in my office tomorrow afternoon. I'm glad you're on this one, to be honest. I think I'll finally get a win in my column against you."

His words were like chum in the water. For a moment, it spurred my interest in the case far more than Beth Chapman's sack of cash.

Chapter 5

IT WAS seven o'clock before I made it back to the office. Miranda had long since gone home. And yet, I saw a single light still on in my second-floor office window.

I found Killian Thorne waiting for me there, eating from a Styrofoam to-go container. It smelled delicious and the loud growl of my stomach betrayed me.

"Sit," he said through a mouthful of food. He was sitting in one of the chairs I kept for clients in the corner. A second Styrofoam to-go box sat on the coffee table in front of him.

"Chicken chop suey," he said.

"Thanks," I said. I could think of a thousand reasons to decline the offer. My having dinner with Killian would piss off just about every person in my life who cared about me. But I was starving. And he was already here.

I picked up the container and the plasticware beside it and dug in.

"I was skeptical," Killian said after another bite. "Drive-through Chinese food has no business tasting this good."

He wasn't wrong. I devoured my chop suey. Every bite helped me clear my head.

"So," I said. "Why don't you tell me why you're really here? And how'd you manage to convince Miranda to let you stay?"

The moment I said it, I realized there was another distinct possibility to explain his presence in the building after hours. He may well have figured out how to let himself in.

He waved his fork at me. "I'm not without my charms."

"Great," I said. "So you didn't break in. Glad to hear it."

"How was your day, dear?" He smiled at me. That used to undo me. Now? I had half a mind to throw my plastic fork at him.

"You didn't answer my question. In point of fact, you haven't answered any of my questions since you showed up this morning."

"Yes, I have," he said. "I told you I have business nearby. It serves my purpose to keep a low profile while I'm conducting it."

"I don't even want to know what that means anymore, Killian. Plus, low profile for you is pretty high profile for me. You being here is causing me problems I'd rather not have."

He put his empty food container down. "And yet you haven't thrown me out."

"Would that work?" I asked. "It's never worked before."

Killian sat back, making himself comfortable in my leather chair. Making himself comfortable in my life again.

"I miss you," he said.

"Don't."

"Don't miss you? Or don't tell you I've missed you?"

"Either," I answered.

"You look good. I like your hair this way. You've lightened it."

I stabbed my fork into a juicy piece of chicken, then chewed it with gusto.

"I'm sorry," he said. "I'm not trying to make trouble for you."

"Liar," I said. "You relish it. How'd your visit with my brothers go?"

Killian laughed. "About as well as your visits with my brother go."

I put my food down, beginning to lose my appetite. "Killian, I'm tired. It's been a long day. You're not going to tell me what business you have. Quite frankly, I guess I really don't want to know. If you really need a place to stay, you're welcome to crash here. That couch against the wall pulls out."

"I'm sorry," he said abruptly.

He'd done it. He'd finally done it. Killian Thorne had rendered me speechless. I recovered.

"For what?"

"I really don't mean to cause trouble for you. I wouldn't have darkened your door if it hadn't been necessary."

I closed my eyes, steeling myself for the next answer he might give me. Every instinct in me told me not to ask. I opened my eyes.

"The truth," I said. "How bad is the trouble you're in?"

His face changed. He grew serious. He paused for a beat and it confirmed my fears. "The truth?" he said. "The truth is it's nothing I can't handle in time."

"But you're hiding out," I said. "That's really the business we're talking about."

"I just need to be off the radar for a day or two. I promise. That's the extent of it."

"There are probably a hundred other places you could have gone to do that. I find it a stunning coincidence that you just happened to show up on a night Eric was at my house."

It wasn't just *a* night. It was *the* night. After everything we'd been through, Eric and I had taken a critical step in our relationship last night. We'd shared a bed for the first time.

"Have you been watching me?" I asked.

Killian let out a breath. "No. A rúnsearc. I'm not watching you."

"Swear it," I said. "On your mother's grave. Swear it."

He straightened in his chair, leaning forward. "I haven't been watching you."

My head started to pound. I went to the bookshelf in the corner. Behind one of the books I kept a bottle of whiskey. I generally hated the stuff, but long ago, Jeanie convinced me any respectable lawyer kept one for situations just like this. I pulled out two glasses from the cabinet against the wall and poured a shot for me and for Killian.

Jeanie was right. She was always right. As the liquor warmed me, it was just what I needed.

"Are you happy?" Killian asked. He swirled his glass but didn't drink.

"What?"

"Wray. Does he make you happy?"

I put my glass down. "Can we not do this?"

"I want you to be happy. It's all I've ever wanted."

I glared at him. "Killian, we've known each other far too long, been through far too much together to start telling lies. My happiness was never your top priority. My loyalty was. My complicity. My ... submission."

It was a little of the whiskey talking. "My willingness to go along. Look the other way," I said, emboldened now. "We weren't equals."

He smirked. He got this twinkle in his eye that still got to me. He took a sip of his drink. "You didn't always mind submitting, if I recall."

"Stop it," I said. Even as I did, it was as if he flipped a switch in my brain. A memory flashed. When it was good between Killian and me, it was very good. Good enough that even now, a little spike of heat went through me. If I closed my eyes, I could be right back there with him. Killian had given me something he never gave to anyone else. His vulnerability. For a long time, I thought we fit together. Physically and otherwise.

"I miss disappearing with you," he said. "I won't pretend that I don't wish we still could. You know I still have the house in Helene. I never sold it."

Helene, Michigan. A tiny little town at the northern tip of the state on Lake Michigan. He'd surprised me with it. A Victorian-era historical home that sat on a bluff overlooking the water. Once upon a time, it had been our dream house. When I balked at his plans to throw an epic wedding, I asked him if we could just get married there. The two of us. My brothers. His. I'd once dreamed of saying vows with this man under the stars with the lake in front of it.

We'd spent hours talking about it. I'd felt safe with Killian in Helene. Tucked in the crook of his arm where I used to fit. I traced circles on his chest as he made me promises. I'd gotten to know his body and his scars by heart. The puckered skin right above his heart where he'd been badly cut. A patchwork of old scars tore through his skin like claw marks. Faded now, but part of him. It was part of his violent past growing up in Belfast. He had others. A bullet wound through his left shoulder. He would flinch when I pressed a finger against it. But he let me. Together, I'd helped him heal those scars. And he helped heal mine. Only now, that felt like a million years ago.

"You should," I said. "Sell it, I mean. It was an illusion, after all. You told me you took me there because it reminded you of Ireland. But that wasn't true, was it? You took me there because there was a threat to your life. You were at war with another family. The Feds. It was never about me."

He finished his whiskey. To Killian's credit, he denied nothing.

"I've never outright lied to you," he said.

I laughed. "Be still my heart."

"Cass."

"Yes," I said.

He put his glass down. "Yes?"

"Yes," I said. "Eric makes me happy."

"Are you going to marry him?"

"That's none of your business."

"You may not believe me, but I really didn't come here to make trouble for you or disrupt your life. I came because I needed to. That's all."

"Delphi can't be your refuge, Killian," I said.

"It won't be."

"But I know what I owe you. For Eric."

"He seems to think that's his debt to pay," Killian said.

"And we both know it isn't. You didn't do it for him. You did it for me."

"I'd do it again," he said. "Though it rips my guts out to think of it, I'd do it again. Someday, you'll believe me, maybe that all I want is for you to be happy. If this man makes you happy, then I'll kill for him too if that's what you ask."

"I won't," I said. "But ... thank you." It was as close to a blessing as I'd ever get from Killian Thorne. I would have to figure out whether it was something I needed. I realized in that instant, I could never be fair to Eric if I didn't.

"I'm going home," I said. "I keep some essentials in the bathroom across the hall. You can stay here tonight. That's all. Miranda usually gets here by seven thirty every morning. I would appreciate it if you were gone before that."

"Wait," he said. "I'll be gone by morning. You won't see me again if you don't want to. I'll honor your wishes. But do me this favor."

Killian took a small flip phone out of his pocket and handed it to me. I'd been through this with him so many times before. There would be a single number saved on it where I could contact him if I needed him. Or he could contact me without anyone being the wiser.

"Killian ..." I started.

"Just take it," he said. "I promise, I'll be out of your hair in the morning."

I took the phone. I ran my thumb over the hard edge of it, then tossed it under some loose papers in the top drawer of my desk.

"Thank you, Cass," he said. By the look on his face, I knew he had more to say. Only I didn't. I gathered my things and left him there.

My house was empty when I arrived. I'd hoped Eric would be there. At the same time, I was far too tired to answer any more questions. I needed a good night's sleep if I were going to make a solid decision about Tyler and Beth Chapman in the morning. Much of it would depend on the file Rafe Johnson promised to give me. Then Ty's bail hearing was set in front of Judge Colton just after lunch.

Chapter 6

KILLIAN WAS GONE the next morning by the time I made it into the office. Miranda suspected something. She gave me a pointed stare when I passed by her desk, but didn't lay into me. So there was that.

"Tori's upstairs in the conference room waiting for you," she said. "Johnson's office couriered over Ty Chapman's paperwork."

"Thanks, Miranda," I said. She busied herself with whatever she had on her computer screen. That was it. No more small talk. No discussion of what I had going on the rest of the day. Oh yes. Either she came in early enough to run into Killian, or she had a nose on her that told her all she needed to know. I took the opportunity to quickly get out of her sight. She'd cool off soon enough and there was work to be done.

I found Tori just as Miranda said I would. She had documents organized in piles on the conference room table. She stood over them, brow furrowed, barely hearing me come in.

I poured myself a cup of coffee from the station we kept in the corner and stood next to her.

"How bad is it?" I asked.

"Pretty awful," she said. I grabbed the arrest warrant, blew over the top of my coffee, and took a seat. As I read, Tori started to spell it out.

"Guy walking his dog found Lansky's body on the morning of November 11th. Dog threw his leash and led him right to it. There were crows already picking at him."

I set my coffee down, my stomach starting to turn.

I read the report. Detective Patel had a crew canvassing the area, questioning all the guests staying at the Harmon Arms the night before.

"Hotel manager didn't see anything," Tori said. "But there was a young couple out walking Thursday the 10th. About six o'clock in the evening, so it wasn't full dark but the streetlamps and parking lot lights were already on."

I made a note of that. Lighting could be an issue.

"Where are their statements?" I asked.

Tori pulled two sheets of paper off the table and handed those to me.

"Melissa and Brian Boyd," I read.

"Also guests of the hotel," Tori said. "They were in town for a family reunion. Had their dog with them so they were out walking him before turning in for the night."

According to their statements, they saw a man fitting Ty Chapman's description knocking on the door to room 24.

"That room is at the very end of the row," Tori said. "First floor. It's the one closest to the stairwell and this little outdoor alcove with vending machines and the ice maker."

I read along as Tori gave me the highlights. "Lansky came to the door. They recognized him because Brian Boyd said he'd run into him a couple of times the day before. Various times when they'd both been coming and going."

"They were arguing?" I said, skimming further down Brian's statements. "Lansky and Chapman?"

"Chapman put his hands on Lansky," Tori said. "Brian Boyd says he kind of pushed him backward."

"Says here he didn't think Lansky looked upset," I read. "Brian assumed Lansky knew him."

"Right," Tori said. "Then Melissa and Brian saw Lansky and Chapman walk around the corner, toward the back of the hotel."

"But they never actually saw Chapman head into the woods with Lansky."

"No," Tori said. "And they turned in after that."

"Then that's a problem for Rafe Johnson," I said.

"The Boyds' room was at the other end of the hotel. Number 3. They had an unobstructed view of the woods. Maybe a half hour later, their dog started going nuts, barking. Melissa went out to the car to get something. There's a little path behind the motel where guests with pets are supposed to take them to do their business. When Melissa got there, she claims she saw Tyler Chapman running back out of the woods alone toward the other end of the motel."

"She said he looked rough," I said, reading.

"He was bleeding from a cut over his eye."

"How'd she make the ID?" I asked, sifting through the police report.

"Chapman's phone was found under a pile of leaves in the woods back there. After they brought both Boyds in for questioning, they showed them a photo array. They both independently picked Chapman out right away. They each said they got a good look at him."

"But nobody's claiming they actually saw Chapman with Lansky in the woods," I said. "Only the before and after."

"Right," Tori said. "But the during is pretty grisly, Cass."

She picked up a stack of color photographs and put them in front of me. I sucked in a breath. These were the crime scene and autopsy photographs.

"Oh lord," I said.

The man in these photographs hadn't just been killed. He'd been beaten to a bloody pulp. His face had been smashed beyond recognition. There were no eyes, nose, or even a mouth that I could make out. I'd seen hundreds, maybe thousands of crime scene photographs in my life. These were the most disturbing by far.

"I know," Tori said, reading my grimace.

This wasn't just violence. This was animal brutality. Whoever had done this to Lansky had wanted to obliterate the man off the face of the earth. I tried to envision the stoic, handsome, reserved man I'd met yesterday carrying out such an act of unchecked, primal rage. It was hard to think of any human being doing something like this.

"How did he seem to you?" Tori asked. "When you met with Chapman?"

"Calm," I said as I flipped through the photographs. Lansky was in pieces on the medical examiner's table. The photos taken in the woods were telling as well.

"Rocks," I said. A series of the photos showed different-sized rocks laying on the ground near Lansky's body. They were covered in blood. "His head was caved in by rocks."

"And not just once," Tori said. "Lansky's face got pulverized."

One by one, I laid the photographs back on the table, face down. At the bottom of the stack were pictures of Ty Chapman. They'd been taken during his booking. He had a small, but fresh, deep cut over his right eyebrow. In another photograph, he had some bruising on his right knuckles. Finally, the sheriffs had taken a photo of Chapman naked from the waist up. His chest, just above his left nipple, was covered in deep, jagged cuts and scratches.

"He looks like he was mauled by something," I said, tilting my head to the side to try to make sense of what I was seeing.

"He wouldn't answer any questions about his injuries," Tori said. "He wouldn't answer any questions at all."

"And his phone was found at the scene," I said, rereading it from the police report.

"Did he report it lost or stolen, maybe?" Tori offered.

"He didn't answer many of my questions, either. He just kept saying over and over he didn't want to spend the rest of his life in prison."

"Wow," Tori said. "That's not really a full-throated proclamation of innocence."

"No," I agreed. "I don't know. He just seemed so ... normal."

"What are the odds Detective Patel will talk to you?"

"Nil," I said. "He barely likes talking to Rafe Johnson."

"I've been looking into Chapman a little bit," Tori said. "Did he tell you he was former military?"

"No," I said. "But it's what I suspected. Just something about the way he carried himself."

"He was a Marine," she said. "Served in Afghanistan back in the early days. I asked around a little. He's spent some time at the Veterans Center just outside of town. I used to date one of the guys who runs that place. Chris Dvorak. Anyway, I called him. He knows Ty. Actually, Chris was pretty upset when he heard Ty'd been arrested for this. He's anxious to talk to you."

Tori handed me a piece of paper with a phone number on it.

"Tori, this is really helpful. You're saying Chris thinks all this is out of character for Chapman?"

"Chris isn't a very emotional guy. It's one of the reasons I stopped seeing him, to be honest. He can be like talking to a brick wall. Anyway, Cass, he was beside himself on the phone. I've never heard him like that. When I told him I was working for you now, he just kind of crumbled with relief. He's hoping you can help Ty out. He said the rest of the gang at the Veterans Center would be really happy to hear you were on Ty's side. He's anxious to do anything you need to try to help. He said they're working on raising funds for Ty's defense. You should talk to him."

"That's great Tori," I said, pocketing the slip of paper. "Thank you."

"He's there for the next couple of hours."

"Do you know anything about Lansky?" she asked.

"I really don't," I said. "He just looked really familiar from the photo the police put out. I know I've seen him somewhere before."

"You probably have," she said. "Matty knew who he was right away."

Tori and my brother had been seeing each other for the past few months. They were getting ready to move in together. I wasn't sure how I felt about Tori discussing firm business with him. She read something in my face.

"I didn't tell Matty anything," she said. "Cass, you know I'd never talk about clients or potential clients with him. He saw Lansky's picture on the news."

"My brother knew him?" I asked.

"Actually, Vangie does. Matty said she hired him to do some work around the house for her. He was recommended to her by one of her neighbors further down the lake. Lansky was pulling docks for people at the end of the season, doing yard work, house washing, just whatever kind of work he could get. Matty said he thought the guy did good work."

"Thanks," I said. "I guess I need to have a conversation with my sister, too. I really appreciate this, Tori."

"Glad to help," she said. "Do you want me to go with you to the Veterans Center when you talk to Chris?"

"No," I said. "I think if you've got a history with him, it's better if I take this one solo."

"Good call," she said. "Just let me know what else I can do. And look, things didn't work out for Chris and me, but he's a great guy. I trust his opinion. I also trust his judge of character. If he thinks Tyler Chapman is worth defending, I kind of hope we do."

"Thanks," I told her, gathering my things. If I hurried, I could make it to the Veterans Center in about twenty minutes.

Chapter 7

THE BUILDING HOUSING the Delphi Veterans Center used to be a fire station. A squat, square, two-story brick building that had ironically burned completely out leaving only the outer walls intact. This was after they'd built the new, fancier fire station closer to downtown. The place had expanded over the years, as the organization had managed to buy up the adjacent property, to the delight of the whole county. They had basketball hoops, a tennis court, and a hiking trail through the woods behind the property.

Chris Dvorak met me at the front door. For his day job, he was a corrections officer at Jackson State Prison. Last I heard, he refused to draw a salary for his work here at the center, preferring to donate it back.

"Thanks for meeting with me," I said as we walked into the empty building. The first floor was a common room with cozy tables and chairs and a coffee station and kitchenette. There were two big-screen televisions against one wall where the members could watch whatever sporting events were on. Upstairs, Chris told me, they had meeting rooms and two apartments where they sponsored select veterans needing temporary help with housing. Tori had told me it was Chris's dream to be able to build and open up a full shelter on a parcel of land just down the road.

Chris began turning on the lights and started brewing the coffee. I followed him to the kitchenette.

"It's just great what you're doing out here," I said.

"Well, your donations have been very much appreciated over the years," he said.

"I can think of few organizations more worthy than yours, Chris," I said.

"Have you talked to Ty?" Chris asked, jumping right into the crux of my visit.

"We've met, yes," I said.

Chris finished with the coffee machine and ushered me to a grouping of plush chairs and a table in the corner of the room.

Almost as soon as the scent of freshly brewing coffee hit my nose, the door opened and a few young men started filing in. They waved to Chris but went to the opposite end of the room where the big-screen TVs were.

"We'll start getting the old guys in here in a few minutes," Chris said. "They play a weekly Euchre game. It'll start getting pretty loud."

"I imagine," I said. "Can I ask you? How well do you know Ty Chapman?"

"He's been coming here for a little over a year," Chris answered. "Just walked in one day and asked me if there was anything he could do to help out. Fixing up this building has been a DIY project from the get-go. Ty offered his services to upgrade the HVAC system in here. He helped me get a new furnace at pretty much cost. He was a godsend."

"I see," I said. "What's your impression of him?"

"Ty's a solid guy," Chris said. "Not much of a talker."

I smiled. "That was my impression, too."

"But like I said. He's solid. Ty does whatever he says he's going to do. He's well liked around here. A lot of the younger, newer guys look up to him. He's helped a few get jobs with some local construction crews."

"That's great," I said. "When's the last time you saw him?"

"Ty was coming in every Wednesday evening," Chris said. "We do a couples' game night. He started bringing Beth, his wife, maybe six months ago. Those two are polar opposites, I swear. You can't get Ty to talk and you can't get Beth to shut up. But I mean that in a good way. Beth is as sweet as they come."

"Would you consider yourself close with the Chapmans?"

"Not socially, no," Chris said. "I didn't really see Ty outside the center here. But that's nothing to do with Ty. I just don't have a lot of spare time. I'm either at the prison or I'm here. Plus, with me being single, we were just in different places in our lives. But I just can't believe any of this. You know? What they're saying Ty did."

"You don't think he had anything to do with John Lansky's murder?" I asked.

The door opened and a familiar face walked in. Ted Moran served as a bailiff in Judge Moira Pierce's courtroom. At six foot seven, Ted had to duck to clear the door as he walked in.

Chris waved him over. Ted was still wearing his suit and courthouse credentials. He'd be on his lunch break now.

"You know Moran?" Chris asked me.

"Of course," I said. I'd known Ted since he was a little kid. He was friends with my younger brother, Matty.

"Hey, Cass," Ted said. As I rose, he pulled me into a bone-crushing hug.

"I asked Ted to come down. He knows Ty about as well as anybody," Chris said.

Just then, the phone at the front desk started ringing. "I gotta take that," Chris said. "I'm here by myself until after six today. But whatever you need, Cass. I'm glad you're going to help Ty. I don't know what's going on with him, but I know you'll make sure he gets the best defense possible."

"I haven't ..." Before I could finish, Chris waved me off and headed for the ringing phone.

Ted sat down in front of me and promptly fell apart. "Can you help Ty?" he asked, a tremor rippling through his whole giant body.

"I'm still trying to figure that out," I said. "Chris says you were close."

"We're friends, yes," Ted said. "And my wife Bridget is close with Beth. God. Cass. They're having a baby. Did he tell you that? Beth's like three months pregnant. They've been trying for a long time."

"I do know that, yes."

"He just didn't do this. Ty would not throw his whole life away by beating up some guy in a motel. It just doesn't make sense."

"Where did you meet Ty?" I asked. "Here?"

"No," Ted said. "Actually, I'm the one who asked Ty to see if he could help Chris out with the furnace issues he was having here. I met Ty pretty soon after he and Beth moved to Delphi."

"When was that?" I asked.

"Gosh. Three years? Maybe going on four. He works for Bo Bonham. His company has the HVAC contract for Lancor Construction. That's who built our house in White Oak."

The White Oak subdivision was one of the newer developments going in on the east side of Delphi. Upscale, but cookie cutter homes in what used to be three hundred acres of corn fields.

"Ty and Beth bought the house three doors down from ours. Bridget and Beth met doing the first neighborhood garage sale. They clicked right away, and so did Ty and me."

"You both have a military background," I said.

"Yeah," Ted said. "That was the start of it. And we both served in Afghanistan around the same time. Though I was Army. Ty was a Marine."

"Doing what, do you know?" I asked.

"He was a corporal," Ted answered. "Had a couple of fire teams under him. They worked embassy security mostly. In and around Kabul. Back in the late aughts."

"What else do you know about his background?"

"Ty's from northern California originally, I think," Ted answered. "Never went to college. Got his HVAC certification and I think he worked for a company out there for a while before he joined the Marines. Did ten years. Got out like six years ago, I think. Just a couple of years before he and Beth moved here."

"Ted, can you think of any reason why Ty would want to hurt this John Lansky? Did you know him at all?"

"Lansky? No. Never heard of him before. As far as I know, Ty doesn't even know him."

"You never saw them together? Ty never mentioned him?"

"Never," Ted said.

"Was there anything unusual going on in his life recently? Were he and Beth getting along?"

"Yes," Ted said. "Ty's crazy about Beth. And they're both so excited about this new baby. She's had all kinds of trouble getting pregnant. They just started telling people because she's past twelve weeks or whatever it is. He showed me an ultrasound picture. He had tears in his eyes. You have to know. That's pretty unusual for Ty. So yeah. You said unusual. That's the only thing. He's been unusually happy."

"What does Bridget have to say about all of this?" I asked. "What's Beth telling her?"

"She's a mess," Ted said. "A wreck. She knows Ty couldn't have done what they're saying. Or if he did, he had a damn good reason. What's he telling you?"

"Ted ..."

"Yeah. I know. I know. You can't say."

"But maybe," I said, "it would help if you could encourage him to trust me."

"I get it," Ted said. "He's not saying anything, is he? Not even to help himself. I knew it. Cass, I tried talking to him too. Beth called me when the cops started questioning him. Then when they came to search his house. I begged him to get a lawyer. I told him to call you. He should have done it weeks ago."

"I appreciate the vote of confidence. Ted, do you think Ty might have been triggered by something? I don't know. Something that might have happened overseas?"

"I don't know," Ted said. "I asked him that too. This whole thing. It's just not Ty. He doesn't have a temper that I've ever seen. Not even watching football or anything. He's as cool as they come. But I don't know."

"Have you ever talked to him about what he might have seen in Afghanistan?"

"Some," Ted said. "But it's just not something we do. If you're asking me if he's been through some shit. Yes. Of course he has. He was involved in some pretty hairy situations in Kabul. He lost men."

"Was he seeing anyone? Like a therapist?"

"I don't know," Ted said. "God. I feel like I don't know anything. It's just none of this makes sense. I'm telling you. Ty and Beth were in a good place in their lives. There's just no reason why Ty would go bludgeon some guy to death over nothing. There had to be something. You've got to get him to tell you whatever it was."

Ted's eyes filled with tears. I reached out and touched his knee.

"We're raising money," he said. "Cass, please. Please tell me you'll defend Ty. I know if you do, he'll get a fair shake. I know you can't promise anything. But this is actually me begging you. Whatever Ty's not saying. Stick with him. Even if he won't admit it. He needs you. If it's money, we'll raise it. Everyone here loves Ty. Beth too. If you need us lined up at his bail hearing tomorrow or trial, we'll be there. He's one of us."

"I appreciate that," I said.

"You're taking his case then? It would really help morale around here to know that much."

I still had far too many questions than answers. Ty Chapman was one giant puzzle. Everything I'd seen on paper told me this guy was likely going to prison for the rest of his life, regardless of anything I did. But as I looked into Ted Moran's tear-swollen eyes, I knew my answer.

"Yes," I said. "God help us both, but yes. I'm on board."

Ted pulled me into another of his crushing bear hugs and sobbed into my shoulder.

Chapter 8

TED MORAN and Chris Dvorak came through the morning of Ty Chapman's bail hearing in front of District Court Judge Mark Colton. As far as I could tell, at least half the veterans in Woodbridge County showed up in Ty's corner. They filled the gallery in a silent show of solidarity. The majority of them, former Marines honoring their pledge to leave none of their members behind.

For his part, Ty stood mute beside me, rod straight, stoic as Rafe Johnson detailed the horror of John Lansky's death.

"Your Honor," he said. "This is perhaps the most violent murder I've ever seen. In my estimation, it's the most violent one you've seen. The autopsy showed virtually every bone in Mr. Lansky's face was crushed. Mr. Chapman's propensity for violence knows no bounds. He is a trained killer. A master killer, if you will."

Ty stiffened beside me. I heard rustling from the members of the gallery. Johnson had just made no small amount of enemies with that. They would remember. So would I.

"Furthermore," Rafe went on. "Mr. Chapman and his wife are recent transplants to Woodbridge County. He's lived all over the country and all over the world while deployed. He doesn't have significant ties to the community and with the funds being raised for his defense, he poses a significant flight risk. Quite frankly, there's no clearer case for a denial of bail that I've ever argued."

"Ms. Leary?" Judge Colton said.

"Your Honor," I said. "I take great offense to Mr. Johnson's characterization of Mr. Chapman as a master killer by virtue of his military record."

"As do I, Mr. Johnson," Judge Colton said.

"As to the issue of him being a flight risk, Mr. Chapman's wife is carrying a fragile pregnancy with a history of miscarriages. She's not going anywhere and neither is Mr. Chapman. Mr. Chapman has no criminal history and his military record, as Mr. Johnson so callously invoked, happens to be exemplary. We ask that a reasonable bail be set pending the outcome of these proceedings."

Judge Colton took a moment to gather his notes and his thoughts. Then, he delivered the ruling I'd told Ty to expect.

"Mr. Chapman," he said. "The court thanks you for your service. I hold the utmost respect for it, as I do for the sacrifices of all members of the military and their family. To those back in the gallery, thank you for coming and for your service, too. However, I cannot deny the severity of this crime and the singular violence committed in its perpetration. As such, I'm going to deny bail pending the outcome of these proceedings and bind you over to the Circuit Court for trial. The defendant is remanded back into the custody of the

Woodbridge County Sheriff's. Counsel, if you'd like a few minutes to confer with your client before he's transferred, you're welcome to it. That is all."

Judge Colton banged his gavel. Behind me, Beth Chapman sobbed. From the corner of my eye, I saw Chris Dvorak go to her and carefully usher her out into the hallway.

The deputies led Ty into the adjoining conference room where we'd have maybe ten minutes to talk before they led him back to his cell.

"I want to see Beth," Ty said as soon as he sat down.

"You'll have a minute," I said. "I'm sorry. But we pretty much predicted how that would go in there."

"What happens next?" he asked.

"There will be a probable cause hearing in Circuit Court. It's a formality. Your case will be set for trial," I said. "I'll confer with the prosecutor to try and gauge where his head's at."

"You think he's going to offer me a plea deal?"

I sat down and folded my hands in front of me on the table. "He might," I said. "Johnson's under a lot of political pressure. He was appointed to his position after Jack LaForge died. He's got to earn it in the next election outright. Johnson's an outsider. He'll have the advantage of incumbency, but he didn't do himself any favors in there with a large, well-respected chunk of his constituency. I'm sorry that this boils down to political motivations when it's the rest of your life we're talking about, but that's how it goes, Ty."

"I understand."

That was it. His tone stayed flat, his expression, almost blank.

"Ty," I said. "I agreed to put on the best defense I can for you. I'll keep that promise. But if you think I can work some kind of miracle without ..."

"I'm not asking for a miracle," he said. "Your best effort is more than enough. I'd just like to not spend the rest of my life in prison."

There was that line again. He said it as a mantra, almost.

"If you want my help. If you really want the best of my help, you have to give me something."

"We're paying your premium hourly rate," Ty snapped. It was the first sign of anything resembling anger I'd gotten out of him.

"You can throw all the money in the world at me," I snapped back. "At a certain point, you're going to have to tell me what happened out there."

Blank stare. Nothing more from him. I envisioned reaching across the table and shaking him, just to get a reaction.

"You asked about a plea deal," I said. "Even if Rafe offered one and you were willing to accept it, you understand that's not the end of it."

"What do you mean?"

"I mean ... you would have to stand up in open court, on the record, and explain what happened out there."

"They can't make me do that," he said. "That's self-incrimination."

"Not in this context, it isn't," I said. "It's part of the deal. You'll be asked what you did. In detail. And if you refuse, your plea would be rejected and you'd be back to facing life in prison, Ty."

The door opened a crack behind me. Beth poked her head in.

"I'm sorry," she said.

"No," I said. "Come on in. We're just about done here. You two should take a few minutes together. You need to be prepared. It's the last time you'll have a chance to speak privately for a very long time. But Beth, I need a minute with you first."

I rose, gently took Beth's arm, and brought her into the hallway with me out of Ty's earshot.

"You have to talk some sense into him," I said. "Make him understand that he's got to start leveling with me. I'm on his side. And I'm the only person in a position to do him any real good with the fix he's in."

She nodded. "I'll try."

"And that's all you should say," I said. "Do you understand? You're a witness in this case too."

"But they can't make me testify, can they?"

"They can't," I said. "But I will if I have to."

Fear made her pale.

"One thing at a time," I reassured her. "For now, just try to get your husband to talk to me. I'll make arrangements to visit him next week. Try to stay positive. There's hope, Beth. He needs to get that. So do you."

She hugged me, her body falling into mine. Her mental and physical state was no small worry of mine. But I'd have to put it aside if I were going to truly help her husband.

"I've got to get back to the office," I said. "The deputies are going to want to get Ty back to his cell pretty soon. You have maybe ten minutes. Be strong, okay?"

She nodded.

"Thank you. You're all we have, Cass. I know nobody else would waste their time with this. With what happened to that poor man ..."

That poor man. As I said my goodbye to Beth Chapman, I was off to learn as much as I could about John Lansky.

Chapter 9

"HE WAS A SWEETHEART," my sister Vangie said. That evening, I met her at her place just down the lake from me. Her daughter, my niece Jessa, was having dinner with a friend. I'd asked Vangie to invite as many neighbors from around the lake as she could who'd had dealings with Lansky. She'd corralled six of them. We sat in Vangie's living room as she served wine, tea, and an impressive charcuterie board.

"He put all of our docks in last spring and pulled them a few weeks ago," Rick Bowman said. He and his wife Iris lived on the north end of the lake.

"I had him paint my deck," Vangie said. "Matty and Joe were busy with work and I didn't want to bother them all the time anyway. John was power washing Louise Sidney's place across the street and I asked him if he'd do mine. When he offered to do the painting too, I said sure."

"Did he talk much?" I asked. "Tell any of you about his personal life?"

Mary Leroy shook her head. "I got him to have lunch with us one afternoon after he did some yard work for us. It was the end of the summer. September. The temps hit the high nineties and I was worried he was going to pass out from heat stroke. So, we sat at the picnic table and had sandwiches. He said he was from the Lansing area."

"He told me he was from Detroit," Vangie said.

"I asked him if he had a wife or kids," Iris said. "He said he hadn't gotten around to it."

"He told me he wasn't fit for a wife," Mary said, smiling. "Said something about him being too feral yet."

"And none of you knew where he lived?" I asked.

They all shook their heads.

"I just assumed he lived around the lake," Vangie said. I glared at her. Joe and Matty were already furious that she'd let the guy into her house without either of them there.

"Do you know who first hired him?" I asked.

No one did. By all accounts, John Lansky had just sort of showed up doing odd jobs around the lake at the end of the summer.

"I think he told me he was a mechanic," Rick said. "Said he got laid off from one of the Big Three."

They all had similar stories. Lansky was just trying to earn extra cash between jobs. Everyone was impressed with his work ethic and the job he did.

"I even saw him down at the public park and the boat launch. Doing some weed whipping and picking up trash," Mary said.

"We had a whole conversation about that. We can't get the township to do anything about what goes on at the park. So John took it upon himself to help out."

"I just don't get it," I said. "He didn't live here. He was living over at the Harmon Arms. That's six miles from the lake."

The group agreed, but no one had any new light to shed on the mystery of John Lansky. As the meeting wound down, I helped my sister clear plates and tidy up her kitchen. I packed up her leftovers as she said goodbye to the Bowmans, the last of her guests. Then she joined me at her kitchen table.

"Cass," she said. "You don't think Lansky was trouble, do you? Like a pedophile or something? I never left Jessa alone with him. In fact, she was never here when he was. He didn't start doing work for me until after the school year started. He was always gone before Jessa came home."

"I don't know what to think about him," I said. "I just don't ever want to hear about you letting some drifter do handyman work for you again. You hire a professional service or you wait for Matty or Joe. Or Eric, for that matter."

"I know, I know," she said. "I just hate asking them all the time."

"They don't mind," I said. "In fact, they insist. So do I."

I wanted to say more, but Jessa tumbled in through the front door.

"Man," I said. "Stop growing already, will you?"

At ten years old, my niece hurtled toward adolescence. Gone were her baby face and chubby cheeks. In the last few months, her legs had grown long and thin. She was almost five feet tall. Jessa gave me a quick hug, then scuttled off to her room.

"Homework before screens," Vangie called out. Jessa mumbled something that might have been a yes but was hard to tell.

"How'd she get so beautiful?" I said, putting the last of Vangie's plates in the dishwasher.

"She's ten going on thirty," Vangie said. "All attitude these days."

"Hmm," I said. "Kind of like her mother was at that age."

"Don't remind me," she said. "You warned me Mom always said this was God's sweetest revenge. Giving us kids that acted just like or worse than we did."

"She's amazing," I said. "And so are you as her mom. You didn't do anything wrong with Lansky. I just want you to be careful. I'm going to find out who this guy was."

Vangie nodded. "I'm sure you will. And I'm sure everyone in town will have an opinion, like always."

"They're already starting," I said. Social media had already taken up the Lansky murder. But so far, even the internet couldn't figure out any more than I had.

Once again, I had more questions than answers about this case. But they would have to wait.

Tires crunched on Vangie's gravel driveway.

"My ride's here," I said, smiling. Eric pulled up in his brand-new Ford Bronco.

"Nice wheels," Vangie said as he headed up the walk.

Eric leaned down to kiss me. With the Chapman case taking up most of my time, I hadn't had much of a chance to see him. Now, it was Friday night and I was all his.

"Don't let her talk work stuff," Vangie said. Eric had a quick hug for her, too.

"I heard you had a day," Eric said. Word of Chapman's bail hearing had no doubt already made its way through the town gossip mill. His tone was light, but there was a hard edge to his expression. I knew that look. He had something to tell me. And it would be something I wouldn't like.

Eric held the door for me, then took my elbow and led me outside to his waiting car and whatever bad news he'd brought.

Chapter 10

From the moment we sat down, I knew Eric had something on his mind. He fiddled with his watch. Smiled a little too big when the waiter came to take our order. And he'd brought me to Claudio's, the most expensive restaurant in Delphi. The only fancy one, really.

"You might as well tell me," I said as soon as we had our Greek salads in front of us. I caught him mid-chew. He feigned confusion at my question. Poorly.

"You've been bouncing off the walls since you picked me up. Making small talk that's not like you. So you're trying to avoid talking to me about whatever the thing is you want to talk to me about. It's no good, Eric. I know you too well."

He took a sip of his draft beer. "Sorry," he said. "I'm that obvious?"

"To me you are," I said. "To everyone else, including our waiter, you're extra charming."

He laughed. "You win. I was going to wait until later to talk to you about this. I know you've got a lot on your plate."

"Oh stop," I said. "We both do. We always do."

"I'm taking my old job back," he blurted. "It's official. I'm going back to the police department. And I feel bad about it. I know you're gearing up with the Chapman case."

My heart fell just a little but I kept my smile in place.

"Are you sure?" I asked.

"I am," he said, putting his napkin down. "It's what I want."

"Your pension's already vested," I said. "You can start drawing it any time. The Chapman case is going to be an earner for the office. I can give you a competitive fee. You know I've already had a ton of other attorneys ask me if you're ready to freelance as an investigator."

"I know," he said.

"It's not exactly the greatest time to be a cop right now," I said. "I worry about you."

"I know that too. But it's also one of the reasons why I have to be a cop right now, Cass."

I reached across the table and grabbed his hand. "I love you for that."

"I know," he said, flashing me that crooked smile that always got me.

"Stop trying to be charming," I said.

"You're not mad?"

"Of course I'm not mad. A little disappointed maybe. I was looking forward to working with you on another case. But if this is what you want, then I'm happy you get to do it."

Eric's brow went up. "I gotta say. I'm not used to that kind of reaction. I can't tell you how many arguments I had with Wendy when we were married over my career."

I took a sip of my wine. "I'm not Wendy. And you were a detective before we got involved. Just like I was a defense lawyer. Are you planning on ever asking me not to be? Even if that's easier for you?"

"No," he said. "Never. It's your calling. Sure. It'd be a lot easier if you did something else. Anything else. But it's who you are."

"Exactly," I said. "This is who you are right now too."

"I do feel bad though," he said. "You've got your work cut out for you with this one."

"And now I can't bring you into it," I said. "Which sucks because your brain is exactly what I need."

"You'll do fine without me," he said.

"I'm happy for you," I said. "I really am. It's been a long year and you've had so much taken away from you."

He met my eyes and it warmed me. "I've gained a lot more than I've lost," he said.

He'd trusted me with the truth about what he wanted. I knew I had to be honest with him too.

"What is it?" he asked, reading me.

"It's nothing," I said. "But since we're laying everything out. Killian."

Eric took a breath, bracing himself. "I thought he was gone."

"He is," I said. "At least, I think so. But the other night, I let him crash at my office. It was just for the one night. I told him I expected him to be gone before Miranda came in. And he was. But that's it. I let him stay there."

Eric took another sip of his beer. "Are you planning on letting him do it again?"

"He hasn't asked. In fact, I haven't seen or heard from him since I left him there. Which, quite frankly, I find odd."

"Are you worried about it?" he asked.

Again, Eric could read me. "Yes," I said plainly.

"Killian can take care of himself," Eric said.

"Normally, I agree with you. This time though, I don't know. He seemed spooked by something. Desperate, almost. Something's going on he's not telling me about."

"Good," Eric said. "I'm sorry, Cass, but I'm glad. Whatever Thorne's involved in, he shouldn't be dragging you into it. You think he's got your best interests at heart, he hasn't."

"I don't think that," I said. "Believe me. I'm fully aware that Killian will always look out for Killian when his back is to the wall. But I do feel like I owed him that one thing. Now it's done. He came asking for a favor and I gave it to him. End of story."

"You sure?" Eric asked. "Because he made it pretty clear to me the other day that I'm in his debt for life."

"You aren't," I said.

"Cass!" My brother's voice pulled my focus away from Eric. I turned. Matty had just walked in with Tori. The two of them had been serious with each other for the better part of the last year.

"You clean up nice," I told Matty. Freshly shaven, with a new haircut, my little brother wore a red tie, white dress shirt, and khakis. I'd rarely seen him this dressed up unless we were at a church wedding.

Tori looked absolutely stunning in a little black dress that hugged her small frame. Though I worried constantly where my brother was concerned, the two of them looked adorable together.

"Are your guests joining you?" Our waiter materialized. Before any of us could properly respond to the question, Matty gushed.

"That would be great!" He plopped himself in the chair next to me. Tori's smile faltered a bit and she looked to me for guidance. Eric was already holding the chair out for her.

"Way to crash," I said to Matty under my breath. "You mind telling me what you're avoiding?"

"I'll just have an iced tea," he told the waiter, ignoring me. "Tori?"

"Uh ... that sounds fine for me too."

Eric shot me a look. He'd picked up on the same vibe I had. What bullet was my brother trying to dodge here?

Whatever it was, our waiter provided impeccable service and within a few minutes, the conversation was easy and our entrees came.

My brother remained antsy though. He kept knocking my knee under the table. For her part, Tori seemed overly hyped up. She kept repeating things, distracted.

Eric sat back, amused, watching the two of them try to act comfortable when they were anything but. Finally, Eric couldn't take it anymore. He made up some excuse about wanting Matty to go look at the craft beer selection with him. This was doubly weird as Matty was sober. Even so, Matty practically tripped over himself leaving the table.

I put my napkin down and leveled a stare at Tori. She sipped her tea, but couldn't escape.

"What's going on?" I asked.

"Nothing!"

"Stop it. I know you. But I know Matty even better. You're both acting weird. And he's wearing a tie. Is he planning something tonight?"

The second I said it, I knew I'd hit on it. "Holy crap," I said. "Is he working up to proposing to you tonight? He chickened out. Is that why he invited himself to our table?"

Tori's hands were shaking. "I can't say. I shouldn't say. Oh, Cass."

There were tears in her eyes. I moved over so I was sitting across from her. "What happened?"

She shook her head so fast I thought it might fall right off. "I got some news this morning. Matty did too, actually. Cass ... don't be mad. It's just ... I'm pregnant."

Her words hit me right in the chest. I couldn't breathe.

"Pregnant," I said. "With Matty's ..."

She nodded. "Yes."

"How?" I asked. "I mean, don't tell me how. But aren't you? Isn't he?"

"Careful?" she said. "Of course. It just happened." She was full-on crying now.

"Are you happy? Is Matty happy?"

A million thoughts raced through my head. Matty wasn't ready. He had almost two years sober, but this was major. He was living in a rented house. He worked construction, but it was cyclical. He didn't have great benefits. Tori got hers through me, but even I had to admit they weren't stellar.

"Yes," she said. "That's the thing. We didn't plan it. Of course we didn't plan it. But yes. I'm stupidly happy. But Matty's freaking out a little. The tie? This place? Yes. I think the idiot was working up to asking me to marry him tonight."

"Don't you want him too?" I asked.

"No!" she practically shouted. "I mean ... not yet. Not because of this."

"Well, it wouldn't be his worst idea," I said, feeling proud of my brother.

"I don't want him to feel obligated. I want to make sure it's what he really wants. What he's ready for."

"I think it's a little late for that," I said. "Are you okay? Are you feeling okay? Have you seen a doctor?"

"I've got an appointment next week," she said. "It's all so new."

"Are you keeping it?" I asked, feeling like an idiot that I'd already bungled this with a million assumptions.

Tori took a breath. "Everything is on the table at the moment. I'm still trying to process everything. That's why I really don't want Matty to propose just yet. I need a second to breathe."

"Of course." I reached for her. "But you're okay?"

"Yes." She smiled. "Weirdly. Yes. I just want some time to sit with it all."

I looked over my shoulder. Matty and Eric were sitting at the bar. Eric shot me a quick glance and his expression said everything. He'd gotten Matty to fill him in already. I just prayed Eric gave him good counsel.

"Let's talk about something else," Tori said. "Lord. Anything else. Oh! I know. I was going to text you tonight anyway. I got a call back from the Boyds. You know, the couple who saw Ty Chapman with John Lansky at the Harmon Arms. The night Lansky was killed?"

"They talked to you?" I asked.

"They agreed to meet with you," she said. "Tomorrow morning, actually. They're coming into the office."

"How did you persuade them?" I asked. "They've been dodging my calls."

Tori shrugged. "Thank Miranda. Turns out she knows Brian Boyd's aunt from church. She leaned on her a little. Don't ask me how. Anyway, they'll be there at nine. First thing in the morning. Though Melissa Boyd told me you weren't going to be at all happy with what she had to say."

"Well that's fantastic," I said.

"That's what I said," Tori said. "If anyone can poke holes in their stories, it'll be you."

"Thanks for the confidence," I said, wishing I could pass some along to Tori. The color had returned to her cheeks, but barely.

Matty and Eric made their way back to the table. I met my brother's eyes and his jitters came back in full force. He knew I knew what was going on. Suddenly, he moved to avoid his next confrontation.

"Well, we better head out," he said, taking Tori gently by the arm. The pair of them were a walking train wreck. All nerves and fluster. Matty fumbled with his wallet.

"My treat," Eric said, laying down his credit card.

Matty thanked him and took the opportunity to make a clean getaway with Tori on his arm.

"Good Lord," Eric finally said.

"Yeah," I agreed, having the sense a freight train was coming straight for me. One with my brother's name painted across the side.

Chapter 11

BRIAN AND MELISSA BOYD would make fantastic witnesses.

For the prosecution.

Melissa was a schoolteacher for Ann Arbor-Pioneer. Pretty. Dark hair, bright eyes. She sat with perfect posture and her hands folded in her lap. Any jury would believe her as she gave me clear, direct answers with no equivocation.

Brian was an even bigger problem. A wedding photographer, he had an eye for detail and knew how to give a physical description. He eyed me with suspicion, but the fact he'd agreed to meet with me told me a lot about his character. Just like it would Rafe Johnson. The Boyds didn't have to meet with me like this. They would have been within their rights to make me get a subpoena and depose them.

"There just wasn't anything unusual about it," Melissa said. "I wanted to walk Victor, our mini Aussiedoodle. Brian didn't want me going alone. So we took the walking trail around the motel. That's when we saw Mr. Lansky talking to that other man."

"Just talking?" I asked.

"Just talking," she said. "They were standing right outside Mr. Lansky's room. Though I didn't know it was his room at the time. We found that out later."

"What was their demeanor?" I asked. "The two men you saw."

"Casual," Melissa said. "Right, Brian? At first anyway. Then later, Lansky was poking the other man in the chest. I wouldn't say it was aggressive really. I just thought they knew each other."

"Yes," Brian agreed. As a couple, they were made for each other. Brian too had dark hair. Fit and trim, he wore freshly pressed khakis and a button-down with an open collar. Straight female members of the jury would be attracted to him, for sure. He volunteered with Big Brothers and with their church outreach program for at-risk youth.

"Could you hear what they were saying?" I asked the pair of them.

"I couldn't," Melissa said. "But I wasn't really listening to it. Victor was pulling on the leash. Got his nose on a squirrel."

"He was barking," I said.

"No," Brian said. "The dog had his nose down. He's a good hunter. Won't bark at anything unless he's inside the house."

I made a note. For Melissa's part, I could make the case that her attention was primarily on the dog, not the men in the parking lot.

"I kept my eye on them," Brian said, as if he could read my mind. "Force of habit."

"He's always thinking of how he'd frame people," Melissa offered.

"I'm curious," I said. "Why the Harmon Arms? It's not the best hotel in or near Delphi. It's actually got a bit of a reputation."

"He's cheap," Melissa said, her voice taking an edge. It was the first sign of any discord between the two of them. I watched as Brian's back went stiff.

"It's close to the highway," Brian said. "Easy on and off. We were just staying a couple of nights. Through the weekend."

"Right," I said. "You were in town for a family reunion. Whose family?"

"His," Melissa said abruptly.

"But you're less than an hour away from Ann Arbor. Why stay overnight at all?"

"I don't like driving at night," Melissa said. "I wanted to be someplace close so Brian could have a few beers with his brothers if he wanted to. The reunion was out on Finn Lake. His brothers rented a house there for the week."

"But you didn't stay there?" I asked.

Once again, I sensed tension between them. My guess? Melissa didn't care for Brian's brothers and their drinking one bit.

"I just like having our own place," she answered.

"Your family isn't from Delphi though," I said to Brian.

"We're from the Cheboygan area originally," he said. "But we're scattered now. One of my brothers lives in Indiana.

Another one near Milwaukee. We're in Milan. My parents are at Lake St. Clair. This was just as close to a central location as we could find. My one cousin lived on Finn Lake for a while. His mom, my aunt, still lives in town."

"I see," I said. "I just want to be clear on what you saw. You told the police you saw Mr. Lansky and this other man talking?"

"On the way out, yes," Melissa said. "We walked Victor for maybe thirty minutes. Thirty to forty. On the way back, we didn't see Mr. Lansky or Mr. Chapman. I'd left Victor's dog bed in the car, so I asked Brian for the keys so I could go get it. He went back to our room. I waited by the car with Victor. That's when I saw Mr. Chapman come out from behind the hotel."

"How far away were you?" I asked.

"The police asked me that. I'm so bad at judging distance. Our car was parked right by our room. Brian always insists on that when we stay in motels."

"About a hundred yards," Brian said, growing irritated. "Melissa was standing by her car. Mr. Chapman came running around the opposite end of the building. We're talking a hundred yards."

"Yes," Melissa said. "A hundred yards or so. He was running. He was a mess."

"The man you say was Mr. Chapman?"

"It was Tyler Chapman," she said. "I saw him. Saw his face. The clothes he was wearing. A pair of jeans and they had blood all over them. His shirt too. It was a white tee shirt. There was blood on the shoulder. A little spot of it. He had a different shirt on when we saw them talking in the parking lot earlier. He took his button-down shirt off. He was just in his tee shirt the second time I saw him. He was sweating."

"He was running," I said.

"She got a good look at him," Brian said. The urge to cross-examine her burned through me. I'd get my chance for that later if this thing ever went to trial. For now, I knew I had to just let their story come out naturally. I couldn't tip either of them off about the questions I might ask if they took the stand. Rafe Johnson would do that enough as it was.

"Was he running toward you or away from you?" I asked.

"Well, both," Melissa answered. "At first, he was running a little toward me. But he kept on going so then I saw him from the back."

"You didn't call out to him?"

"No," she said. "I was shocked."

"Where were you during this?" I asked Brian.

"I came out and by then, Chapman was running further down by the road."

"You didn't see him get into a car or anything?"

"He disappeared down the road," Brian said. "Melissa was upset so I went to her and made sure she was all right. I thought maybe Chapman had said something to her or approached her. That was my focus. But I recognized Chapman from seeing him a little while before that. It was the same guy."

"All right," I said. "But you went to your family reunion later that night, right?"

"We did," Brian answered.

"Were you drinking that night?"

"Later," Brian said, irritated. "I had a few beers but it wasn't until after nine o'clock that night. We saw Chapman and Lansky at approximately six p.m. on the night of November 10th. Then again at approximately six forty-five. It was fairly light out. We left for the reunion party just after seven."

"Got it," I said. "When did you get back to the motel?"

"Super late," Melissa said. "After two in the morning. We slept in until, what, nine, Brian?"

"Nine thirty," he said.

"We were just going to get up and go home," Melissa said. "That's when the police knocked on the door. They'd found Lansky in the woods behind the motel. So we told them everything we knew. Just like we just told you."

"Did either of you go behind the motel with the police?" I asked.

"Of course not," Brian said. "It was an active crime scene. I spoke with the detective on scene, told him who I was. Gave our statements."

"And here we are," Melissa said. "That poor man. It was just awful what Chapman did to him. I don't understand it. They were just talking."

"Not arguing," I said. "You're sure?"

"Just talking," she insisted. "I assumed they were friends. Actually, I assumed they were staying together in the hotel. They looked friendly. At least, they didn't look adversarial. I mean the one poked the other in the chest. But like I told you. It didn't seem overly aggressive to me. But I didn't hear what they were saying."

"Mr. Lansky didn't seem upset?"

"Not at all," she said. "I don't think he was smiling. Was he smiling, Brian?"

"Not smiling," Brian answered. "I'd describe his expression as grim. So no, I didn't get the impression they were friends or not friends. I had no impression of that at all."

"Got it," I said. "And the police brought you in for a line-up?"

"A few days later," Melissa offered. "We got a call well after we went home. We both took off work and came back. They showed us pictures. I picked Tyler Chapman out right away. Plus, he had that cut above his eye."

I made a note. If Tyler was the only person in the photo array with a cut above his eye, that could help his defense.

"I think we're done here," Brian said. "I respect you have your job to do, but we've said all we're going to say."

He rose, pulling Melissa up by the elbow. She quickly grabbed her purse and the pair of them hustled right out of my office. I heard the door slam downstairs as they left.

"Well then," Miranda said, materializing in the doorway as she often did.

"Indeed," I said.

"You think they're lying?" she asked. She held a folded pink slip in her hand.

"No," I said. "They said a few things that might be helpful, but I don't think I'm going to be able to prove mistaken identity."

She fanned herself with the piece of paper. "Well, I'm rooting for the Chapmans on this one. I just refuse to believe that boy could hurt anyone like that."

"That boy is almost forty years old, Miranda."

"Hush," she said.

"Did Tori come in yet?" I asked her.

Miranda's face fell. "She, uh ... I forgot to mention it. She's at a doctor's appointment this morning. She'll be in later."

"It's no good, Miranda," I said. "I already know. Tori told me about her, um, condition last night."

Miranda smiled. "Quite the pickle those two have gotten themselves in. Are you angry?"

"I don't know what I am," I said. "Worried, I guess. Matty isn't ready to be a dad yet."

"Oh, honey," she said. "Nobody's ever ready. And he sure is crazy about Tori. They make each other happy. Maybe that's all you need."

"Food," I said. "You need food. And a stable job. And a roof over your head. A college fund. How about health insurance?"

She waved me off. "You're in a mood today."

"I'm just worried. Like I said."

"You're always worried," she answered. "Here. Something to take your mind off it."

She handed me the pink note. She was right. The name on it sure took my mind off my brother's impending fatherhood.

Special Agent Lee Cannon.

"That's that handsome FBI agent who sniffs around you every now and again, isn't it?" she asked.

"Sniffs around me?" I asked.

"You know what I mean."

"I do," I said. "That's the problem."

"Well he said it was urgent. Wanted me to interrupt your meeting. That's his personal cell."

Puzzled, I picked up the office landline.

"I'll scoot and leave you to it," Miranda said, closing the door behind her.

Cannon answered on the first ring.

"Cass?" he asked.

"Cannon," I answered. "What's going on?"

"Has he checked in with you?" Cannon asked.

I could have played dumb or coy. But he knew I knew what he meant.

"No," I said. "Is there something wrong? Did something happen?"

Lee fell silent.

"No," he finally said. "But it's in my interests ... it's in Thorne's interests ... for us to have a conversation. If you're in contact with him, it would help me out a lot if you could get a message to him from me."

"I'm not your go-between," I said. The burner phone Killian gave me was still hidden beneath a stack of papers in my desk drawer. I'd never taken it out. I also hadn't told anyone else about it.

"Fine," Lee said.

"What message?"

"You'll reach out?" Lee asked.

"I didn't say that," I answered. "But I'm curious enough to ask. What message, Lee? What's going on?"

"It's nothing," Cannon said. "Probably. Just ... if you talk to him, let him know I'd like a conversation."

"If he calls me, I'll tell him," I said.

More silence. "Thank you," Lee said. "And Cass ... just ... for now ... stay away from the guy. Okay?"

Cannon hung up before I could ask him again what he meant. I'd been down this road dozens of times. Lee Cannon warned me almost every time we spoke. Somehow, this time, he seemed legitimately worried. I pulled the burner phone out of my desk. I flipped it open and saw the saved number. I let my fingers play over the buttons. Then, I flipped the thing shut and tossed it back in the drawer.

Chapter 12

WEEKS WENT by as I readied myself for the Chapman trial. I interviewed Ty's neighbors, co-workers, other guests at the Harmon Arms that weekend, my own neighbors around the lake. No one had anything unusual to tell me. Lansky had seemed like a decent guy. A hard worker.

A picture began to emerge though. Lansky seemed to have told different people different things about his background. One neighbor said he came from the Lansing area. Another, Detroit. He'd gotten friendly with a waitress at the diner on Blackmun Street. She said he'd mentioned a brother in Wyandotte. Only no brother actually existed when I looked further into it.

It could have all been harmless. Lansky was new to Delphi. He kept mainly to himself. It was possible the people I interviewed didn't remember correctly. Most of them admitted that these were casual conversations. They were being polite. It was small talk. It just seemed the more I tried to figure out just who John Lansky was, the more elusive he became.

There was one small break. John Lansky had done jail time himself for assault. I had a meeting set up with his probation officer the week after next. As far as I could tell, his P.O. might know more about Lansky than anyone else on the planet.

Ty Chapman was another matter. His trial was set to begin the first week in April. The date loomed before me once we'd cleared the holidays. Rafe Johnson, so far, wasn't even hinting at a possible plea deal. He wouldn't take my calls.

I had a birthday. A big one. Forty. I spent it quietly with Eric. Until my brothers, sister, and nieces descended on the lake, bringing me cake and decorating my yard with fake headstones.

The first week of February, I met with Ty again at the county jail. As always, he remained calm and stoic as I reported back everything I'd learned from interviews and evidence I combed over.

"They can put you at the scene, Ty," I said. "Your blood. Your DNA. We have no explanation for any of that."

"They have to prove I killed him," Ty said. "Right? The prosecutor has to prove I planned to kill him."

"For first-degree murder? Yes."

"The jury has to give me the benefit of the doubt. If they can infer I'm not guilty, they have to."

"Yes," I said. "But they're going to have questions. Ones I can't adequately answer for them. You were hurt when you came out of those woods. Bleeding. Yes, Brian and Melissa Boyd can positively identify you. But they can also tell the jury about your visible injuries. If you were in a fight. If you were trying to defend yourself ..."

"But they have to prove all of that. The prosecution. I don't have to say anything," he said in his usual, frustratingly flat tone.

"I have to give them a reason for all of this, Ty," I said. "You're right. I don't have the burden of proof. Rafe Johnson does. But the jury is going to want some alternate theory, an explanation for what happened out there. They are *going* to see the pictures of John Lansky's mutilated body. I may be successful in keeping some of the photos out. But not all of them. Not enough of them. They're going to ask why someone would do something like that."

Ty looked toward the wall. In the weeks I'd known him, I recognized the gesture for what it was. A signal that Chapman was done answering my questions. Done talking. Done doing anything that might be useful in his own defense. If I pressed him on it, he'd say the same thing he always said.

"Just keep me from a life sentence," he'd say. Not an admission of guilt. Not a denial.

"How is Beth?" he asked.

"She's holding her own," I said. "They've been helpful at the Veterans Center. One of the other military wives has been going to her doctor's appointments with her. Ted Moran's wife."

Ty nodded. "She told me. That's good. She'll be all right. The baby will be all right."

I bit my tongue. I wanted to scream. Shake him. Beth Chapman was not in any way, shape, or form all right. Her husband was on trial for murder. He barely seemed to care.

"Ty," I said. "When are you going to tell me what really happened? I've told you a thousand times. What you tell me is privileged. I can't tell anyone else. Ever. You can't be forced to testify at your trial. It would stay between us. Forever."

"You should go," he said.

"Ty ..."

"We'll talk next week," he said. "After you've met with Lansky's P.O. Isn't that what you said? Relax. I know Beth's checks have cleared. You're doing your job. If I was dissatisfied, I'd let you know."

Ty rose. He went to the door and tapped on it to let the guard know he was ready to leave. As he always did, Chapman left me sitting there bewildered and frustrated.

I didn't get a chance to stew over it though. My phone rang. Once again, I recognized Lee Cannon's number. The call dropped when I tried to answer. The interior of the Woodbridge County Jail didn't get the greatest cell reception.

I gathered my things and went outside. As I did, a text from Lee came through. Simple. Cryptic. Enough to get me worried about something else.

"Can you meet? I'm at the coffee shop around the corner from the jail."

How the hell did he know where I was? Sure enough, I saw the black SUV Cannon usually drove parked at a meter one block over. Slipping my phone back in my pocket, I went to meet him.

I hadn't seen Lee Cannon in a couple of years. In my mind, he looked like what might happen if you transplanted a Viking into the FBI. Tall, white-blond, strapping. He had, at various times in my life, been a thorn in my side and my would-be savior. I knew the next five minutes would dictate which one he'd be today.

Lee stood as I approached the table. He'd picked one way in the back away from the lunch crowd, but right next to the kitchen.

I heaved my leather messenger bag in the booth beside me.

"You look great," Lee said. "I like your hair that way."

My hand went to the side of my head. About a year ago, I'd gone lighter blonde.

"I guess it has been a long time," I said. "How's the Chicago Field Office treating you?"

"Busy," he said.

"I would have thought you'd have put in for a transfer for something more conducive to a home life by now."

As long as I'd known him, Cannon had worked white collar crime. He'd served on a task force responsible for taking down several high-placed members of various organized crime families. It had been Cannon who first approached me to serve as his confidential informant against the Thorne family. For years, I declined. When I finally couldn't look the other way anymore, Lee and I established an odd friendship.

"You aren't the first person who's mentioned that," he said, smiling.

"Let me guess," I said. "Mona's starting to lay down the law? Threaten your inheritance?"

Mona Cannon, Lee's mother, was part of the Hamptons, country-club elite. She never wanted her only son to pursue a life of public service. She would have rather he go to work for a prestigious Manhattan law firm. I knew Lee had plenty of offers over the years. We both had. And yet, here we were.

Lee's face darkened. "Mona's no longer with us. She passed away a few months ago. Massive stroke after a plastic surgery procedure we all told her she didn't need."

"Oh, Lee," I said. "I'm so sorry. You should have called me. I would have liked to pay my respects."

Lee smiled. "There weren't any respects to pay. My mother didn't want a funeral."

"Well still," I said. "I'm your friend. I think, anyway. And I'm sorry for your loss."

"Thanks," he said.

"Now," I said. "What's going on? Why the hurry-up-and-meet? Why are you stalking me?"

"I'll be blunt," he said.

"You always are."

"I'll ask you the same thing I asked you a few weeks ago. When's the last time you saw or spoke to Killian Thorne?"

I waved the server off when she offered to take my order. I stuck with coffee.

"Why do you ask?"

"Come on, Cass," he said. "Let's not dance. Has he reached out to you recently?"

Old conflicts rose within me. In the past, even meeting with Lee would have been a betrayal of Killian and his brother's law firm. Then, one dark day, it almost got me killed. I hadn't thought about it much over the years. I'd tried to shove it out of my mind. But Liam Thorne, Killian's brother, my firm's senior partner, had arranged to scare me back to loyalty. He'd threatened to send me to the bottom of Lake Michigan from the deck of the family yacht.

That was the day I left Chicago. I came back to Delphi to put all of that behind me. Except it kept coming back. "First," I said. "Tell me what's going on."

"So he did reach out to you," Lee guessed. "When, Cass? How long ago?"

I sat still, reading Lee's face. His eyes flicked over to me. He carried tension in his shoulders. He didn't know Killian had showed up on my doorstep last fall. He didn't know about the burner phone I kept in my desk. Old loyalty kept me from saying a word.

"We think something's going down," he said. "Something big."

"Is it something I need to worry about?" I asked. "I haven't set foot in Chicago in years. I don't stay in contact with anyone from the Thorne Law Group. I'm out. Completely." These things were true. And yet, I still couldn't bring myself to tell him about my most recent contact with Killian. Not yet.

"He still thinks you belong to him," Lee said. "You get that, right? He makes that pretty clear to his associates."

My heart turned to ash.

"How closely are you watching him?" I asked. "Lee, do you have Killian up on a wiretap?"

He stared at me, unmoving. I knew he could neither admit nor deny anything if there was an ongoing investigation.

"Lee," I said. "Is there something I need to worry about?"

"He's missing," Lee said. "No one has seen or heard from Killian Thorne in over a month. There have been meetings. High-level meetings he didn't show up for. It doesn't look good."

It got hard to breathe.

"Lee," I said. "You need to tell me what you know. You wouldn't be here if there wasn't something. You knew I'd ask questions."

"You first," he said. "Has he reached out to you?"

"Do you have eyes on him?" I asked.

"We did," he answered plainly. "But like I said, about a month ago, Thorne didn't show for a meeting he was supposed to have in Detroit. It made some waves. You know there's a limit to what I can say. But you also know me well enough to know I wouldn't be here if I wasn't worried."

I sat back against the cushioned leather seat.

"He's not your client anymore," he said. "You're not breaching confidentiality by telling me whether you've seen or talked to the guy. Do you know how to get a hold of him?"

"Yes," I said. "I've seen him. Last November. He showed up on my doorstep asking for a place to stay."

"He's with you?" Lee asked.

"No. He came to the house. I turned him away but let him crash overnight on my office couch. He was gone the next morning. Like I said. That was before the holidays. I haven't seen him since."

"Cass," he said. "What did he tell you?"

"Lee, it would really help me if you clued me in as to what's going on. You're right. Killian's no longer my client. But you have to know talking about him like this with you. After all these years. It still feels like a betrayal."

A shudder went through him. When Lee spoke again, his voice was so low I almost couldn't hear him.

"You may not believe me, but I'm trying to keep the guy alive."

"What's going on?" I insisted.

Lee sat upright. He looked out the window, deciding for himself what he could say.

"You're here," I said. "You called me. Not the other way around. You say you're worried about Killian. Give me a reason to believe you."

"Because despite our past dealings, it serves my interests to keep Killian Thorne right where he is. In control of Chicago. Lesser of several evils, you might say."

"Is he working with you?" My pulse quickened. "My God, Lee. That's it, isn't it? And whatever it is, you've lost control of it now. He's in danger. You put him in danger!"

"Calm down," Lee said. "And lower your voice. It's not like that. It's complicated."

This didn't make sense. The Killian I knew would never work with the Feds. Being a snitch of any kind violated a code. It was a line Killian would never cross. And yet here Cannon was, worried about protecting him.

"You need to level with me," I said.

"Do you have a means of getting in touch with him?" Cannon asked.

"No," I lied. "Not anymore. When he calls me, it's usually from a burner phone."

"But you can get a message to him," he said. "If you called the Thorne Law Group and told them you needed to talk to Killian, they'd convey it to him. Wouldn't they?"

"No," I said. "If anything, that would put Killian in even more danger than whatever he's currently in. You'll have to trust me when I say Killian and his brother aren't on the best terms anymore. Liam is the last person you'd want to tip off about anything amiss with Killian."

Lee nodded. "You're right. Listen, you know I can't say much. I'm violating about twenty different protocols even meeting with you like this. If anyone finds out, it's gonna cost me my job."

"Then why are you? Why risk it?"

"I already told you. Killian's dangerous. He's a criminal. Through and through. But there are worse out there trying to get a foothold."

"And you're afraid they have," I said.

"I just need to find Thorne, that's all."

"Do you think he knows you're looking?"

"I don't know. There's a war brewing. Rumor has it, Killian's about to make a play against one of the more powerful families in the Detroit crew. Russian mobsters, Cass. He's been moving pieces. I can't get into specifics. But these meetings he missed? They were a big part of that. If he's gone to ground, I need to know where."

"No," I said. "Lee, this doesn't make any sense. If Killian were in real danger, he wouldn't come to me. He'd never risk exposing me to whatever he's caught up in. He wouldn't bring it to my literal front door. There's something else going on. If Killian can't be found, it's because he doesn't want to be. Believe me, the man can take care of himself."

It sounded good. I wanted to believe it. At the same time, Killian's behavior the last time we spoke felt like a goodbye.

"I hope you're right," Lee said.

"So do I."

"I have to get going," he said. "I've been here long enough." Lee pulled a business card out of his pocket and handed it to me.

"In case you lost ... or tore up the last one."

I smiled. Point of fact, that's exactly what I'd done with the last card Lee Cannon had given me.

"Lee," I said. "You know I can't promise you I'll use this. Over the years, I've found out I'm better at looking out for my own interests than the Bureau could ever be. I can promise that if I do talk to Killian, I'll tell him we met and why."

"Do that," he said. "And don't let him crash on any more of your couches."

I smiled. "Yeah. You're not the only one giving me that edict."

Lee raised a brow. "So that's still going on? You and the detective?"

I thought about getting indignant or evasive. But in his own weird way, Lee wanted good things for me.

"Yes," I said. "It's still going on."

"So was he there when Thorne showed up at your front door?"

I couldn't help it. I laughed. It was an answer.

"Man," Lee said. "I can imagine how that went over. Here I'm thinking the Detroit mob is Thorne's biggest problem. Seems to me he's got something more home grown to worry about. Damn, Leary. You sure have a knack for hot messes."

"Just for that, you're paying for my coffee," I said.

Cannon was still laughing as I rose.

"Lee," I said. "If you find him first, you'll get word to me?"

His face grew serious. "Yes," he said. "That's a promise. As long as you promise to call me if you hear from him."

I stayed silent. It wasn't a promise I could make.

"Someday your loyalty to this guy is going to get you into trouble that I won't be able to help you get out of."

"Would you?" I asked. "Now? Have you ever?"

He let out an exasperated sigh. "I'm on your side. I've always been on your side. But I see I'm wasting my time with you as far as Thorne is concerned. At a certain point you're going to have to trust me. I need to talk to him. It's important, Cass. Think about what I said."

"I always do," I answered. That, at least, was the truth.

"In the meantime, take care of yourself. Stick close to Wray. He seems like a stand-up guy."

"He is," I said.

"You going to tell him about this?" Lee asked, gesturing between us. "Our meeting?"

It was a good question. One I didn't yet know how to answer. Cannon seemed able to read that dilemma in my face as well. For once, he didn't comment on it. He put two bills on the table and shook his head as he left the diner.

Chapter 13

I WAITED until late that evening, sitting alone in my office. Miranda, Tori, and Jeanie had all gone home. Eric was working afternoons for the rest of the month on a new task force. I wouldn't see him until tomorrow morning over coffee.

Lee's words echoed through me. His worry too. I knew this was a mistake. I knew the safest course was to simply throw Killian's phone to the bottom of Finn Lake.

I pulled it out of my desk, feeling the slight weight of it. Would he still answer? It had been weeks since he handed the thing to me. Could I assume he'd keep the phone connected to the number he'd left on his person?

This wasn't my problem anymore. Whatever entanglements Killian had with the Russian mob or business in Detroit or Chicago or Ireland ... weren't my problem anymore. And yet, when he'd handed me this phone, it felt like a lifeline. I just didn't know if it was supposed to be for him or for me.

I found myself dialing the number. It rang six times. I was about to give up when the line clicked over. He was there. Breathing. Waiting for me.

"Cass," he said. Relief washed over me. Though maybe it should have been dread.

Now that I had him, I realized I hadn't worked out what to say. "Well," I settled on. "So you're still alive, I take it."

He laughed. It felt hollow though. Should I lie? Downplay my worry? But if I did, then I'd be telling lies or half-truths to too many people. Lee Cannon. Killian. And Eric. He still had no idea I kept this phone or what it meant.

"Killian," I said. "Lee Cannon sought me out. He said he's concerned you might be in over your head on a business deal that's caught the Bureau's attention."

He didn't answer at first. In the distance, I heard a rush of sound. Water. Seagulls. I didn't let my mind fully go there, but I had a hunch where he might be. Instinct told me it was better not to ask him to confirm it.

"Killian," I said. "Do you need help? Are you finally in the kind of trouble you can't fix?"

"Is that worry I hear in your voice?" he asked.

"Yes," I said. "No games. Yes. I'm worried. You show up out of nowhere. You hide out in my office then disappear. You give me this phone. Now Lee says you're AWOL. Agent Cannon has practically made a career out of telling me to stay away from you. Now he's asking me to reach out to you. It means he's desperate. It means he's legitimately freaked out by something. So yes. I'm worried, Killian."

"I'm touched."

"Don't be," I said.

Silence. I heard the birds in the distance. Definitely seagulls. If I had to guess, Killian was actually holding the phone out so I could hear them clearly. A message. A signal. A warning?

"Killian ..."

"There's nothing for you to worry about," he said. "Nothing I can't handle. Relax, Cass. It's just business."

"My ass," I said. "I know you. This is different. Killian, if it's time ..."

"Time for what, a rúnsearc?"

"Time for you to make a deal. To get out. You can trust Cannon."

Killian laughed. "If I recollect, Lee Cannon nearly got you killed."

"Your brother did that," I said. "Have you forgotten?"

"Never," Killian said, his tone cold.

"Killian, what do you want me to do? Cannon asked me to get a hold of him if you reached out to me. So do you need to?"

"What do *I* want you to do? When was the last time you ever listened?"

"I'm worried about your life, you idiot. About whatever mess you've gotten yourself into."

"Would you come with me?" Killian asked bluntly.

"What?"

ROBIN JAMES

"This parachute. This lifeline Lee Cannon thinks he can make me. Would you come with me if I asked you? Would you come with me if I retired once and for all?"

"Killian ..."

"It's all right," he said. "I'm not asking. You don't have to answer. And you've done your duty. If you speak to Cannon again, you can tell him you conveyed his warning."

"If I tell him I spoke to you, he's going to want to know how. He won't be the only one. I can't lie for you, Killian," I said. But we both knew I'd been doing just that. Again.

"Take care, Cass," he said. "I appreciate the call."

"Killian, wait." But he'd already hung up. He left me staring at the phone in my hand. Though he hadn't said it, I expected he'd destroy the one he'd been holding now. He hadn't instructed me to do the same. I didn't know what that meant. I didn't know anything anymore where he was concerned.

I let a few minutes pass, then I tucked the phone back under a stack of papers and locked it in my desk drawer.

Chapter 14

Two DAYS LATER, I stood in the kitchen sipping my coffee as Eric walked back from the barn. We had a dumping of snow and he'd just finished shoveling the drive so I could get out in an hour.

He smacked the snow off his boots before leaving them on the mat outside the door, then came inside.

"Thanks," I said. "Coffee's still warm. I poured you some."

His hands were red from the cold. He warmed them on the outside of the mug. "We might get another three inches by this afternoon. I'll text Joe and have him come over."

"I can handle a shovel," I said. "But thanks."

"He likes to do it," Eric said. "So do I." He leaned in and kissed me on the cheek.

"Your lips are like ice!" I laughed. "Seriously though, don't text Joe. He's mad at me and I'm not in the mood to deal with it."

Eric sat on one of the stools in front of my kitchen island. "Tori and Matty still? He's not mad at you. He's just worried."

"So am I," I said. "So is Matty."

"Have you talked to him?"

I shrugged. "My little brother has been avoiding all of us. And I'm making a concerted effort not to bring personal stuff up with Tori at work. The whole thing has just been very strained. She had a rough go of a first trimester and it hasn't gotten better into the second. Miranda keeps making different soups and things and bringing them in, trying to find something that doesn't make Tori nauseous. Jeanie's gone into full-on military commander mode, trying to plan out the rest of Tori's life and financial decisions. It's just been ... a lot."

Eric kept a hard gaze on me. I tried to look away, knowing he wasn't buying a word I was saying. I was worried about my brother and Tori. But that wasn't what was really on my mind.

"You still haven't heard from Thorne?"

"Eric," I said. "We don't have to talk about him." I told him about my conversation with Cannon. I had yet to tell him about my conversation with Killian himself. But apparently, I had a *look w*here Killian was concerned.

"I think we do," he said. "You barely sleep anymore. You're up at all hours pacing down here. Ruminating."

I smiled and set down my mug. "I thought you were sleeping."

"Sometimes I am. But you're not and you can't keep going like this. Killian Thorne's not your problem anymore. Let Cannon worry about him. No news is good news. If something has happened to Thorne, they'll let you know."

"Like Hoffa?" I said. It was a weak joke and I instantly regretted it. Eric's expression went grim. He came to me.

"I'm sorry," I said. "I know it's not fair to you that I'm using brain space to worry about my ex."

"It's your nature," he said. "And as much as I hate the guy, the fact that you *do* care is one of the reasons I love you, Cass. Only you can't fix this one. It's unfixable."

I touched his cheek. "I love you too. But I *am* sorry."

Eric collected my mug and his and put them in the dishwasher. "Are you going to be late tonight?"

"Maybe," I said. "I'm headed to Wayne County to meet with John Lansky's probation officer."

"You think that's going to go anywhere?" Eric asked. "Johnson's never going to let you introduce evidence of the victim's criminal record."

"I'm just trying to get a clearer picture of who he was," I said. "It might be a dead end. Or it might lead somewhere."

"What's his name? The probation officer."

I picked up my phone and pulled up the email exchange I'd had with the guy. "Luke Todd."

"Big guy? Thick head of red hair? I think I worked with him on a couple of cases a few years back."

"I'm not surprised," I said. "He's apparently been around forever. Anything I should know? How's he feel about defense attorneys?"

"He's pretty even keeled from what I've seen," Eric said. "Big Cleveland Browns fan."

"Something I should hold against him?" I asked.

"I would." Eric winked.

"Thanks for the tip," I said. I collected my messenger bag and slipped my phone in the outside pocket.

"Great," Eric said, turning to the window. It had just started to snow again. "I really wish you'd let me call Joe. 94 is gonna be slick. Why don't you take my car? It's got the four-wheel drive."

"So does my Jeep," I said. "Quit worrying. I'm a Michigan girl. I know how to drive in the snow. What about you though? You staying here tonight or at your place?"

Eric had succeeded at selling his house well over asking price. He'd been renting an apartment downtown, but in the last couple of weeks had stayed more here than there.

"Not sure," he said. "I'll text you."

We said our goodbyes and Eric left ahead of me. I watched him go, then slipped behind the wheel of my Jeep, headed for my meeting with Luke Todd.

———

THE MAN WAS EXACTLY as Eric described. A tall ginger with a beefy, strong handshake and Browns memorabilia covering the walls of his small office inside the Southwest District probation office. Like most probation officers in the county, he was overworked and underpaid. I thanked Todd for meeting with me and agreeing to share his thoughts.

Todd shifted a few stacks of papers and picked up a battered file folder, opening it to the top page.

"When was the last time you met with John Lansky?" I asked.

"Last summer," he said. "From what I knew, he was doing pretty well. Getting his life back on track."

"How did you find him?"

"Personality-wise? Real quiet. Respectful. Docile, actually. I got the impression something bad happened to him when he was inside."

I looked at my own notes. "Lansky did time for aggravated assault though."

"Yeah," Todd confirmed. "Sentenced to a year by Judge Patterson. Ended up doing a little north of eight months. He had little jail stints before that. Mostly related to robberies. He'd been a low-level dealer in his teens and twenties. The agg-assault stemmed from a bar fight in downtown Detroit. Cut the other guy with a broken bottle. Freak thing. The guy got some kind of blood infection from the wound and damn near died."

"But he got out what, five, six years ago?"

"Yep," Todd said, referring to his notes. "Five years' probation. We were done. He moved out of the county down your way and the last I heard he was doing odd jobs. That was always the thing with him. I helped him find work here in Wayne County a couple of different times. As a maintenance man mostly. Factory work. He was good at it. He just never stayed in one place for very long."

"Was there any specific reason for that?" I asked. "Did you speak to any of his employers?"

"They all said he was a good worker. Kept to himself. Didn't cause trouble. After a while, though, maybe three or four months, he'd just stop showing up. We'd meet. Holding steady work was a condition of his probation. As soon as it started to become an issue, he'd find another job and start the cycle all over again. But he was getting by. Paying his bills. Lansky just wasn't one of my problem children, if you know what I mean."

"Do you know what brought him to Delphi?" I asked. "So far, I haven't been able to find any connection he might have had there. He just basically showed up there a few months before his murder."

Todd shrugged. "I don't know. The last time we spoke, during his exit interview, he told me he and a friend were going to head up north to work on an oil rig. He seemed excited about it. At least, as excited as I ever saw Lansky get about anything. He had a pretty flat affect."

"What about mental health issues?" I said.

"He was introverted," Todd said. "He had psychological assessments in prison. He'd been treated for mild depression. There was evidence he was learning disabled. He had reading difficulties. But there was nothing he wasn't able to overcome on any of that. John Lansky was just a pretty basic, boring guy who had some troubles in his younger days but seemed like he was trying to straighten it all out. It was kind of like he lived two different lives."

"What do you mean?" I asked.

Luke Todd let out a sigh. "Look, the guy I knew. The guy who used to come in here and meet with me because he was court ordered to was, like I said, pretty boring and docile. The bar fight he was involved in was pretty vicious."

Todd took some photos out of his file and laid them on the desk. They depicted the apparent victim of John Lansky's assault. The right side of the man's face looked like hamburger meat where Lansky had sliced him with the broken beer bottle.

"Before that," Todd said. "There was another incident, another assault. Charges were dropped."

"I'm not familiar with that one," I said, looking through my notes.

"You wouldn't be," he said. "Like I said, it never went anywhere. Wasn't part of Lansky's criminal record. But about a year before the bar fight that landed him in prison, he was suspected in a rape case."

I sat back hard in my seat. "What can you tell me about it?"

"The allegation was he followed this woman home from another bar just outside of Flat Rock. I don't know if she got in his car willingly or if he forced her in. Her story changed several times. That was part of the problem. But the woman had been pretty badly beaten and raped. A neighbor saw her coming home. She collapsed on her front porch and the neighbor called an ambulance."

Todd took out several more sheets of paper and laid them in front of me. It was a police report taken by the Wayne County Sheriff's Department six years ago. It detailed exactly what Todd had just told me. I slowly flipped through the pages.

"What happened?" I asked.

"Victim recanted her story," Todd said. "She identified Lansky in a lineup. Then a couple of weeks later she said it wasn't him. They never formally charged him. Then the woman pretty much dropped off the face of the earth. Went inactive on all her social media accounts."

"But it was the same bar where he got into a fight the following year?"

"Yep," Todd said. I flipped to the last page in the police report. It showed a picture of a woman, her face swollen on one side. She was covered in cuts and bruises. Her name, according to the report, was Ellen Colby.

I couldn't stop staring. There was something eerily familiar about her. I'd have to find a better picture of her, one where her injuries didn't distort her face as much, but there was no mistaking it. The resemblance between Ellen Colby and Beth Chapman was uncanny.

Chapter 15

IN SIX WEEKS, I would stand in front of a jury and argue to keep Ty Chapman out of prison for the rest of his life. Today, his pregnant wife sat before me and every instinct in me told me she was lying to me.

Well into her third trimester now, Beth started to grow uncomfortable in her chair. I met her at her house. The Chapmans' newly built, three-thousand-square-foot gem sat on one of the most desirable lots in the White Oak subdivision. She had woods behind her. That was a rarity here as most of the homes abutted other neighbors. I laid a photograph of John Lansky in front of her. A mugshot from almost a decade ago, but it was the best one I had. Beside it, I laid a picture of Ellen Colby, the woman who had accused him of sexual assault and then recanted. It was a picture she'd posted on her own social media account. Todd was right though. The woman hadn't posted anything in more than two years. As much as the police photo resembled Beth, this one from Ms. Colby's personal account looked even more like her. There was no mistaking it.

"Do you know this woman?" I asked.

Beth sat with her arms folded protectively in front of her.

"No," she said.

"You don't notice anything familiar about her?"

Beth shook her head. "Does she live around here?"

"Beth," I said. "You might as well be looking in a mirror. Can't you see that?"

She shrugged. "I mean, her hair is reddish like mine and sort of styled the same way. But I've never seen her. Who is she?"

"About five years ago, she accused John Lansky of raping her. They met at a bar. He followed her home."

Beth leaned over the table, peering at the picture even closer. "How awful. Is she okay?"

"She changed her story just before they were going to arrest him."

Beth nodded, but showed no other reaction.

"You swear to me, you'd never seen John Lansky before?"

Beth pulled her pink cardigan sweater tighter around herself. "No. I told you. I told the police. I've told everyone who will listen. I don't know John Lansky. Ty doesn't know John Lansky."

"Think," I said. "Could you have run into him when you were shopping? Getting gas? Running other errands?"

"Cass," she said. "I don't know how many times I can say it. I'd never seen this man before in my life. Not until they arrested Ty and his picture started making it around online. I'd never heard his name before."

"Ty has given me next to nothing," I said. "You know that, right? No explanation for what he was doing in that hotel parking lot the night Lansky was murdered. No rationale for why the police found his cell phone in the woods a few feet from Lansky's body. Nothing on how he got injured that night. In every way that matters, the prosecution will be able to prove the elements of murder. The only thing ... and I mean the *only* thing I might be able to argue is that this wasn't premeditated."

"And that will keep Ty from spending the rest of his life in jail?"

"I have no idea," I said. "I really don't, Beth. At this point, I need to be honest with you. I'm regretting even getting involved in this case."

"We paid you," she said. "We paid you more than you've ever been paid to defend a murder case, Cass. Is it more money that you need?"

"What I need is a plausible explanation for what happened out there. John Lansky was a violent man. Rafe Johnson will put up a fight, but I think the jury will hear that."

"Then we'll win," she said. "Ty was defending himself."

"Has he told you that?"

"No," she said. "He won't say anything to me either. But it would make sense, wouldn't it? He had all those bruises and scratches on him."

I tightened my fists in frustration.

"Do you think maybe Lansky was trying to hurt someone else? Another woman maybe? You're right. She does look like me. If he was capable of hurting this Colby woman, maybe he'd moved on to someone else."

"I can't prove that," I said. "Not yet. And my client has been basically mute on the subject."

Tears filled Beth's eyes. "I can't lie. I know I can't lie."

"I'm not asking you to," I said. "In fact, I'm specifically telling you not to."

Beth buried her face in her hands. She was holding something back. I had no doubt of it. For as mute as Ty was, Beth had always been downright cagey.

"Did John Lansky approach you?" I asked her. "Did he try to hurt you too, Beth?"

Nothing. She said nothing. She didn't confirm it. She didn't deny it. I wanted to punch the wall.

"You can't quit on us," she said. "I know you can do a good job for Ty at trial. I know you're the only one who can. He needs you. We both need you."

"And I need the truth. All of it."

"If Ty says nothing, you can still do your job," she said. "You can still make sure Rafe Johnson can't prove his case beyond a reasonable doubt. You'll find the holes. I know you will."

I slapped my hand flat against the table. "With nothing," I said. "The jury has to believe something else besides cold-blooded murder, Beth. Right now, I'm not sure I would if I were them. That's the problem."

"He was violent," she said. "Lansky has a history of hurting people. Johnson can't prove what really happened out there."

I squeezed the bridge of my nose. Beth was infuriating. One minute, she seemed dense and befuddled. The next, she knew exactly what burdens of proof the prosecution faced and the specific hurdles that might benefit her husband. She sounded eerily like Ty just now.

"I can pay you more money," she said. "If that's what it will take."

"I'm not here to shake you down," I said, gathering the photos. "That's not what this is."

"I'm sorry," she said. "But we trust you."

I shoved my things into my bag. I felt worse than if I hadn't come at all. At the same time, I knew there was something this woman wasn't telling me. But her secrets might land her husband in prison forever.

Chapter 16

ON THE NIGHT before the start of the Chapman trial, I stared at the whiteboard. It was the sparsest trial outline I'd ever had. Late on Saturday night, Tori and Jeanie hung out with me, staring at the same thing.

"They know the odds," Jeanie said.

"The Chapmans expect me to work miracles," I said.

"No, they don't," Jeanie said. "They expect you to work the prosecution."

Tori stood up and walked over to the whiteboard. At nearly twenty-seven weeks along, she still was barely showing. You couldn't tell if you looked at her straight on. Only if she turned to the side. But you could see her pregnancy in the hollowness of her cheeks. Her hair, a pale blonde, had a new luster. So far, she and Matty clammed up when we started asking questions. I opted for quiet support. And prayers.

"The jury is going to have the same questions you do," Tori said. "Why? What on earth would make Ty Chapman snap like that? He's got everything going for him."

"Have you decided who you're going to call in your case in chief?" Jeanie asked.

"Probably Ted Moran," I said. "He knows the Chapmans as well as anyone. He can provide great character evidence."

"It's so thin though," Tori said.

"Johnson can't prove premeditation," Jeanie said. "He can prove brutality, but that's not the same thing."

"He can prove Ty Chapman was standing in the parking lot talking to John Lansky for nobody knows how long. He can prove he walked back into the woods behind the Harmon Arms with him and only one of them came back out."

"But maybe the brutality is the thing that will make the jury think it wasn't premeditated," Tori offered. "Angry. Yes. Rage. Yes. But if Chapman, for whatever reason, decided John Lansky needed to be dead that day, he clearly didn't plan it. He simply grabbed the nearest thing he could, a rock."

"Several rocks," I said. "And premeditation doesn't have to be hours or days in advance. It could be minutes. Arguably even seconds."

"Still," Jeanie said. "The Boyds said they saw Chapman with Lansky. They aren't eyewitnesses to a murder. You can hit that hard. Nobody knows what happened in those woods. What led up to it. John Lansky can't say and Ty Chapman doesn't have to. I still say at best he's looking at second degree. Which is bad enough ..."

"But what Chapman expects," I said. "It's the thing he's said to me like a mantra from day one. He just wants me to keep him from a life sentence."

"Well, then," Tori said. "Odds are good that's what he'll get. Johnson isn't offering a plea deal yet? That's the part I don't understand."

"He wants a win," I said. "He thinks this case is a sure-fire victory against me and can help set him up for his election next year."

"Hell of a gamble, just to satisfy his wounded ego," Jeanie said.

I kept staring at the crime scene photos of John Lansky's remains. The jury would see them. All of them. All the hair-splitting legal arguments in the world wouldn't stop regular people from being horrified by them. I still was.

Tori was dead on her feet. She kept trying to suppress a yawn.

"No reason to keep staring at this with me," I told her. "Go home. Sleep in tomorrow. I'll need you plenty next week and there's nothing else to do here. We're pretty much just jumping off a cliff."

"At least it's a very well-funded cliff this time," Jeanie joked.

Tori didn't argue. She simply thanked me, grabbed her things, and headed for the parking lot.

"I should have had Matty come pick her up," I said.

"She won't break," Jeanie said as soon as we heard the downstairs door shut. "That girl's tougher than she looks."

"She has no idea what she's in for, Jeanie," I said. "Neither does my idiot brother."

"Would you have preferred if she hadn't kept the baby?"

"No," I said quickly. "Of course not. As much as I'm worried about them, I'm excited for me. I get to be an aunt again. It's my favorite."

Jeanie smiled. "Good. Because I can't wait to get my hands on that little nugget. We could use another baby around here. Unless you're planning on getting busy, this one will have to do."

I laughed. "Bite your tongue!"

"How's that going?" Jeanie said, diving right into the heart of things as she always did. "You and my favorite defective detective?"

"Good," I said. "Slow and steady. Drama free. It's been nice to just ... be ..."

She nodded while pursing her lips. "No drama, huh? What about the other one? Any word from the Irishman?"

I started gathering my things. "No," I said.

"You worried?"

"I'm trying to stay too busy for that."

"You think he's dead?"

Jeanie's blunt words went through me like a gunshot.

"Jeanie!"

"I'm sorry! But I have to ask. The guy leads a dangerous lifestyle. That kind of thing is bound to catch up with him. I'm not wishing for it. I'm just trying to be practical."

I rose, heartbeat thundering. "I don't know," I said. "No. I don't think he's dead."

"Based on what?"

"Based on ... I don't know. I just think I'd know."

"Well," Jeanie said, rising with me. "As long as everything's drama free and going okay with you and Wray."

"Stop it," I said.

"I love you, kid. You know that. But you've got your mind on more than this trial. I know you. And I'm not the only one. Eric's playing it cool. He certainly brought enough of his own baggage into your relationship. But at a certain point, you're going to have to stop jumping every time those Irish eyes start smiling at you."

"I can be concerned," I said. "It's not the same thing as jumping. And I do not jump."

Jeanie laughed as we walked out to our cars together. "Well," she said. "You at least hop to a little."

"Cram it," I said, heaving my bag into the backseat of my Jeep.

She was still laughing at her own joke as she drove away.

Chapter 17

"COLD. That's the kind of person who committed this crime. Cold and calculating. Inhuman. And the evidence you're about to see? What happened to John Lansky will shock you. Horrify you. Members of the jury, I've been prosecuting murder cases for twenty years. I can tell you, this is one of the most brutal crimes I've ever seen."

Rafe Johnson hit his stride right out of the gate. He stood at the lectern, making eye contact with every member of the jury in turn. We had an even split. Six men. Six women. Four baby boomers. Four Gen Xers. Four millennials. Rafe held their attention as he laid out his case.

Beside me, Ty Chapman sat expressionless. He was handsome though. Beth had picked out a smart blue tailored suit with a red tie for him. He was clean-shaven with his hair cut in the short, military style that favored his strong, square jaw. Behind him, his very pregnant wife sat, looking like she'd just stepped off a runway in a white suit accented with a blue scarf tied at her neck.

"John Lansky wasn't just murdered. He was mutilated. Beaten into something that barely looked human. The police couldn't even rely on dental records to identify him. Every bone in his face was shattered, ladies and gentlemen," Rafe continued.

"You'll hear how the defendant, Tyler Chapman, lured Mr. Lansky into the secluded woods behind the Harmon Arms. How he beat this man using his fists and rocks as weapons."

I made a quick note on the pad in front of me. Ty kept staring straight ahead.

"Then he fled," Rafe said. "John Lansky put up a fight. He tried to defend himself. Tyler Chapman bears the scars from that fight. You'll hear how he ran from the crime scene and tried to cover up this heinous act. Cold. Calculating, but ultimately, ineffective. The defendant thought he'd silenced John Lansky that night. Took away his voice. He was wrong though. The evidence, and there is a mountain of it, I assure you, will show how Tyler Chapman left a literal trail of breadcrumbs leading away from the scene, right to his front door."

Rafe never moved. He stood rod straight at the lectern. "The defense ... well ... they have none. There is simply no other explanation for what happened out behind the Harmon Arms than what I've just told you. Tyler Chapman went to the Harmon Arms. He spoke with John Lansky at length. Then he took him behind the motel. We don't know why. That's true. But we don't have to. It doesn't matter. What matters is what happened next. The defendant, Tyler Chapman, picked up a rock and caved John Lansky's head in. Lansky fell to his knees. Pleaded for his life, perhaps. But those pleas were ignored. Mr. Tyler beat the man to a bloody pulp, spraying evidence all around. So violent were his actions, Mr. Chapman's phone flew out of his hand or his pocket. It was found just a few yards away from Lansky's body. The evidence will show how he tried to find it, but failed. Because he knew. Tyler Chapman knew the evidence out at the crime scene would allow the police to catch him cold. And that's just what they did. Once you've heard all the evidence. Once you've endured the horrific account of John Lansky's final moments, you'll be able to give him back his voice. You'll be able to deliver justice for him and find Tyler Chapman guilty of the cold, premeditated killing of John Lansky. Thank you."

From the corner of my eye, I saw Beth Chapman begin to cry. Ted Moran's wife Bridget sat beside her. As a potential witness, Ted wasn't in the courtroom but Bridget's presence had a calming effect on Beth.

Ty leaned forward, folding his hands, and resting them on the table. As he did, I saw crescent-shaped marks in the meat of his palms where he'd dug his nails into his skin.

"Ms. Leary?" Judge Able Hughes said. "Are you prepared to deliver your opening statement?"

"I am, Your Honor," I said. I put my pen down on my notepad and walked up to the lectern.

"Good morning," I addressed the jury. "My counterpart, Mr. Johnson, is right about a lot of things in this case. He's right that what happened to Mr. Lansky was horrific. He's right that it's one of the worst crime scenes there is. Believe me, I want to find justice for John Lansky too. I want answers. Regardless of the kind of man John Lansky might have been, he deserves answers and justice for what happened."

I moved to the side of the lectern, making sure the jury had an unobstructed view of both Ty and Beth Chapman.

"Your job," I said, "isn't easy. You're being charged with deciding a man's fate. You're being asked to review the evidence in this case. Evidence that will be difficult to bear. But Mr. Johnson is going to ask you to render a decision on that evidence *because* it is so difficult to bear. Not because it points to my client's guilt beyond a reasonable doubt.

"He will play on your emotions, your sense of decency. You'll want to give into that. There is no denying the brutality of John Lansky's death. But here's the problem. Mr. Johnson can tell you a lot about what caused John Lansky's death. That's not in dispute. But he will not be able to tell you what happened in those woods. He cannot prove that Tyler Chapman is guilty of John Lansky's premeditated murder. He cannot prove Mr. Chapman killed him. Plain and simple."

I walked back to the defense table, pivoted on my heel, then took my place back at the lectern. "It looks bad," I said. "That, members of the jury, will be the entire crux of the prosecution's case in this matter. It *looks* bad. Mr. Lansky's fate, certainly. We cannot spare you having to witness the aftermath of that. It *looks* bad.

"But that isn't enough," I said. "The state must prove each and every element of the crimes charged beyond a reasonable doubt. That means, among other things, that if there are alternate interpretations for the facts of this case … interpretations that would not incriminate Mr. Chapman … then you have to give him the benefit of the doubt.

"I'm asking you to keep an open mind. Mr. Lansky is not who the prosecution wants you to think he is. Mr. Chapman is not who the prosecution wants you to think he is. And it is up to Mr. Johnson to prove to you that his interpretation of the facts is the correct one. It cannot just look bad."

They kept eye contact. That was a good thing. But years of jury trials and my own instincts told me this panel would be particularly hard to read.

Tori sat on the bench behind Ty Chapman, just to the left of Beth. She scribbled on her own notepad, trying to record any and all observations she had of the jury members' body language. I'd come to rely on her keen eye.

"The judge will instruct you on just how high a burden reasonable doubt is," I said. "But once Mr. Johnson is done presenting his evidence, I challenge each and every one of you to ask yourself this simple question. Is this real proof of guilt? Or does this just look bad? I'm confident that by the end of this trial, you'll see Mr. Johnson's case won't pass the test. Tyler Chapman is not guilty of the crimes for which he's been charged. Thank you."

"All right," Judge Hughes said. "We'll take a brief, fifteen-minute recess, then reconvene."

The deputies ushered Ty and me into the conference room next to the courtroom. Beth was able to quickly squeeze her husband's hand but she would not be permitted to wait with us.

"The hard part is coming," I said to Ty once the door was shut.

"I hate that she's going through this," Ty said. His voice cracked. It was the first time I'd ever seen even the hint of emotion in him. "Beth looks so tired. Can you promise me that however this turns out, you'll make sure she's okay? I have some other money saved. I can take care of her."

"Let's just get through the day," I said. "Beth has support. She's going to be okay."

"But I trust you," he said. "You can look out for her. Just promise me you'll stay close to her."

"You're my client," I said. "You're my priority. But the Morans. The other families from the Veterans Center. Believe me, they are looking out for Beth."

"She doesn't have anyone," he said. "No family. Neither of us do. That's why we were drawn to each other initially."

"Ty," I said. "There will be time to worry about all of that later. Trust me."

He met my eyes. "I do," he said. There was gravity in his tone that unsettled me for a moment.

"Good."

"Who is he going to call first?" he asked. "The first witness."

"He'll either call the lead detective or the first deputy on scene," I said. "He's going to start with the crime scene. He'll want to get those photographs of Lansky's body seared into the jury's mind right up front. That's what you have to prepare for."

"What do you need from me?" he asked. "Should I react?"

Still, he kept that laser stare on me. "I won't coach you on your reactions, Ty," I said. "Anger from you is the only thing I'm worried about. The jury is going to need to believe you're capable of beating John Lansky to death. Try not to give them any help."

He nodded. "I understand."

There was a knock on the door. Tori poked her head in. "They're ready for you," she said. "I've asked Bridget Moran to take Beth down to the coffee shop. She's feeling a little nauseous. We can't have her losing it when those crime scene photos come up."

Tori's pregnancy worried me on that score as well.

"Are you going to be okay?" I asked her. "Frankly, you losing your lunch in there is far worse than Mrs. Chapman doing it."

Tori gave me a weak smile. "I'm okay. I've seen them before."

The bailiff appeared at her shoulder. "Judge is ready to go," he said. Ty rose. He held the door for Tori in a gentlemanly gesture. She looked so tiny standing beside him. The man's hands were huge. As we made our way back into the courtroom, I advised Ty to keep his hands folded in his lap and out of sight. It would be far too easy for the jury to imagine him holding a large rock in his palm.

And then caving John Lansky's skull in with it.

Chapter 18

DEPUTY DETECTIVE RODNEY PATEL usually left an impression with juries before he uttered a single word. Reedy, thin, tall, with a pair of menacing dark eyes, he rarely, if ever, moved from his straight-backed posture, perched at the edge of the witness chair. It made him seem serious, intense. He was that. But Deputy Patel also had a literal stick up his back. A seven-inch titanium rod fusing his spine together after an on-duty car crash that left him in a coma for two weeks. That was ten years ago. He'd refused to take a desk job and instead poured himself into his work until he got promoted to one of two homicide detectives working for Woodbridge County.

"Detective," Rafe Johnson said. "Can you describe what you're seeing in the photographs marked for identification?"

He did.

"Mr. Lansky was found lying on his left side in a fetal position," Patel said. "At first, I thought he'd been decapitated. I couldn't ... I couldn't see what was left of his head."

The photographs came next. Much as I wanted to keep the jury ... or all of humanity ... from ever seeing them, there was no way around it.

"The victim's head had been essentially pulverized," Patel went on. "The area where he was found ... it's a small clearing about four hundred yards from the rear of the Harmon Arms Motel. The motel doesn't own the land. It's actually owned by the county. There's a drainage ditch to the northwest. A cell phone tower sits on the northeast quadrant of it. Mr. Lansky's body was located maybe three hundred yards from that."

"What else struck you about the crime scene?" Johnson asked.

"It's a relatively flat area. There's actually a small walking trail back there. Made from use, not intention. A lot of the motel guests use it to walk their dogs, jog, that sort of thing. There has also been drug activity. Anyway, I noticed several large rocks strewn along the path. That was unusual because like I said, we're talking about a fairly worn path in the thickest part of these woods. I shined a light on them and saw a dark, reddish-brown staining that later turned out to be the victim's blood."

"And what did you conclude from that, if anything?"

"I was looking at the murder weapon," he said. "Or several of them. We found bits of bone and gray matter embedded in several of the larger rocks. Mr. Lansky was beaten to death, sir."

"What other investigative steps did you take, Detective?"

Patel led Johnson through his investigation. He had officers canvassing the area, questioning every guest staying at the motel as well as the night manager. No one had seen or heard anything until Patel himself knocked on Brian and Melissa Boyd's door.

"What did the Boyds tell you?" Johnson asked.

"Well," Patel started. "I asked if they'd seen or heard anything unusual the night before. At the time I questioned them, we were still trying to establish a timeline. Mr. Kennedy, the man who discovered the victim's body, had been out walking his dog at five in the morning. I'm not a medical expert. But my experience at that point told me that Mr. Lansky's body hadn't been there that long."

"Based on what?" Johnson asked.

"Based on the fact that the blood on those rocks looked fresh. It was still wet in places. Also, and I don't know how to put this more delicately, but the bugs hadn't gotten to him yet. It was November, but we hadn't had a good frost yet. Anyway, the night manager started his shift at six p.m. the preceding evening. He reported having seen Mr. Lansky getting something from the lobby vending machine just after he punched in. The security cameras in the lobby confirmed that. They showed a man loosely fitting Lansky's description at 1813 hours. Or six thirteen p.m."

"What do you mean, loosely fitting his description?" Johnson asked.

"Well, sir," Patel said. "I didn't know what the victim looked like at that point. On account of the fact, he pretty much didn't have a face when I saw him. But the man in the security footage was wearing the same clothes. Blue flannel checkered shirt, jeans, and a pair of tan work boots. So I was pretty sure I was looking at my murder victim at that point. So, I theorized the murder had to have taken place between six thirteen p.m. and approximately five a.m. the following morning."

"Objection," I said. "Foundation. We don't have a murder, Your Honor."

Johnson merely nodded. I knew it was a nitpick of an objection, but my whole defense rested on the idea Johnson wouldn't be able to prove the elements of his most serious charge.

"Sustained," Judge Hughes said. "Let's have the word murder stricken from the record and the jury is instructed to disregard it. You may proceed, Mr. Johnson."

"Thank you, Your Honor," Rafe said. "So you were able to establish that Mr. Lansky died sometime in a roughly twelve-hour period from the evening of the 10th to the morning of the 11th."

"Yes, sir," Patel answered.

"All right. So, what did you do next?"

Patel described how the night manager identified Lansky as his tenant from room 24. From there, Patel was able to find Lansky's mugshot from his robbery arrest. By the next day, Patel was able to positively identify Lansky from his fingerprints. From there, the Boyds identified Lansky as the man they saw talking to Chapman from that mugshot.

"We found a cell phone registered to Tyler Chapman," Patel explained. "I brought Mr. Chapman in for questioning and he was unable to establish his whereabouts for the evening in question."

"Objection!" I said, standing. "The witness is assuming facts not in evidence!"

"Counsel, approach," Judge Hughes said.

Ty Chapman kept his poker face in place. So did Detective Patel.

"Your Honor," I said. "Ty Chapman, as is his constitutional right, gave no statement to the police. What this witness just said is tantamount to a comment ... a judgment ... on the defendant's right against self-incrimination. He can't refer to it. He can't project guilt because of it."

"Mr. Johnson?" Judge Hughes said.

"We're talking mountains and molehills here," Rafe said. "Chapman *didn't* establish his whereabouts that evening."

"He doesn't have to," I said, getting hotter. "And your witness knows that. You know that. He just telegraphed to the jury he thinks Chapman is guilty by omission. The lead detective in your case. It's grounds for a mistrial."

"Are you making that motion now, Ms. Leary?" the judge asked.

"I am," I blurted. It was a big swing.

"Your Honor," Johnson started.

"Save it," the judge said. "I'm not granting a mistrial over that. But Detective, you know better. Do better."

On brand, Patel's face didn't change.

"I'll instruct the jury to disregard the last bit of Detective Patel's answer. You may proceed, Mr. Johnson. With caution."

I wanted to storm back to my table. Instead, I regathered my cool and took my place beside Ty as Rafe finished his direct examination.

"Detective Patel," he said. "Did Mr. Chapman give a statement?"

"No, sir," Patel said. "But I observed some scratches on his hand. A fresh cut above his eye. Also, he was wearing a button-down shirt and I could see the edge of a bandage poking out near his collar. As if he had a wound on his chest."

"What did you do next?"

"Mr. Chapman asked me if he was free to leave. I took his picture. I then arranged for the Boyds to look at a photo array. They identified Tyler Chapman as the man they saw talking to John Lansky. And the man they saw running away from the scene with visible injury to his face and chest. That, coupled with finding Chapman's cell phone at the scene, I felt I had probable cause to arrest Tyler Chapman. I secured an arrest warrant and search warrants. We brought Mr. Chapman in and documented his injuries in accordance with booking him."

Johnson introduced the photographs of Ty Chapman's wounds. He had a cut above his right brow. Several scratches on his hands, and the worst. Deep gouges to his chest on his left pectoral muscle just above his heart. They looked, unmistakably, like claw marks.

"Thank you, Detective," Johnson said while that final image of Ty with his marred chest displayed on the overhead. "I have no more questions."

"Ms. Leary?" Judge Hughes said. "You may proceed."

I knew I'd never get Rodney Patel to contradict himself on the stand. My best strategy would be to get him away from the jury as quickly as I could, seeding the questions I would raise in my closing arguments.

"Detective," I started. "You indicated that Mr. and Mrs. Boyd said the man they saw running from the Harmon Arms parking lot had injuries to his face and neck area, correct?"

"That's what they said, yes."

"This photo array you arranged for them to view, isn't it true that Tyler Chapman was the only person depicted with cuts to his face?"

"They recognized Mr. Chapman from when he was speaking to the victim in the parking lot. They saw him walk behind the motel with Mr. Lansky."

"That's not what I asked you," I said. "Please refer to exhibit twenty-seven. This is the photo array you showed the Boyds, isn't it?"

"It is," he said.

"Tyler Chapman is the only man in this array with a visible cut to his brow, isn't that correct?"

"Yes," Patel said.

"Isn't it also true that you were never able to establish any kind of prior connection between John Lansky and Tyler Chapman?"

"In what way?"

"Well, you have no evidence that they knew each other."

"Not specifically, no."

"Not specifically or generally, correct?"

"Well, no."

"You have Mr. Chapman's phone. You have Mr. Lansky's phone. There were no calls or texts between them."

"No, ma'am."

"In fact, you weren't able to find a single witness who ever saw Chapman and Lansky together prior to the events of November 10th."

"Prior to? No."

"And isn't it true that the night manager ... well ... in fact ... any manager at the Harmon Arms, had never seen Tyler Chapman before, had they? Or did you even ask?"

"I asked," he said. "They'd never seen him before. But as I testified, the Boyds saw them together."

"Detective," I said. "I just want to clarify. You said in your direct testimony that the area behind the Harmon Arms is known for drug activity. What do you mean by that?"

"I mean it's a spot where historically, dealers have met up with clients."

"In fact, you're aware, aren't you, of specific drug stings targeting the Harmon Arms and the area around it, right?"

"Sure," he said. "We've run stings there. It's actually been better over there in the last year because of those stings."

"And yet," I said, "you never questioned any dealers in connection to John Lansky's death, isn't that right?"

"There was no evidence of drug activity back there that night," he said.

"Because you didn't ask," I said.

"Objection," Rafe said. "Counsel is giving speeches now?"

"Sustained," Hughes said.

"I'll move on," I conceded. Patel had said enough for me to draw on in my closing remarks later. "To be clear, Detective, you said you had to rely on DNA and fingerprints to positively identify John Lansky. Correct?"

"That's right."

"He didn't have ID on him, did he?"

"He didn't, no."

"And you didn't find ID in his hotel room either, did you?"

"No."

"His wallet was missing, wasn't it?" I said.

"Correct."

"Got it," I said. "Thank you. Detective, how many homicides have you worked?"

"I don't know the exact number, but it's been dozens and dozens."

"More than a hundred?"

"Probably shy of that."

"And you've worked plenty of assault cases, haven't you?"

"Yes."

"How would you compare the scene where Mr. Lansky was found with other similar cases?"

"What do you mean?"

"Well," I said. "Did you draw any conclusions about the type of person who might have committed this act?"

"Of course This was an unusually violent killing."

"Unusually violent," I said. "So the perpetrator was likely enraged?"

"Undoubtedly," he said. "We're talking explosive anger here. Whoever did this didn't just want to kill John Lansky. He wanted to obliterate him off the planet. This was some intense rage."

I paused. Beside me, Tyler Chapman stayed stock still.

"Thank you," I said. "I have no further questions."

Rafe Johnson apparently felt no need to redirect. That surprised me. I wondered if it was more about his desire to rattle me than anything else. It didn't work.

"Detective," Judge Hughes said. "You're free to go. With the lateness of the hour, let's adjourn until tomorrow morning."

Judge Hughes banged his gavel, dismissing the jury.

I gave Ty a nod of encouragement as the deputy led him away. Behind me, Beth Chapman waited. When her husband left the room, she grabbed my arm. "Cass," she said. "We need to talk."

Chapter 19

I HAD ONLY a few minutes with my client before they took him back to lock up. Beth Chapman took the opportunity to follow me into the room next door. The deputy stood at the door while Ty took a seat.

"Beth," he said quietly. "You don't look well. You should go home and get some rest."

Her face was flushed. She grabbed at her throat as I closed the door behind her.

"How can you sit there?" she said. "The both of you. How can you sit there and let them say all of those things? You have to do something, Ty. Cass, you have to make him do something."

I took a breath, trying not to state the obvious. What exactly was it that she expected me to do? As long as Ty refused to give me any explanation for what happened behind the Harmon Arms, I was left with holding Rafe Johnson to his proofs as our best defense.

"Beth," Ty said. "I really think it's time for you to go home. It's not good for you and the baby to sit inside the courtroom day after day."

"Maybe not," I interjected. "But it's the only thing that's doing you any good at the moment."

"This was a mistake," Beth said. "This whole thing. Ty, you have to ..."

"Enough," he said, the word sharp and cutting.

"No," Beth said, crying. "It's not enough. It's not nearly enough. I've sat quietly. I've let you handle this the way you wanted. I've ..."

"You've sat quietly?" Ty said. He looked at Beth, then stared at a point on the wall. The dynamic between them shifted. With her eyes, her body language, the tension that poured off her, Beth Chapman was trying desperately to convey something to her husband.

"You have to stop this," she said. I didn't immediately know if she meant it for me or for Ty.

He said nothing. He kept staring at the wall.

I took a seat at the table opposite him. "Ty, Beth's not wrong. Detective Patel's testimony was rough. I got in a few hits, but not nearly enough. If there's something you're not telling me. Please. There's still time to help yourself. Did John Lansky threaten you? Did he threaten Beth?"

Beth stopped pacing. She clutched at her gold necklace. Hard enough I thought surely the clasp would break. She craned her neck until tiny veins began to pop out along the column of her throat. She seemed almost to be trying to speak to Ty telepathically.

"Do you two need a moment alone? I can ..."

"No," Ty said. "I need to go back to my cell. I'm tired. It's been a long day."

"Ty," she said.

"I said it's been a long day," he repeated.

"They're calling the Boyds first thing in the morning," I said. "They'll definitely put you at the scene the evening Lansky was killed. I'll make an issue of the way the photo array was conducted, just like I did with Patel. But that's the thinnest of straws and not enough for reasonable doubt."

"It is," Beth said. "It has to be. They said they were looking at someone with a cut on his face. Ty was the only one with ..."

"They saw him before he was cut, Beth," I said. "They each picked him out independent of each other. But to think ..."

"They were coached," she said. "You argue they were coached by that detective."

"Right," I said, nodding. "Only Ty's phone was found at the crime scene. His blood was found at the crime scene. Even if Melissa and Brian Boyd never saw a thing, we'd be in the same place we are now."

"Go home now, Beth," Ty said. "Don't come to court tomorrow. You need to get some rest."

"I don't think that's a good idea," I said. "Whether you like it or not, appearances matter. If Beth isn't in the courtroom the day after Detective Patel testified, the jury is going to wonder why. They might assume that Beth finally, after hearing that testimony, decided she can't stand by you anymore."

"I'm not going anywhere," Beth said. "I'm going to do my job."

Her job. It was an odd way to put it. Accurate, yes, but colder than every other thing Beth had said. She put emphasis on the word my. At first, I thought it was a dig at me. But the entire time, she kept her eyes locked on her husband's.

"I don't care what they think," he said. "You need to stay home, Beth."

"You need to care what the jury thinks," I said. "It's the only thing that matters. The judge will instruct them to regard only the admitted evidence in this case, but they won't. They will judge every single thing they see and hear this week. What you wear. What I wear. Your facial expressions. The noises you make. You won't be testifying so the only way you get to tell any part of your story is how you conduct yourself in there. How I conduct myself in there."

"Ty, please," Beth said, crying again.

Finally he met his wife's gaze. I watched as his eyes flicked over her face. He'd been like a statue. Now, a tiny muscle jumped in his jaw. Then he looked away.

The deputy poked his head in. "Time to go, Chapman."

Ty rose.

"No," Beth said. "Please. Just a little more time."

"See that she gets home," Ty said to me. "I don't think Beth should be driving."

Ty put his hands together, holding them in front of himself so the deputy could easily put his cuffs on. He led him quietly out of the room, shutting the door behind him.

Beth broke down. She sank into the chair her husband had just vacated. I gave her a moment to collect herself. After a few minutes, she slowly raised her head and met my eyes.

"Beth," I said. "You know something. Don't you? What was it you wanted to talk to me about?"

She blinked rapidly. "I just ... I wanted Ty to know how I felt."

"He knows how you feel," I said. "But that's not what you said. You specifically said you wanted to talk to me. You're holding something back. I know he is."

All of a sudden, something came over Beth. She stared at a different point on the wall like her husband had before her. She'd been ready to tell me something. And now, after a few moments in Ty's presence, she had changed her mind.

"Beth," I said. "Do you understand what's happening?"

She looked at me. "My husband is on trial for murder. Of course I understand."

"No," I said. "Your husband is going to be convicted of first-degree murder. As of right now, if this trial were to go to the jury today, he's done. He will go to prison. No opportunity for parole. He won't be here when your child is born. Your child won't know him at all except for random visiting days."

"If you do your job ..." she started.

"I'm doing my job," I said. "I'll argue nobody saw Ty kill John Lansky. I'll create some kind of alternate story. A fantasy.

Praying the jury somehow takes pity on you or on Ty and brings in a verdict for a lesser charge. Second degree murder, probably. That was my point with Detective Patel. I got him to admit that the injuries inflicted on Lansky were made by someone in an intense, violent rage. People don't usually plan for that type of violence, Beth. It comes on suddenly. They snap. Something happens. A crime of passion. Heat of the moment. That's the argument. But even if I succeed, it's likely the judge would sentence Ty to the maximum. That's twenty years. Twenty years. Your baby's entire childhood. That's if Ty survived it. If you did."

"I know all of this," she said. "Don't you think I know all of this?"

"No," I said. "I think you came to me expecting some kind of miracle because of my reputation. Because I'm friends with Ted Moran. Because I successfully defended Aubrey Ames."

"I have to go now," Beth said.

"What is it?" I said more forcefully. "What aren't you and Ty telling me? Lansky did something to you. Or he did something to Ty. I have to know what it is. If he was defending you, I can use that, Beth. Were you with him? Did Lansky approach you? Hurt you? Try to hurt you like he did Ellen Colby?"

She wiped a tear from her eye. "I really have to go."

"Who are you protecting?" I asked. "Ty? Not telling me the truth is going to bury him, Beth. Your child's father. If you have the ability to stop that, don't you want to?"

She rose. "I don't have anything that can help you."

"But you have something. You know something. I saw the looks between you. Ty's keeping you from saying something. Is he trying to protect someone?"

A tremor went through her, but Beth kept on walking toward the door. Her step quickened. Earlier, she'd seemed desperate to talk to me. Now, she was desperate to get away.

I banged my fist against the table. "Beth!"

"I'll see you tomorrow," she said. "Ty's right. I don't feel very well. Maybe I'll stay home."

"You can't."

Beth hustled down the hallway, leaving me frustrated and confused in her wake.

Chapter 20

When I got back to the house, Eric was waiting with a glass of wine and some reheated shrimp hibachi from my favorite food truck.

"I love you," I said.

He smiled. "I figured you need it."

"You heard about Patel's testimony?"

"He's unshakable," Eric said. "Other than myself, he's one of the guys I'd trust to handle the investigation if anyone I cared about was murdered."

His face fell then. Someone he cared about had been murdered.

"Anyone else?" he said quietly.

I kicked my feet up. Eric took them in his lap and started rubbing my arches. I let out an involuntary moan of pleasure.

"You have no end of redeeming qualities, do you?" I asked.

He gave me a suggestive waggle of his eyebrows. I snorted wine as I laughed.

"I'm not ashamed to admit it," he said. "But I'll be glad when this trial is over. I wish you hadn't taken it."

I leaned my head back on one of the couch pillows. "Detective Wray, for once, I agree with you on all points. I should have followed my gut, not my bank ledger. It's not too late for you to jump ship and join me though?"

He laughed. "Now, she says. When her ship is actually sinking."

I playfully kicked at him. "I'm not done yet," I said. "I have a few tricks up my sleeve still."

He nodded. "Lansky. He wasn't just a mild-mannered handyman."

"You've looked at his record," I said.

"It's out there," he said. "But you know you won't be able to use a lot of it. Or any of it, maybe. If there was something I could do to help ..."

"Could you try and help me find someone?" I asked.

He didn't answer right away, but gave me a dubious glance. I pulled my feet out of his grasp and set my wine glass on the coffee table. Reaching over, I grabbed a notepad out of my bag and tore off a page. I handed it to him.

Eric read the name. Ellen Colby.

"Allegedly, Lansky assaulted her. Raped her and pretty much left her for dead."

Eric scowled. "That's not on his rap sheet."

"She recanted," I said. "But I saw a picture of her, Eric." Grabbing my phone, I pulled up the screenshot I'd taken at the probation officer's.

Eric held my phone out so he could make out the photo. "I mean ... a little? Maybe? Redhead, pretty ..."

"It's more than a little," I said. "Anyway. My attempts to find her have all been dead ends."

Eric handed the phone back to me. "Johnson would never let you call her to the stand anyway. It's irrelevant."

"I just want to talk to her. See what she has to say about Lansky and why she changed her story. She might not even know he's dead now."

"I don't know," he said. "I feel a little funny about it. She's a crime victim."

"Just a conversation," I said. "That's all. I'm not trying to upend this woman's life or anything."

"I'll see what I can find out. But no promises. This didn't even happen in Delphi, did it?"

"No," I said. "Flat Rock."

"Text me that picture." I did. Eric watched as I finished my dinner. Then he took it all from me and loaded the dishwasher.

"Thanks for all of this," I said. "It's nice having you around. It's nice coming home to you."

I hadn't quite planned to say that last bit. At least, not with the weight I'd said it. But once I had, I knew it was true. Eric paused as he held my empty wine glass in his hand.

"You heard from Agent Cannon lately?" he asked. His question had weight too. Eric knew my concern for Killian's whereabouts were on my mind. It hung there between us, an unspoken barrier. He hated that I still cared. He wouldn't say it.

"No," I said. "I'm trying to take that as good news. Like you said."

"Unless he's Hoffa, like you said," Eric responded. I knew he meant it as a joke, but he saw the change in my face before I could stop myself.

"Cass ..."

"It's okay," I said, smiling. I held up a hand.

"I'm sorry."

Nodding, I took his hand. I was too tired to argue. Too tired to say another word. I would have to do plenty of both in the morning as Rafe Johnson showed the blood trail leading straight to Ty Chapman, cementing his guilt if I couldn't find him a way out.

Chapter 21

"Detective Rayburn," Rafe said, first up the next morning. "Can you explain how you came to be involved in this case?"

"Sure," Emily Rayburn said as she leaned closer toward the microphone. "I'm assigned to the Crime Scene Unit for the Woodbridge County Sheriff's Department. I was contacted by Detective Patel, the lead investigator on this case, to assist in processing an area behind the Harmon Arms motel, where the victim's body was found."

Johnson then went through Emily Rayburn's extensive background in criminal forensics. She was new to the Delphi area, having served in the same role at the Wayne County Sheriff's Department. Her hire was a feather in the cap of Sheriff Lubell. Part of an election promise he'd managed to fulfill. Within a few minutes, Johnson got to the meat of Detective Rayburn's testimony.

"There were several distinct blood patterns found out at the scene," she said. "The largest concentration of blood was pooled beneath the victim, John Lansky. It came from a massive wound he had to his head."

Once again, the jury was treated to the grisly crime scene photos showing what was left of Lansky's face.

"Additionally, we located a few splatter patterns on the fallen leaves and surrounding trees, here and here." She used a pointer to illuminate several areas where blood had fallen.

"Were you able to identify whose blood this belonged to?" Rafe asked.

"Oh yes," Detective Rayburn said. "What I'm showing here in exhibits thirteen through twenty-one, the splatter pattern on the leaves and tree trunks, those belonged to the victim, John Lansky. They were consistent with him being struck on the right side of the head. Based on the trajectory and the position of the body, I believe, to a reasonable degree of scientific certainty, that Mr. Lansky was struck while he was on his knees and facing his assailant. You see here, in the next photograph, Mr. Lansky was found lying in a fetal position on his left side, the most significant wounding to his head having occurred on the right side. The blood pooled beneath him, but then we have another splatter pattern on this tree just a foot from where the body lay."

"Why is that significant, in your opinion?" Rafe asked.

"Well," she said. "The victim was already on the ground. I believe that he was struck again several times after he was either already mortally wounded, or had already died."

"What other significant findings did you make out there, Detective Rayburn?"

"Well, here," she said, scrolling through the photographs. "Beginning approximately five feet from the victim, there is a distinct trail of blood leading away from the victim's body."

"Can you describe it to the jury? For the record."

"Of course," she said. "These are droplets of blood. They occur in a more or less straight line."

"Why is that significant?"

"Well, what you have here is evidence that this person suffered an injury and was bleeding enough that the blood dripped down while he walked or ran away. The droplets occur at intervals which suggest the defendant was running, or at least walking briskly."

"Objection," I said. "The witness is assuming facts not in evidence." Ty Chapman kept his hands folded on the table in front of him. He had a fresh scar across his right knuckles that would come into play momentarily.

"Sustained, Mr. Johnson," Judge Hughes said.

"My apologies," Detective Rayburn said.

"Detective," Johnson continued. "Were you able to determine who might have shed that second pattern of blood?"

"Yes," she said. "Upon his arrest, DNA samples were taken from the defendant, Tyler Chapman. They were a match with this smaller blood trail leading away from the crime scene. As you can see in the photograph, this trail led all the way to the northwest entry point to the parking lot of the Harmon Arms."

Later, I knew Rafe would tie Detective Rayburn's analysis to the exact location where both Melissa and Brian Boyd claimed they saw Ty emerge.

"And then they disappear?" Rafe asked.

"First the droplets become less frequent. But yes, then they disappear."

"Thank you, Detective, I have nothing further."

"Ms. Leary?" the judge asked.

I rose. "Thank you. Detective Rayburn," I said. "You can't say for certain what type of injury would have caused this droplet pattern, could you?"

"Not for certain, no," she said. "It's one that was actively bleeding. Profusely, I might add."

"Profusely," I said. "So you think this person was hurt badly?"

"He was wounded, yes," she said. "I couldn't answer whether he was hurting. Those are two separate issues."

"Fair enough," I said. "You indicated that this blood trail, as it were, led away from the victim. Is that correct?"

"It is, yes."

"But none of the defendant's blood was found on the victim himself, correct?"

"That's correct."

"And none of Mr. Chapman's DNA, no skin, hair, nails, nothing like that, was found on or near the victim, correct?"

"That is correct."

"You didn't find skin under Mr. Lansky's fingernails, did you?"

"No."

"And you agree that the presence of Mr. Chapman's blood in those woods doesn't prove he killed the victim, does it?"

"Alone? No," she said. "If that's all you had, that would be problematic. But it isn't."

"And that's not the question I asked you," I said. "I asked you specifically. The presence of these blood droplets near where Mr. Lansky was found only proves that these blood droplets were near where Mr. Lansky was found, correct?"

"It proves that blood belonging to your client was found within a few feet of a man who was violently murdered, yes."

"Detective, you also cataloged the personal effects found on Mr. Lansky's body, didn't you?"

"Yes," she said. "That was within my purview."

"But you never found a wallet on Mr. Lansky, did you?"

"No."

"No money?"

"No. His pockets were empty."

"Empty," I said. "Not so much as a hotel key?"

"No," she said.

"To your knowledge, Mr. Lansky's wallet and room key were never found, isn't that right?"

"To my knowledge, that's true," she answered.

"In fact, Mr. Lansky had no valuables on him at all when he died, did he?"

"On him? No. We did find a ring belonging to the victim a few feet away from the body. It had his DNA on it."

"A ring," I said.

"Yes," she said. "Exhibit forty-nine."

"This ring?" I said, picking up the baggie containing the odd, silver ring found laying near Lansky's body. It was silver, with a domed top, much like a class ring.

"That ring," she answered.

"So I'm clear, the victim's wallet was missing. And you believe this ring was ripped from his finger?"

"I didn't say ripped," she said. "I just said it was found near him. I have no idea how it got there."

"Might have been dropped," I said.

"I'd say most likely it was dropped," she answered.

It might be inconsequential, but later I planned to argue to the jury that robbery might have been a motive for Lansky's killing. I would let them wonder whether Ty could have just been unlucky enough to happen upon a robbery or a drug deal in progress. A stretch, to be sure, but worth a shot.

"Thank you," I said. "I've got no further questions."

When I headed back to my chair, Ty Chapman was almost smiling. I had a vision of braining *him* with a rock.

"Your Honor," Rafe said, buttoning his suit jacket. "The state calls Deputy Paul May to the stand."

Rayburn and May passed each other coming and going. I knew May had one job and I knew it might be the most damning evidence of the entire trial next to the photographs of John Lansky's battered body.

"Deputy May," Johnson began. "I'd like to draw your attention to the photograph that's been marked as State's Exhibit fifty-eight. Can you describe it for me?"

"It's a picture of Tyler Chapman's torso," he said.

"Who took that picture? Under what circumstances?"

"I did," May said. "I was responsible for booking Mr. Chapman after his arrest for the murder of John Lansky."

"And is that photograph a fair and accurate representation of Mr. Chapman's appearance at the time of the booking?"

"It is," May said. "It's him."

"Your Honor," Johnson said. "I'd like to move for the admission of State's Exhibit fifty-eight into evidence."

"Ms. Leary?" he said.

"I object," I said. "Counsel has still failed to establish that this photograph's probative value outweighs potential prejudice to my client. As it was taken during Mr. Chapman's police booking procedure, it was, as such, taken many days after the victim was killed."

"Overruled," Judge Hughes said. I expected this. I'd made the same motion in a suppression hearing several weeks ago. But I had to renew that motion now that we were at trial. For all the good it would do.

Rafe went back to his laptop and displayed the photograph of Tyler Chapman, naked from the waist up as he stood against a solid blue wall, his expression blank.

In the photo, Ty's chest, above his heart, was raw and angry. Scratched and clawed. The center of the wound was particularly deep. Something, someone had gouged him there.

I knew what the jury saw. I knew what they might think. These were the wounds made by someone who had tried to kill Ty Chapman with his bare hands. It was the blessing and the curse of these photographs.

"Deputy May," Johnson said. "I'd like to direct your attention to the photograph that's been marked as State's Exhibit fifty-nine."

We went through the dance with five more photographs. Each time, my objections were overruled and the jury was allowed to see them.

A close-up of Ty Chapman's face showed the cut above his brow. Another photo showed fresh scabs on the cuts over his right knuckles. He'd punched something. Hard enough to rip the skin off. Deep enough that even common sense would dictate he had bled from these wounds. I knew the jury could easily imagine Ty's wounded hand, hanging by his side, dripping blood all the way back to the parking lot.

There was nothing more I could do. Those photographs would stick in the jury's mind. Something happened to Ty Chapman that night, just like it did John Lansky. And not even I knew what.

I took my seat at the table after the judge excused Deputy May.

"Mr. Johnson?" the judge said. "I think we may have time for one more witness."

"Yes, Your Honor," Johnson said. "At this time, the state calls Christopher Dvorak."

Ty stiffened beside me, surprised as I was. Dvorak was on my witness list, not Rafe Johnson's. I put a light hand on Ty's shoulder, encouraging him not to react. Then I fought like hell to do the same.

Chapter 22

"Mr. Dvorak," Rafe started. "Would you tell me how you know the defendant?"

Last week, Chris had stood in the courtroom with a contingent of Ty's supporters from the Veterans Center. Those men and women, including Chris, had stood in quiet, stoic solidarity with their brother in arms. Today, Chris was pale, shaky even. What on earth had changed?

I wrote a quick note to Ty. "What's he going to say?"

Ty waited a moment before writing back. When he did, he slowly picked up the pen and simply wrote a question mark. Terrific. We were heading up the top hill of the rollercoaster. I could almost hear the rickety wheels ticking up.

"I met Ty Chapman probably a year and a half ago now," Chris said. "I run the Delphi Veterans Center over on Holly Street. We're a non-profit."

"What's the purpose of the center?" Rafe asked.

"Lots of things. Basically, we're a community outreach program. Veterans from all military branches, active or retired, can enjoy the benefits of the center. It's a place to gather socially. We have game rooms. Televisions. Conference space. A coffee bar. We installed a fitness center last year. All of this was made possible through private donations and grant money. We provide resources for our membership. Whether it's counseling, or assistance with benefits, access to medical care. I mean, we don't provide health care, but we have staff members who can help counsel and guide veterans who are running into red tape with the V.A. or their private healthcare providers, that sort of thing."

"I see," Rafe said. "So back to my initial question, how did you become acquainted with Mr. Chapman?"

"Initially," Chris started, "I had some issues with the air conditioner and the furnace in the building. We renovated it ourselves. Again, all from volunteer work and donations. I was looking for somebody to come in and look at the HVAC system. I put a request out to the membership. Posted it on social media. Anyway, one of our members, Ted Moran, said he had a neighbor who might be able to help. A retired Marine. That was Ty. Again, we're talking about a year and a half ago now. Ty came out."

"He fixed your furnace?"

"He did," Chris said. "Installed a new one. Did some duct work. I got the materials through a private donation. I just needed someone to do the install. That was Ty. After that, he started coming to the center on a more regular basis. Socially."

"Socially," Rafe said. "Can you be more specific?"

"I work with a lot of people," Chris said. "I can't specifically recall when and what function or service Ty first availed himself of. I know we had a cookout and cornhole tournament that summer. Ty was there. He came with his wife, Beth. That's probably the first time I can recall really talking to Ty on a personal or social level. We became friendly. After that, he started hanging out at the center. He'd come to poker nights. He volunteered for the building maintenance crew. You know, just started doing some work around the building as it needed it."

"So you and Tyler Chapman became close?" Rafe said.

"I don't know what you mean by close. We were friends. We *are* friends."

"Did you see Ty Chapman outside of the center?"

"You mean around town? Sure. It's Delphi."

"Did you hang out with him socially outside of the center?" Rafe asked.

"Not really one on one, if that's what you mean. We did some outings, like to the Casino down in Toledo or in Detroit. Ty and Beth went to some of those. I had a party at my house for the Michigan-Ohio State game. I seem to recall Ty coming to that. If you're asking me how many times we hung out, I can't tell you that. But I'd consider him a friend. Ty's a good guy."

"A good guy," Rafe asked. "Did you and the defendant ever discuss his time in the military?"

"What do you mean?"

"I mean, did Tyler Chapman ever tell you where he served, what he did?"

"I told you," Chris said. "He was ... is ... a Marine. Retired as a Corporal. He served in Afghanistan."

"Do you know what he did as a Marine Corporal in Afghanistan?"

Ty stiffened beside me. I had an objection to this line of questioning on relevance. It could backfire though. It might not be the worst thing in the world for the jury to hear about Ty's military record.

"Ty didn't talk about that much," Chris said. "Which is understandable."

"Why is that?" Rafe asked.

"Because it's nobody's damn business but Corporal Chapman's."

"Sergeant Dvorak," Judge Hughes said. He was a retired Army, just like Chris. "Let me remind you you're in a courtroom. My courtroom."

"Sorry, sir," Chris said. Hughes might be wearing a robe, but to someone like Chris Dvorak, he would always be a commanding officer first.

"Let me rephrase," Rafe said. "You indicated Mr. Chapman didn't discuss his military service with you often. But he did discuss it with you on occasion, didn't he?"

"Some," Chris answered. He grew pale again, squirming in his seat.

"He told you he served in Kabul, didn't he?"

"Objection," I said. "Counsel is leading the witness. Also, I'm not sure how the defendant's exemplary military record is relevant to the issues in this case." I figured if I objected just enough, Rafe would take the bait and fight harder to get Ty's record in.

"I'll get to that in just a moment," Rafe said. "If Your Honor would allow me a bit of leeway, these are foundational questions."

"Very little leeway, Counselor," the judge said.

"Of course. Mr. Dvorak, to your knowledge, what was Mr. Chapman's role when he served in Afghanistan?"

"He was with an MEU. Marine Expeditionary Unit. They did what Marines do. He would have been in charge of embassy security once it was reestablished during Operation Swift Freedom."

"Embassy security," Rafe said. "Mr. Dvorak, isn't it true that Ty Chapman once told you how he killed a man with his bare hands?"

"Objection!" I shot up.

"Up here," Judge Hughes said, coming in hot.

I charged up to the sidebar. Rafe calmly took his place beside me.

"What the hell are you up to?" Judge Hughes asked.

"Your Honor," Rafe said. "The defendant confessed to this witness about a particularly violent episode in his past. One that bears a striking resemblance to the events of this case. It's within my rights to explore it."

"That's crap," I said. "And Rafe knows it."

"This witness is privy to a conversation, a firsthand account from the defendant, which has a chilling similarity to the events of this case. It's relevant. Ms. Leary will have the opportunity to cross-examine Mr. Dvorak to her heart's content."

"This is ridiculous," I said. "We've had no discovery on these allegations."

"Mr. Dvorak was on your witness list," Rafe said. "It's not the state's fault if you didn't do your due diligence."

Anger rose. I saw white spots in front of my eyes.

"Ms. Leary's objection primarily results from the fact she's been figuratively caught with her pants down in the middle of the trial," Rafe went on. "But this line of inquiry is relevant and has direct bearing on the events of this case."

Judge Hughes rubbed his temple. "Cass," he said. "He's right. I don't have to like it either. But Mr. Johnson will have the opportunity to ask his question. If it's what he says it is, this is a statement made by the defendant against his own interests. It's admissible."

"But he's never ..." I clamped my own mouth shut. When I looked over, Chris Dvorak had gone even whiter. I could have killed him. His pained expression was, I think, meant as some sort of apology.

"Additionally, Your Honor," Rafe said. "I'd like permission to proceed with Mr. Dvorak under the hostile witness rule. He's already stated he's a friend of the defendant's. His presence here today was compelled according to a subpoena."

"Which I never received a copy of," I said.

"It was delivered to your office early this morning."

"Likely after I was already here, Rafe," I said.

"Again, Dvorak is on your own witness list. You can't claim surprise here."

I got an angry glare from Judge Hughes. I was stuck. Blocked. In deep trouble. When I turned on my heel, Ty Chapman's expression had turned to stone.

As I sat beside him, the question mark he drew on my notepad earlier just made me that much angrier.

"Mr. Dvorak," Rafe started. "Isn't it true that Ty Chapman once told you he killed a man, an insurgent, with his bare hands?"

"What Ty Chapman told me, he told me in confidence," Dvorak said. "It was never meant to leave the room."

"You're not a therapist. Not a priest. Not his lawyer. You understand no privilege or expectation of privacy attached to this statement. And he made it, didn't he?"

Dvorak looked desperately at the wall. There would be no help there.

"Where is he getting this?" I wrote to Ty. "Who else heard this?"

Ty reached over and tapped that infuriating question mark again.

"Is he lying?" I wrote.

Ty folded his hands in front of him.

"Yes, okay?" Dvorak snapped. "You need to understand the context. The climate. This would have been a year ago maybe. Ty trusted me. We were talking. He was having a tough time. Beth had just had a miscarriage. I could see something was eating at Ty. We had a beer or two watching a hockey game at the center. It just came out of him. He told me there'd been a fire fight near the embassy. I don't know the circumstances. I don't know when it happened."

"What did Ty Chapman say?"

"He said he sees the guy's face sometimes. In his nightmares. He asked me if that ever happened to me. I told him yes. He was hurting. You have to understand."

"He said he sees the man he killed in his nightmares," Rafe said. "What did you say to him?"

Chris went blank.

"What did he say to you then, Mr. Dvorak?"

"I don't know what you mean," Chris said.

Rafe said. "In fact, I think it bothered you greatly, what he said. Didn't it?"

"I don't know what you mean," Dvorak said again, tight-lipped.

"Isn't it true you tried to make Ty Chapman feel better. You tried to empathize with him. You told him what he was experiencing was normal. You told him you had nightmares too."

"Your Honor," I rose. "We've gone so far beyond the pale here ..."

"Mr. Dvorak," Rafe said, shouting over me. "Tell the truth. What did the defendant tell you about the man he killed in Afghanistan?"

Someone had overheard them. It had to be that. Rafe had found a witness to the conversation. I had no doubt he'd drag that person to the stand next if he felt Chris was changing his story now. I just couldn't believe Dvorak never thought it necessary to clue me in on this bombshell of a conversation.

Dvorak shook his head. Ty simply stared straight ahead.

"Your Honor," I said, still waiting for a ruling on my objection.

"He told you how he killed that man, didn't he? When his weapon jammed. When they'd resorted to hand-to-hand combat. He told you, didn't he? In exacting detail."

"Counsel is testifying," I shouted.

"Yes!" Dvorak yelled over all of us. "Yes. Yes! Ty said he smashed his face in with a rock. Said he pummeled him until there was nothing left. But he's alive. It was something he had to do to survive. This isn't the same."

"Thank you," Rafe said. "I have no further questions."

I should have. I wanted to lay into Chris Dvorak, ask him why he'd never bothered to tell me any of this during the times we spoke prior to trial. I wanted to move for a mistrial. What Dvorak said veered so far out of the realm of relevance. At the same time, as Chris Dvorak crumpled with the guilt of what he believed was betrayal, he had just opened up a line of defense I'd never seen coming.

"Ms. Leary?" a weary Judge Hughes said to me.

"Your Honor," I said. "I have no questions for this witness. Though I reserve the right to recall him later." A gamble. A big one. But I could see no upside in attacking Chris Dvorak right now.

"Mr. Johnson?" Hughes asked.

Rafe stood. He took a slow, deliberate breath. Then, he locked eyes with Judge Hughes and said, "Your Honor, at this time, the prosecution rests."

If I'd stunned them by not further cross-examining Chris Dvorak, Rafe Johnson had just stunned me more. I just prayed my gamble would pay off.

Chapter 23

I HAD precious little time with my client before he was taken back to his cell. The stark, cold, cement walls of the county jail lawyer's room seemed to close in on me. Ty sat before me, stoic as always.

"You understand what's happening," I said. "You get what Rafe Johnson tried to do today."

Nothing. Not so much as a blink from Ty. My blood ran hot.

"He's trying to establish you're a killer, because you've killed before."

Still nothing.

"Ty," I shouted. "Did you say those things to Chris Dvorak? Did you confide in him?"

"I've never lied," he said.

"That's not what I asked you. Chris did. Or he withheld the truth from me. Did you tell him to? If it comes out that you in any way tried to influence his testimony ..."

"I never tried to influence anyone," he said. "Chris is free to say whatever he wants."

"I need to know what happened out in those woods," I said.

He turned to stone again, staring at a point on the wall just over my left shoulder.

"Do you even remember? Is that what this is?" I asked. "Ty, you have to talk to me. It has to be now."

Still nothing but a blank stare from him.

"We have a chance," I said. "For the first time since this whole thing started, I can see a path, Ty. A way to at least raise reasonable doubt on first-degree murder. But more than that, if you snapped. If something happened where you reacted to something that wasn't really right in front of you ..."

"You want to tell the jury that I'm crazy?" he said, his tone devoid of any emotion.

"No," I said. "Not crazy. Not in the slightest. I can't even begin to imagine the things you've seen in your life. The things you were forced to endure ..."

He turned his gaze back to me. I searched for even the tiniest flicker of understanding, of emotion. I saw none.

"Rafe Johnson's plan may have backfired today," I said. "He put Chris Dvorak on the stand to try to show the jury that you're a trained killer. That you knew what you were doing. That you were executing some objective and maybe John Lansky got in the way. He's trying to prove you're a monster, Ty. But I don't think that's what's going on."

I saw the slightest arch to his brow. "You think I'm a monster, Cass?"

"No," I said. "But I think you're being tortured by something. I think you're clinging to some sense of duty. To your country. To Beth. It's time you told me who you're trying to protect. Because it's not serving you. If you don't tell me the truth, I won't be able to help you. The thing you asked me to save you from ... I won't be able to. That jury is going to put you in prison for the rest of your life."

He looked back at the wall.

"He said something to you—Lansky," I said. "Or he reminded you of something or someone. Is that it?"

"I thought lawyers were never supposed to ask questions they didn't already know the answers to," Ty said. There was a slight curve to his mouth. Was he mocking me?

"Fine," I said. "You want to know what I think the answers are? I'll tell you. Yes. I think John Lansky did something. Approached Beth somewhere. I think she's his type. Was it a bar? A store? A parking lot? He scared her. She told you about it. So you went out there to tell him to back off. Maybe you even threatened him. But it went sideways, didn't it? You went into those woods with him and he did something. Said something. Triggered you."

"Triggered," Ty said, his voice filled with contempt. "You know how much I hate that word? People throw it around as an excuse for bad behavior. For oversensitivity."

"But you weren't overly sensitive," I said. "It wasn't a matter of that, was it? You were fighting for your life. It's what you were sent over there to do. Protect. Defend. And John Lansky tried to hurt you. Or hurt Beth. It all came rushing back. Is that it?"

179

"You want me to take the stand and try to justify what it is that I do? What we all did? So you and the people on that jury can sleep safe and warm in their beds."

"You don't have to justify it," I said. "Not to me. Certainly not to the jury. And no. There's no way in hell I can let you take the stand. If you did, you'd have to admit the truth."

"What truth is that?" he asked.

"If you tell the jury that you killed John Lansky ... if they hear you say those words, then you're backed into a corner I can't get you out of."

"You don't think I can handle Rafe Johnson?" he asked.

"No," I said bluntly. "Because you can't. You're good at what you do, Ty. The best at it. But so is Rafe Johnson. And this? This stoicism. What you think is noble? It'll come off as cold and calculating. Premeditated. And it won't matter what you say or what I do. You'll lose."

"Then what are we still doing here?" he asked.

"There are mitigating circumstances," I said. "Lansky provoked you, didn't he?"

He didn't answer.

"Ty," I said. "You have to tell me the truth. Is that what happened?"

Silence.

"Do you remember? You have to be honest with me. Did you black out?"

I couldn't read him. I knew that meant the jury wouldn't be able to either. Finally, he met my eyes.

"What do you think I am, Cass? Tell *me* the truth."

I sat back. "I think you're trying desperately to hold it together. Just like you have been since you came home from Afghanistan. I think you've been pushed to your limits. You've needed help for years but you refused to admit it. You were starting to though, weren't you? When you met Chris. When you started reaching out and getting more involved with the Veterans Center. But then you crossed paths with John Lansky. But no, I don't think you're a monster, Ty. I just think it's time to let other people help you. Really help you."

Ty rose to his feet. "I have to go now."

"Ty," I said.

He tilted his head to the side, regarding me. "Maybe I am," he said.

"What?"

"Maybe I'm just the monster you need."

He knocked on the door, calling the guard. He gave me one last hard look before leaving.

Chapter 24

"IT COULD BACKFIRE," Tori said. It was almost eleven o'clock the same night. I had the weekend. Roughly fifty-seven hours to figure out how to save Tyler Chapman from himself.

"If you take the position that Ty did in fact kill John Lansky," Jeanie said, "that might just be all the jury needs for first degree. Those pictures. The brutality of the killing. Any reasonable person would want to make sure a guy who could do that never sees the light of day again."

"That's exactly why a heat-of-passion argument makes the most sense," I said. "No planning could have gone into that kind of killing. It was a spur-of-the-moment reaction to something."

"There's just no time," Tori said. "If Ty had been forthcoming. If Chris Dvorak had. We could have lined up a parade of PTSD experts. Had Ty examined by a psychologist. Look, Rafe Johnson is a lot of things but he's not unreasonable. He's got to see how he teed you up. Maybe he'd be willing to talk about a plea deal now. If you lay out for him where you're headed."

"Once he sleeps on it," I said, "he'll know where I'm headed. The problem with a plea deal is Ty would have to stand up in court and explain exactly what happened. So far, he's told me that's never happening."

"Even if it could ensure he'd get out of prison in his kid's lifetime?" Jeanie asked.

"So far," I said.

"So now what?" Tori said, looking at the whiteboard of witnesses I intended to call. It was sparse. I'd gotten most of my case in during cross-examination of Rafe's witnesses. It just wasn't nearly enough.

"Putting Ty on the stand is still a hard no?" Jeanie asked.

I sat with my feet up, shoes kicked off, staring at Ty's mugshot taped to the board.

"So far, none of the conversations I've ever had with him make me think he'd make a good witness for himself. He comes off cold, calculating, evasive."

"He comes off like a killer," Tori said. She looked uncomfortable in her chair, squirming, trying to stretch out her lower back. At over six months pregnant now, her hands and feet were starting to swell. It was starting to concern me. She'd worked twelve-hour days over the last few weeks, helping me prepare for this trial.

"You should head home," I said. "Enjoy your weekend. Let my little brother pamper you. And if he doesn't, I'll brain him."

Tori smiled. "We've got plans. Matty wants me to wait to tell you, but I'm just too excited. I think we're going to make an offer on a house."

"What?" I said, dropping my feet to the floor and sitting upright.

"It's this adorable mid-century modern ranch on Windham Street. It overlooks Shamrock Park on the north side. It's adorable. Like a time capsule. It's only had two owners and the sellers left a lot of the original character."

"Ah," Jeanie said. "So it's a fixer upper."

"It's a steal," Tori said. "The backyard is heaven. All private with woods behind it. I don't know what I'll do if we don't get it."

I took a moment to remember to breathe. A thousand worries crossed through my mind. Was Matty ready for this? Would this be the thing that tripped him up and sent him back to the bottle?

"It's okay," Tori said, as if she could read my mind. "Believe me, I wouldn't push for this if I thought Matty wasn't happy about it. He is. I promise."

"Tori," I said. "I'm happy. If you guys are happy, I'm over the moon, actually."

"I can't wait for you to see it," she said. "The wait is excruciating. If we don't get it ..."

"Then you weren't meant to have it," Jeanie said. "I believe in real estate karma. If this house doesn't work out, it means there's another one. A better one."

Tori nodded. She held a protective hand over her swollen belly.

"Matty has such great ideas. He's already figured out an area in the yard where he can put up a little basketball hoop for when the little guy gets ..."

She stopped, her face turning white.

"Little guy?" Jeanie and I said it together.

"Oh," Tori said, realizing what she'd just let slip.

"Little guy!" I said again, joy flooding through me. I went to Tori and enveloped her in a hug.

"Don't tell him," she said. "Oh shoot. I shouldn't have ..."

"Shh," I said. "I won't say a word. It's terrific, Tori. I cannot wait! Now I mean it. Get out of here. Go let my brother spoil you for a couple of days. I'll let you know if I need you."

"Promise?" she said.

Just then, I heard the back door to the office open and close.

"Cass?" Eric called up. I checked my smart watch. It was nearly midnight. I texted Eric an hour ago to tell him I was on my way.

"I think you better let him spoil you too," Tori said, rising. She and Jeanie scooted out the opposite door as Eric headed up to my office.

I met him there, still grinning from ear to ear with Tori's secret news.

"What's going on?" Eric said, reading me.

I went to him. Pulling his head down to mine, I gave him a quick kiss.

"Good news," I said. "I'll tell you later. I'm sorry I didn't call. We just got buried."

He put his arms around me. "I got worried."

"I know," I said.

"But that's not why I'm here. I got a little buried in something myself. I didn't want to tell you until I was sure."

I stepped back out of his embrace. "What? Eric ... what? I've had enough surprises for one day."

"Ellen Colby," he said. "The woman John Lansky allegedly raped and beat up."

"The one who changed her story," I said.

"Yeah," he answered. "I found her."

"You what?"

"I made a few calls. Called in a favor with a detective I worked with on a task force in Wayne County. Anyway, she works at this bar. Usually on Saturday nights. And I got an address."

"Did you reach out to her?" I asked.

"Not yet," Eric said. "But my detective friend. One of his CIs knows her pretty well and told him when she's usually home. We can try to catch her tomorrow afternoon. No guarantees she'll talk though."

"Oh, Eric ..." I went back and kissed him.

"But we go together," he said. "That's non-negotiable. This is a dangerous part of town and this woman has connections that make me nervous."

"Agreed," I said. "I love you!"

He smiled, and using his best Han Solo voice, he said, "I know."

Chapter 25

"Here?" I said to Eric. "You're sure she lives here?"

Of all the shady places I'd ever dragged Eric to in search of a witness, this one reached a new low. We were on a dead-end street in a neighborhood outside of Detroit that looked like it had been firebombed over the last few years. Most of the homes were either abandoned or falling in on themselves, or both. Eric opened my car door for me. He gently pushed me behind him as he kept his right hand resting on his holstered gun as we walked up to a gray two story with boarded-up windows.

"This can't be right," I said.

"It's right," he answered. "My contact just talked to his CI twenty minutes ago. She just got home. He watched her go in the front door."

"Maybe you should hang back a little," I said. "You look like ... well ... a cop. If there's something ..."

"If there's something going on, you're not getting rid of me," he said. "She's home. Let's get this over with."

I knocked on the door and tried to peer through one of the broken windows. Sure enough, I could see movement through the living room in a kitchen off the side. Dishes clanged. I could hear water running.

"Ms. Colby?" I called out. "Are you in there?"

There was a scraping noise as someone or something came to the door. It creaked open slowly. I was met by a pair of beady eyes behind coke-bottle glasses. The woman stood maybe four feet tall. She walked with a cane, which she brandished toward me like a sword.

"We aren't buying," she said.

"I'm not selling," I said. "Does Ellen Colby live here? I was told ..."

"Ellen!" the woman shouted with ear-splitting strength. More dishes clanged in the sink.

"You don't have to shout, Viola," a woman's voice said. She came into view. I recognized her immediately as the woman I'd seen in both the photograph the police had taken after her assault, and her old social media post. She still looked a fair bit like Beth Chapman, but less so than I expected.

Ellen Colby was perhaps forty, though it was hard to tell. She had the deep lines carved around her mouth from a lifetime of smoking, no doubt. Her raspy voice supported my conclusion.

"What do you want?" she asked. Her gaze went immediately to Eric. In an instant, she made him for what he was. A cop.

"We just want to ask you a few questions," Eric said.

"We're not here officially," I said. "My name is Cass Leary. I'm a lawyer. I'm trying a case and it's come to my attention you might have some information about ..."

"Not here," she said. I expected her to slam the door in my face. I could have been far smoother in my introduction. But she didn't slam the door. Instead, she stepped out on the porch, shooing Viola back inside.

"Don't you say anything without getting paid, Ellen," Viola shouted from inside. "They want something from you. And she looks rich!"

"Sorry," Ellen said, smiling. "My sister's got a mouth on her."

"It's okay," I said. "Thanks for coming out."

"Do you need me to sign something?" she asked. "The other lawyer said I'd have to sign something."

Eric and I passed a look.

"I'm sorry," I said. "What other lawyer?"

"You're here about my accident, right? Lord, I've talked to so many lawyers and insurance adjusters."

"Oh," I said. "No. I'm afraid I don't know about your accident."

Ellen rolled her eyes. "You said you were working on a trial."

"I am," I said. "Is there someplace we can talk?"

"Here's fine," she said, beginning to eye both Eric and me with the suspicion I expected when we first rolled up.

Ellen took a seat on a rickety porch swing. There were two other wicker chairs nearby. Both looked like they'd seen better days, much like Ellen Colby. I took one and scooted it closer. Eric stayed on his feet, standing behind me like a gargoyle.

"My name is Cass Leary," I started.

"I heard you the first time," Ellen said.

"I'm a defense attorney," I said. "My client has been accused of a murder down in Woodbridge County. We're actually in the middle of the trial on it. It has come to my attention that you might know something about the victim."

"And what are you, her bodyguard?" Ellen asked Eric.

"For today, yes," he said, unflinching.

I reached into my leather bag and pulled out John Lansky's mugshot. "Do you recognize this man?" I asked her.

Ellen kept her eyes on Eric. I sat for a moment, holding the picture in front of her. Finally, slowly, she let her gaze drop and studied the photo.

Nothing. No emotion. No reaction. She flicked her eyes back to mine.

"His name is ... was ... John Lansky."

There it was. Just the slightest flutter of her lashes. She knew him. She knew something.

"I don't know him."

I took another photograph out of my bag. This was the police photo of Ellen herself. The Wayne County detective working her case had snapped it of her in the hospital.

"This is you," I said.

"I know what it is," she snapped.

"Ms. Colby, this man. John Lansky. You told the police he's the one who attacked you. I'd like to ask you some questions about that if you don't mind."

"I mind," she said. "I've said all I intend to say on that subject. It's over. Ancient history."

"Ms. Colby. Ellen. John Lansky can't hurt you anymore."

A small tremor went through her. I couldn't read her mind, but I would have bet my life savings on the fact she'd just let her last memory of John Lansky flash in her mind.

"He can't hurt you anymore," I said. "Ms. Colby, John Lansky is dead. Did you hear me? I'm representing the man accused of murdering him."

Ellen shook her head. "Are you serious?"

"Yes," I said.

Ellen Colby's eyes filled with tears.

"Do you need something?" I asked. "Would you like your sister out here? A glass of water perhaps?"

"No. No. No. He's not dead. Guys like John Lansky don't die. They can't be killed."

"He was," I said. "I assure you."

I took out my phone and googled Lansky's name. I selected one of the initial news stories from when the police identified his body after the murder. I showed it to Ellen Colby.

Her eyes got big as she scanned my phone screen. She took it from me, scrolling down. "I don't believe it," she said. "I need to see it."

"What?"

"I need to see it. If he's dead. If he was murdered. There are pictures. Show me."

"Ms. Colby, I don't think ..." I started.

"Show her," Eric said.

"You won't be able to recognize him," I said. "What happened to John Lansky was very violent. He was identified through his fingerprints and later DNA. It's him. There's no doubt. He's dead."

She locked her eyes with mine. "I want to see it!" Her words came out dripping with vitriol.

I took my phone from her. Pulling up my cloud drive, I tried to find the least horrible of the horrible pictures taken at Lansky's crime scene. I handed the phone back to Ellen Colby.

Slowly, she put a shaky hand to her mouth. She turned the phone sideways. She tapped the screen to enlarge the photo. Then, she handed it back to me as a single tear rolled down her cheek.

"He can't hurt you anymore," I said.

"Your client," she said. "Is he guilty? Did he actually kill John Lansky?"

I didn't know how to answer her question.

"Probably," Eric answered for me.

"Ellen," I said. "You told the police initially that Lansky beat and raped you. He did, didn't he?"

"What's his name?" Ellen asked. "Your client."

"Tyler Chapman," I answered.

"Tyler Chapman," she repeated. "Good. I'll send him a thank-you card."

"I'd like to show you something," I said. I pulled up one last picture on my phone. This one was of Beth Chapman. It was a shot I thought looked particularly like one of the older photos I'd seen of Ellen when she was younger. I showed it to her.

"This is Beth Chapman," I said. "Tyler's wife."

Ellen understood. Her mouth parted in surprise. "He hurt her too? Of course he did."

"I'm not sure," I said. "That's the truth. But do you notice anything about her?"

"She looks like me," Ellen said. "She's Lansky's type. That's what he told me. He went for redheads. Real ones. He said he always made sure. That's why I bleach my hair now."

My stomach turned. I could only imagine what this woman endured.

"Ellen, will you tell me what really happened?"

"John Lansky was a psychopath," she said. "A monster. I used to hang out at the Blue Rhino. That's a bar out in Flat Rock. I'd go there after work. Usually Friday nights. Lansky started coming in. A real charmer. At first anyway. He'd buy me drinks. We talked. He was interested. I wasn't. Then one night, I had more to drink than I should have. I started getting sick. I found out later he slipped something into my drink. He put me in his car, said he was going to drive me home. He didn't though. He took me to this seedy motel. That's when it happened."

"He attacked you," I said.

"Yeah," she said. "The whole bit. Forced himself on me. He kept hitting me. I told him to stop so many times. I didn't want to be with him, but I told him I'd do what he wanted. I wouldn't fight it. He didn't need to hurt me. I was just trying to make it all stop. I thought he was gonna kill me before it was all over. At a certain point, I blacked out. I woke up in a pool of my own blood. But he was gone. He left three hundred-dollar bills on the bed beside me. Can you believe that? I'm not a pro. And if I were, what he did? Three hundred bucks?"

"You reported it?" Eric asked.

She nodded. "It was bad. Really, really bad. I told you. I'm not a pro, but I know some of the girls that hang out at the Blue Rhino. I didn't want them to get hurt next. It was actually my sister, Viola, who made me realize that. So yes. I went to the cops."

"So what happened?" I asked. "Why did you change your story?"

Her posture changed. She pulled one leg up, hugging her knee. "I knew they weren't going to listen."

"Who?"

"Anybody. The cops. The prosecutor. A jury, if it ever got that far. I said I'm not a prostitute. I left that life a long time ago."

"You spent the money," Eric said. There was no judgment in his tone.

She looked up at him.

"You're not a bodyguard," she said. "You're a cop. That's exactly what they said too."

"Ellen," I said. "The police were getting ready to arrest Lansky. They believed you. I believe you."

"No," she said. "I know how this works. I did my job. Lansky stopped coming around the Blue Rhino. It just wasn't worth it anymore."

"You did the right thing," I said. "When you reported Lansky to the police. I'm so sorry if you felt you wouldn't be believed. I wish I could have helped you then. But now, you have a chance to tell your story. I can give you the opportunity to make sure people know what John Lansky was."

"You want me to testify?"

"Yes," I said. "If you're willing. I'd like you to tell the jury in my case everything you told me. You haven't done anything wrong. You won't get in trouble, Ellen."

The front door opened. "You should do it," Viola said, poking her head out. "Do it, Ellie. Go up there and tell those people what kind of demon that man was. It'll be good for you. She's been a hermit ever since, Ms. Leary. Afraid to leave this house except for work. Afraid to live. If you can promise me she'll get to tell her story, I promise I'll get her to that courthouse."

"You can tell your story," I said.

Viola came out on the porch and sat beside her sister.

"When do you need her?" Viola asked. Ellen let her sister fold her in her arms. She was smiling.

"Are you sure I should, Vi?"

"I'm sure," Viola said. "You have to do this. Praise the Lord, Ms. Leary. Because that's who I think sent you to us today."

"I don't know about that," I said. "But I'm grateful you're willing to help."

"When?" Ellen asked.

"How about Monday?" I said.

Wiping a tear from her eye, Ellen Colby nodded. For the first time since Beth Chapman walked into my office, I believed I might know the way to save Tyler Chapman.

Chapter 26

My first witness Monday morning started the day off by nervously chewing his nails from the stand.

"Mr. Bonham," I said. "Will you please explain how you know Tyler Chapman?"

Roy Bonham took one last chew off the nail on his right middle finger, then mercifully folded his hands in his lap.

"Ty and I work together at my father's company. Bonham Heating and Cooling."

"For how long?" I asked.

"Oh, four years, I think. About that. Ty walked into the office one day looking for a job. I'm actually the one who introduced him to my father."

"For the record," I said. "Who is your father?"

"Oh, sorry. Bo Bonham. He started the company when I was a kid. So we've been in business thirty-five years this year. Anyway, like I said, Ty walked into the office one afternoon and asked my sister Patrice for a job application. Patrice sent him over to me. I walked him in to see my dad. Dad hired him on the spot."

"What do you do?"

"I'm a licensed HVAC technician. So's Ty. We service and install mostly residential heating and cooling systems. We've done some commercial too. But for the last few years, we've been pretty booked up with two new subdivisions going in Woodbridge County."

"Is one of those the White Oak subdivisions?"

"Yeah," he said. "Yes. Actually, that's where Ty and I have been working ... or had been working before all this started. Ty and his wife built their house in White Oak."

"Mr. Bonham," I said. "If I can take you back to the week of or before November 10th, do you recall where you were working?"

"Still White Oak," he said.

"Were you working specifically with Ty that week?"

"Yes, ma'am," he said. "We were under the gun a bit. We were trying to finish up in one of the model homes in the subdivision. It was a corner lot on Birch Street. The developer, Tom Tracy, said that the house was going into the Home Parade and he was worried about delays. So Ty and I worked a bunch of overtime that week to get our piece of it done."

"How was that going?" I asked.

"Oh, things were a mess that week," he said. "The drywallers showed up before they were supposed to. We had issues with one of our suppliers. My dad was really stressed out. He's getting on in years and this project has been good for our bank account, but bad for my dad's blood pressure. Anyway, we were managing it, though."

"So I'm clear, you've worked side by side with Ty Chapman for four years?"

"Sure have. Side by side. On top of. In tight spaces. Hot weather. Cold weather. You name it."

"All right," I said. "I'd like to focus your attention on the morning and afternoon of November 10th. Did you work with Ty that day?"

"Yep. Um. Yes. We were finishing up the last of the ductwork on the model home property."

"How did that go?"

"Smooth. My dad worked out whatever the issues were with the suppliers. The drywallers didn't end up showing up. So it was just the two of us working that day. The weather was mild. We were able to crank through our stuff. Got a good rhythm going. Ty and I can knock stuff out lightning fast when we don't have interference."

"How was Ty's demeanor that day?"

"You mean his mood?"

"Among other things, yes," I said.

"Great," Bonham said. "Like I said, some of the logistical stuff had been causing issues all week. But everything came together that day and we were just able to get in there and do what we do. We banged that stuff out."

"So, his mood was good?"

"It was great," Bonham said. "Upbeat. We were laughing. Joking. Having a good time, actually. Ty was in a really good place in his life."

"In what way?" I asked.

"Ty and his wife Beth had been trying to have a kid for as long as I've known him. So four years. She'd had some trouble. A lot of trouble, actually. She lost a few. Had miscarriages. I felt for him. For them. My wife Leslie too. She and Beth are acquainted. Leslie had a miscarriage her first time. We both know how hard that is. Anyway. Beth had just had a doctor's appointment. An ultrasound. It went really well. Ty was telling me about it."

"And this was on November 10th? You're sure of the date?"

"I'm sure," he said.

"Why?"

"Well, like I said. Beth had her ultrasound the day before. Ty took a couple of hours off to be with her for that. It caused some problems on account of all the other delays and issues we'd been having at the job site. I covered for Ty. So the next day, on the 10th, it was the first thing I asked Ty. How did the ultrasound go? The thing is, Ty's a pretty low-key guy. We've got a nickname for him. We call him the Ice Man."

"The Ice Man?"

"Yeah. Cuz he's so cold. Well, I don't mean cold in a bad way. Probably cool is the better word. He's not super emotional one way or the other. He's got this really dry sense of humor. Deadpan. He's not much of a talker. Which I like. I've worked with other guys I could never get to shut up. Ty's all business. He's there to do the work. He doesn't get angry. There's just no drama with him. Anyway, he was so happy that day. Just psyched about their good news. It was great to see."

"Did he take any phone calls that day at work? Text with anyone?"

"I think maybe Beth called him once when we were taking our lunch break. It was a short conversation though. I think she was just wanting to know if we were working over that day. I assumed they were going to do something to celebrate their good news."

"Objection," Rafe said. "The witness is purely speculating."

"Sustained," Judge Hughes said.

"Sorry," Bonham said.

"Do you recall any other phone calls or texts Ty Chapman took that day?" I asked.

Bonham shook his head. "No. Like I said, Ty was all business most days. Which is really refreshing, if you want to know the truth. It's so hard to get guys who want to work these days. Especially these younger kids."

"Right," I said. "Mr. Bonham, if you recall, when did you finish work that day?"

"Five o'clock," he said. "Oh. That's the thing. I'm not speculating. I remember that. We had a little section we'd almost finished but it was going to take another hour. So it was five o'clock already and we'd been working since eight in the morning. Ty wanted to keep going. I'm the one who said no. It could wait until morning. I told him he needed to take Beth out to dinner and celebrate. I insisted."

"So you both clocked out at five, then?" I asked.

"Figuratively, yes. We don't actually punch a clock."

"Sorry," I said. "But you're sure it was five?"

"It was," he said. "Like I said, I insisted Ty go pick Beth up and take her someplace special."

"Was he going to?" I asked.

"I don't know. He was just really happy. He showed me the ultrasound pictures on his phone again right as we were leaving."

Behind me, I knew Beth Chapman sat. She was heavy with her pregnancy now. Her due date was in just three weeks. From the corner of my eye, I saw her put a protective hand over her swollen belly. Several members of the jury looked her way, too.

"Thank you, Mr. Bonham," I said. "I have no further questions."

"Mr. Johnson?" the judge said.

Rafe made his way to the lectern.

"Mr. Bonham, you said you only met Tyler Chapman four years ago, correct?"

"Yes."

"He never spoke about his military service, did he?"

"What? Um. No."

"Isn't it true you didn't even know he served?"

"Not specifically, no," Bonham said.

"In fact, he never listed it on his job application, did he?"

"Well, he didn't fill out a formal application," Bonham said.

"No written application on file at your father's company?"

"No. My dad just talked to him. That's all he needed."

"So Tyler Chapman was never asked to submit to a background check as a condition of his employment?"

"No," Bonham said. "My dad's a good judge of character. So am I. He cares more about the work you can do. And Ty Chapman is probably the best hire we've ever made."

"So in the four years you've worked with Chapman, you didn't know he served in the Marine Corps."

"No."

"You didn't know he served in Afghanistan."

"No, sir."

"You likewise have no clue the kind of training he received in that role?"

"No."

"You never spent time with Ty Chapman outside of work at all, did you?"

"No. Not really."

"Never went to his house?"

"Socially? No. But I helped install the heating and cooling at Ty's house. He and Beth live in White Oak."

"You ever invite Beth Chapman or Ty Chapman to your home?"

"Yes."

"But they never came, did they?"

Bonham started chewing his nails again. "No. They were going to once. A cookout we were having. But something came up at the last minute and they couldn't come."

"You said your wife Leslie and Beth were friendly. But isn't it true they never actually spent time together in person?"

"They've been around each other, sure."

"But that was only in passing, wasn't it? At the office?"

"I think. I'm not sure. But Leslie reached out to Beth on Facebook. They talked that way."

"So we're clear," Rafe said. "You've never once spent time with Ty and Beth Chapman as a couple, have you?"

"I don't know what you mean."

"What I mean," Rafe said. "You've never gone on double dates with the Chapmans, have you?"

"No."

"You've never even driven Ty Chapman home from work or shared car rides with him, have you?"

"No."

"So in reality, the only relationship you have with Ty Chapman is when you're at work."

"I see him at work, yes."

"So if Ty Chapman had marital trouble, you wouldn't know about that, would you?"

"I think he might have said that," Bonham answered.

"But he didn't, did he?"

"No."

"Likewise, if Ty Chapman were abusing his wife, you'd have no idea, would you?"

"Objection," I said. "Counsel is assuming facts not in evidence."

"Sustained, Mr. Johnson," Judge Hughes said, his tone sharp.

"You know what kind of HVAC technician Ty Chapman is, and that's it, isn't it, Mr. Bonham?"

"What?"

"Your knowledge of Tyler Chapman extends to how he conducts himself at his job, nothing else."

"I wouldn't put it that way, no."

"And you don't have the first clue where Tyler Chapman actually went after he left work on November 10th, do you?"

"I assume he went home to his wife," Bonham answered.

"You assume," Johnson said, his point well made. "Thank you. I have no more questions."

I waived redirect. I had a far bigger hook to bait.

Chewing his nails, Roy Bonham left the witness box.

"Ms. Leary?" the judge said.

"Your Honor," I said, rising. "The defense calls Ellen Colby to the stand."

I expected Rafe to object. I was ready for that. But I'd listed Ellen Colby weeks ago, hoping I'd be able to find her. Behind me, the courtroom doors opened.

I turned, expecting to see Ellen walk through. Instead, it was only Tori, her expression nearly panicked. She put on a brave smile and walked up to me. I leaned toward her so she could whisper in my ear.

"Ask for a recess," Tori said. "We need to talk."

"Ms. Leary?" Judge Hughes said.

"Your Honor," I said, my throat going dry. "Could we have a fifteen-minute recess?"

Judge Hughes eyed me with suspicion, but granted my request. The bang of his gavel pierced through me.

Chapter 27

I DIDN'T WANT to follow Tori. As if some childish part of me thought if I didn't let her tell me what I could plainly read from her face, it wouldn't come true. Eric didn't know her as I did, but even he understood something terrible had happened.

He led the way, making sure the conference room beside the courtroom was empty. I left a bewildered Ty and Beth Chapman behind.

Once the three of us entered the room, Eric shut the door. Tori sank slowly into a chair and folded her hands.

"She's dead," Tori said. "They found Ellen Colby's body on a park bench two miles from her house. A pair of morning joggers thought she was homeless. Or drunk. But when they got closer ..."

I heard the words. But they hovered in the air, refusing to penetrate my brain.

"She's dead, Cass," Tori said. "She's gone."

Dead. I thought of all the thousands of ways a person might die. I don't know why, but my head settled on pills. She had to have taken her own life. Why?

"I don't understand," I said. "She was upbeat when I talked to her. Anxious to get here and tell her story. Viola was going to come with her. Why would she do this?"

Tori met my eyes. "Cass," she said. "Ellen didn't do this. They're not saying it was a suicide. They found her with her throat slit. And ... someone cut out her tongue."

Tori's words went back up to the air. There was a moment before they landed hard within me. Not unlike a physical injury that took a moment before you felt the pain.

"Christ," Eric said. "Someone got to her."

"How?" I asked. "My God. Why? John Lansky's dead. What possible issue could anyone have about what Ellen had to say? It doesn't make sense. Nobody other than the people in this courtroom even knew I was calling her to the stand."

"Somebody knew something," Eric said. "Her sister knew. We don't know who she might have told. Tori, where is she?"

"They're finishing up the autopsy," Tori answered. "I just talked to Viola. She's ... she and Ellen both are at Beaumont. The M.E.'s got her. Cass, Viola's asking for you."

"Can you stall?" I asked. "The judge has given me fifteen minutes and those are about up. Talk to Rafe. He knew I was calling Ellen next. I think he'll agree to a recess until tomorrow morning under the circumstances. If he won't, or if the judge won't, call Bo Bonham to the stand. Just have him back up everything his son said about Ty's demeanor the day Lansky was killed. Ted Moran's at work today in Judge

Pierce's courtroom. You can call him too. That should get us through the day."

"I'll handle it," she said. "I don't see how the judge or Rafe Johnson could stand in the way of a continuance."

"You sure that won't look bad to the jury?" Eric said. "You're about to call a witness, then they get sent home for the day?"

"Just go," Tori said. "I can keep things under control here. Viola needs you. Ellen ... needs you."

I touched Tori's arm, thanking her again.

"I'm coming with you," Eric said. "I can run interference with whatever detective has been assigned to this case."

"Grunwald," Tori said. "Viola said the guy's name was Detective Grunwald."

"Good," Eric said. "I know him. You drive and I'll get him on the phone."

After thanking Tori again, I was on the move with Eric close at my heels.

Chapter 28

In some ways, the hour drive to Trenton seemed like the longest of my life. Eric was as good as his word and by the time we arrived at the morgue, Detective Gary Grunwald was waiting for us. I spotted the small, broken form of Viola Colby sitting on a folding chair in the hallway. Behind her, in a cold examining room, I knew her sister's body lay.

"Go ahead," Eric said to me, gesturing toward Viola. I mouthed a thank you as Eric and Detective Grunwald went further down the hall out of earshot where they could talk.

Slowly, I went to Viola. Squatting down in front of her, I put a gentle hand on her arm.

"Viola?"

She met my eyes. Her face purple and blotchy from crying, she clung to me.

"She didn't tell me she was leaving," Viola said. "I went to bed. Ellen was in the kitchen. I told her she should turn in. Get a good night's sleep. Today was supposed to be a big day."

She hiccupped through most of her words.

"Did she leave with someone? Did she tell you where she was going?"

"She thinks I don't know," Viola said. "She goes down to the gas station down the block to get her cigarettes. She told me she quit. I wouldn't have minded for this though. I knew how nervous she was to go to court and talk about what that man did to her."

"It's okay," I said, then wished I could take it back. It was not okay. For Viola, it might never be okay again.

"She got this suit. Eggplant-colored. I never would have picked it for her. But when she tried it on she looked so pretty in it. She was going to wear it today. For court. She tucked the tags in so she could take it back to the store tomorrow."

All I could do was rub her arm.

"I think I'd like to keep it for her," Viola said. "The man from the funeral home told me I could take my time deciding all of that. But she looked so pretty in it. I think I want to keep it for her."

"Viola," I said. "Is there someone I can call for you?"

"I'd just like to go home," she said. "They told me to wait here. I've answered all their questions. But I'd like to go home."

"I understand," I said. "But I don't think you should be alone. Why don't you let me see if I can get one of the deputies to drive you?"

She nodded. "That would be all right. They want me to show them Ellen's room. They want her cell phone and her computer."

"Of course," I said. "They're just trying to piece together who she might have talked to. Who she might have told she was coming to testify. Do you know?"

"Okay," Viola said. "But we were careful who we told. It was just the neighbors because they were going to let the dog out while we were gone."

Guilt washed over me. I should have warned them. I should have had Eric pull strings and get someone to stay with the Colby sisters until I got her safely to court. If Ellen's death were connected to her decision to testify, it would have only taken one leak to cause a flood.

"Just wait here," I said. "I'll get someone to help you get home."

As I stood, Eric jerked his chin toward me, beckoning me over. I left Viola Colby and joined him down the hall with Detective Gary Grunwald.

"She's pretty shaken," I said. "Do you think you could have a deputy take Viola home?"

"Already arranged," Grunwald said. "I'd like to get a look at the victim's ... Ms. Colby's bedroom and personal effects too. She was just waiting for you to get here. Thanks for coming so quickly. Just give me a second and I'll set things in motion to get Ms. Colby home."

Grunwald disappeared down the hallway leaving Eric and I alone.

"I want to take a look at her," Eric said. It took me a beat to realize what he meant. When I had, I knew it's what I needed too.

"Take me with you," I said. "I want to see her, Eric."

His eyes widened. "Cass, I don't think ..."

"I need to know," I said. "If this happened because of me. Because I talked to that poor woman and convinced her to get involved in something dangerous, I have to see it."

Eric knew me well enough to understand I wouldn't be talked out of it. Setting his mouth into a hard line, he gave me a quick nod.

"Come on," he said. "I suppose it's better to apologize later than ask for permission. Just stay quiet."

Eric went to a set of double doors a few feet from us. He pressed the buzzer and identified himself. A moment later, the automatic lock clicked and Eric pushed through the doors. I followed closely behind.

Chapter 29

We were met by Dr. Grace Chen, the assistant M.E. She had just finished tapping something into her tablet as Eric and I walked into the room. On the cold steel examination table behind her, Ellen Colby's body lay zipped into a black bag.

Dr. Chen looked up. She gave me no more than a curious side glance.

Eric introduced us. Dr. Chen smiled and set down her tablet. "Like I told the other detective, I still have to run more labs but I'll be happy to share what I can."

"I really appreciate it," Eric said. He saved a hard glance for me, telegraphing an *are you sure?* I answered with a curt nod and stepped forward with him as Chen went to the head of the table.

I held my breath as she carefully unzipped the bag. Ellen Colby's dyed blonde hair popped out, looking far more yellow to me than it had in life. It contrasted with her waxen white skin. Her face still seemed pretty. Peaceful. I could almost believe the violence that took her had been merciful. But as

Dr. Chen spread open the top of the bag, exposing poor Ellen Colby to just above her breasts, I knew her killer had shown her no mercy at all.

Ellen's throat was cut from ear to ear. Her lips had an odd, swollen shape to them. Her cheeks sunken in.

"They cut out her tongue, poor thing," Chen said.

"That's what we heard," Eric said.

"Do you know?" I asked, instantly regretting it. "Was it after?"

Grace Chen pursed her lips. "No. I'm afraid not. She was most definitely alive when they did that to her. This girl was tortured. I can't say for how long but there was some clotting around most of her wounds prior to the fatal cut to her throat. She had bruising and lacerations around her wrists. Like I said, I've still got more tests to run, but my best guess, they used zip ties. Also, lividity suggests she died while lying on her back. My understanding is there was very little blood in the area she was found. But she's lost pretty much her entire blood volume."

"She was moved," Eric said.

Chen nodded. "Moved and posed on that park bench."

"Someone was trying to send a message," I whispered.

"Pretty loud one," Chen said.

"What do you make of this wound?" Eric said, pointing to a cut just above Ellen's left breast.

"That's one of the reasons I thought it might be good for you to have a look." I hadn't even heard the doors open. But Detective Grunwald came to join us.

I leaned in closer. Ellen had something carved into her skin. An L shape. I tilted my head. Or a V.

"Well," Chen said. "That wasn't a knife wound. They didn't use the same blade to cut her there."

"How can you tell?" I asked.

"With the neck wound, or really any kind of slashing motion with a knife, you'll have a deeper penetration at the entry point where it breaks the skin. The rest of the cut will vary in depth depending on the pressure used to inflict the wound. For example, she was most definitely sliced from left to right at the neck. But that wound above her breast, it's even at almost every point. It was *pressed* into her."

"Like a cookie cutter," I said.

"Right," she said. "It was pressed into her. Just like a cookie cutter. That's exactly it. But a cookie cutter with razor-blade sharp edges."

"V," Eric said.

"V for victory? Victim? Vengeance?" Grunwald added.

"Voice," I whispered. "She has no voice. They cut out her tongue."

Eric tilted his head. "Unless it's supposed to be read the other way. Inverted?"

"You ever seen that symbol before?" Grunwald asked Eric.

"Nothing comes to mind. But I'll start reaching out my way."

"I'd appreciate you sharing anything you find," Grunwald said. "There's some sick bastard out there. I really hope to God this isn't the start of a pattern."

"You'll keep that detail out of the press?" Eric said. "The wound?"

"Of course," Grunwald assured him.

"Thanks again for letting us in on this," Eric said. He pulled at my sleeve. Slowly, reluctantly, I followed him out of the room leaving Ellen Colby to Dr. Grace Chen's care.

By the time we'd come back out into the hallway, Viola was already gone. My phone buzzed with a text from Tori. She'd put Bo Bonham on the stand, but got the judge and Rafe Johnson to agree to adjourn the trial until the day after tomorrow.

Eric and I were mostly silent as we drove back to pick up his car. I pulled into the empty courthouse lot and parked right behind his Bronco.

"You coming over?" I asked.

"Do you want me to?" he asked. "I'm worried about you."

I found a smile. "I'm fine. Really. But I probably won't be good company."

He nodded. "Yeah. I know you. Your wheels are spinning. Are you planning on letting me in? Tell me what's going on in that brain of yours?"

I wasn't sure myself. But I couldn't push the image of the carving on Ellen Colby's chest out of my mind.

"I don't know yet," I said. "It's just ... there's something. That wound."

"Yeah," Eric said. "Let me do what I said to Grunwald. Reach out to a few people. See what I can scare up on some of the criminal databases we have."

Nodding absently, I waited as Eric got out of the car. He leaned over and gave me a quick peck on the cheek, promising to check in with me later tonight.

I sat there for a moment as he drove away. There *was* something. I felt like the answer was right in front of me, floating in the ether. But the moment I thought I had it, it slipped away.

I pulled out of the parking lot. But instead of going home, I knew there was one other thing I had to do.

Chapter 30

THE ANSWER WAS HERE. I sat in the middle of my office conference room floor, poring over every shred of evidence in Ty Chapman's case.

"What were you trying to tell me, Ellen?" I said. "What didn't they want you to tell me?"

I had the photograph Eric took at the morgue pulled up on my phone. I sent it to the printer and waited. Slowly, the paper curled out. I placed it on the floor with the rest of my mess.

"V for victim," I whispered. "V for victory. Violence. Vengeance. Veritas?"

I didn't notice the sunrise. I didn't hear Miranda or Jeanie or Tori come in. It was only when the scent of freshly brewing coffee hit my nose, I realized how long I'd been at this.

"Cass?" Tori called up. She opened the door and caught herself, about to step right on a pile of papers.

"There's something here," I said.

"Wow," Tori said. "You've ... wow."

She carefully closed the door and took long strides, placing her feet in whatever patch of bare carpet she could find. She squatted down beside me.

"It's a message," I said. "It has to be. What they did to Ellen. Tortured her. Cut out her tongue while she could still feel it. Then posing her on that park bench where they knew she'd be found."

"Cass," Tori said. "We still don't know for sure that this had anything to do with the Chapman trial. What did we really know about Ellen Colby?"

"She didn't learn her lesson the first time," I said. "That's what we know about her. Someone got to her when she was about to report Lansky for rape. She changed her story. She thought now that he's dead, it's over. She was wrong. So the first time was a warning. This time was ..."

"Retribution," Tori said, picking up the picture I'd printed out of Ellen's chest wound. Tori rotated it, cocked her head to the side.

"A vee," she said. "Or a delta. Some kind of symbol. Have you talked to Ty Chapman about this?"

"He's gone even more mute," I said.

Tori tossed the picture in with the others.

"John Lansky," I said. "Mild-mannered handyman by day. Rapist by night."

"Like you said," Tori said. She picked up a photo we had of Ellen Colby from her old social media profile. She laid it against a picture of Beth. "Maybe Beth was his type. He approached her. Stalked her. Threatened her. Something. She tells Ty. He goes to talk to Lansky about it. Warn him. Ty's a big guy. Tough guy. Former Marine. Things get out of hand. Then bam! And Ty's got some red rage going on account of whatever happened to him over in Afghanistan. Plus the thought that Lansky would hurt his pregnant wife."

"Only I can't prove any of that," I said. "Beth isn't talking. Ty's not talking. Even if he were ..."

"You can't put him on the stand," Tori said. "No way."

"Right."

I picked up the file containing Ty's booking photos. There was the mugshot showing the cut above his brow.

"He sure looks menacing," Tori said. "That man has got some cold eyes."

"Yeah," I said. "And I think the jury has noticed that, too."

"But Ellen," I said. "Why silence her? What possible harm could her testimony be to anyone other than John Lansky? He's dead. If he was part of something, protected by someone, there's just absolutely nothing to gain by making this big a show out of her murder."

"Maybe it wasn't Ellen they were trying to send a message to," Tori said. "It's bigger than Ellen. Bigger than John Lansky. Somebody's trying to show that snitches get punished, no matter what. Like even death can't protect you. Lansky's death."

I pulled out the rest of Chapman's booking photos. One showed him in profile; the gash above his eye looked even worse here. His whole temple was swollen.

"Lansky hit him," I said. "Why won't you tell me that?" I was talking to Ty's picture and realized I got about the same out of it as I did the living, breathing, three-dimensional Chapman.

The next photograph was of Ty from the waist up. The most serious wounds he'd suffered were all over his chest. It looked like he'd been mauled, almost. Deep scratch marks cut through his pectoral muscles.

"Lansky sure fought like hell," Tori said.

I stared hard at the image.

"And he ran," Tori said. "God. If only Brian and Melissa Boyd hadn't been there. Do you think they're safe? I mean, if someone's out there killing witnesses ..."

I shook my head. My whole body started to tingle. The Boyds were a problem. Sure. But they'd never changed their story. Not once.

"They recognized him first by the clothes he was wearing," I said. "A blue flannel button-down over a white tee shirt. He'd taken the flannel off when Melissa saw him come back out from behind the motel. She noticed a spot of blood on his white tee shirt."

"Right," Tori said.

I peered more closely at the picture. "Tori?" I said, my heart racing.

I handed her the picture of Ty's naked chest.

"What is it?"

"Ty was wearing two shirts during his encounter with John Lansky."

"Right."

"He fought like hell," I said, repeating Tori's earlier statement. "He tried to erase it."

"What?"

It had been there, teasing the corners of my memory. Ty's wounds. He would bear the scars of it for the rest of his life. He fought like hell. Fought like hell and survived. But he would still bear the scars. If I closed my eyes, I could almost see what they looked like now that they had healed.

The germ of an idea took hold. If I was right, there was someone out there who might be able to put the final pieces in place for Ty Chapman's defense. If he would take my call.

Rising to my feet, I sifted through the rubble, looking for my cell phone.

"Cass?" Tori asked. I held up a finger, gesturing for her to hold on. Then I punched in the number I'd never liked to call.

"Agent Cannon," I said, walking away from Tori.

"Hi, Cass," he said.

"You were right, okay?"

"I was?"

"I'll tell you what you want to know. But first, I need you to do something for me. How soon can you get here?"

"Uh ... I'm in Tallahassee working on a case."

"How soon?"

He let out an exasperated sigh. "First thing in the morning, I suppose."

"Perfect," I said. "Just make sure you're wearing a suit." I clicked off, leaving both Tori and Agent Lee Cannon in necessary confusion.

Chapter 31

"WHAT AM I LOOKING AT?" Lee asked. I'd invited him into the conference room where I had my organized mess of trial-related photos strewn all over the floor.

I handed him the printout I'd made of Ellen Colby's body at the morgue. "She was going to testify for me," I told him. "This is what happened to her. Take a good look."

He did. I watched as his face went through a myriad of emotions as he studied Ellen Colby's gruesome death photo. Slowly, his scowl faded to grim understanding. He put the photo on the table and leaned over it. Cannon rubbed a hand over his mouth.

"Cass ..."

"You've seen that before, haven't you?" I said. "A wound like that. What they carved into her chest. You've seen it. You know it."

"It's hard to tell from just a photo," he said. But he was lying.

"It's not."

"Cass, don't go down this road."

"Cannon, you've seen that wound before. Just like you've seen this one before," I said. I shoved Ty Chapman's booking photo under his nose, the one showing him naked from the chest up.

"I'm telling you," he said. "Don't do this."

"And you know I have no choice," I said.

"Who's the lead detective on this case?" Cannon asked. "I need to talk to him."

"You're coming to court with me," I said. I had my subpoena ready.

"You can't bring this up," he said.

"I can't not," I said. "Lee, you know what that mark on her means. You can tell the jury. It's right here. It's been staring me in the face the whole time. The sheriffs didn't know what they had. I didn't know what they had. But now you do. And you have to tell the jury. They have to understand who John Lansky was."

"You need to be very careful," he said, his anger rising. "You're playing with fire."

"I'm playing for my client's life," I said. "You tell me. Knowing what I think I know about John Lansky, if you'd been the one to meet him in a dark alley, you'd have ..."

"I'd have bashed his damn skull in," Cannon said. "I'd have emptied a clip into his head, Cass."

"Exactly," I said. "What made that mark?"

"Cass."

"Lee! What made that mark?" I stepped over stacks of paper and grabbed the photos of Lansky's crime scene. I laid them all out in front of Cannon.

"Take a good look," I said. "It has to be here. It *has* to."

We combed over the images of Lansky's body. His clothing. His shoes. The bloodied rocks surrounding him.

"His hand," Cannon said. "Do you have a photo of his right hand?"

I found it. Lansky's hand was covered in dirt. Smeared with it, actually. The middle finger was twisted at a wrong angle.

"It would have been there," Lee said, pointing to the finger. "If he'd worn it at all."

I put another photograph in front of Lee. This one showed the only personal item the police had found of Lansky's at the crime scene. A domed ring. His face ashen, Lee looked up.

"Is that it?" I asked him. "Is that what they should have been looking closer at?"

"You have no idea what you're about to unleash," Lee said.

"Too late," I said, sliding Ellen Colby's photograph in front of him once more.

"You want me to do what, exactly?" he asked.

I slid another piece of paper in front of him. As his eyes settled over it, his scowl deepened.

"This is crazy," he said. "If you go down this road, I can't guarantee it won't end badly."

"It already has," I said. "Come on. We're due in court."

Lee picked up his subpoena and crumpled it in his fist.

"All you have to do is tell the truth," I said.

"All you have to do is start," he answered. "You going to make the call?"

I picked up my messenger bag off the floor. As soon as I'd secured Lee Cannon's subpoena, I'd taken the small flip phone out of my desk drawer and slipped it in the side pocket of my bag. I hoisted the leather strap over my shoulder.

"You first," I said. "Let's go."

Chapter 32

I stood at the lectern, arguing for permission to put Special Agent Lee Cannon on the stand. He sat behind me, sour-faced, knowing he'd been had. But I had the thing he wanted. The thing he'd compromise just about everything for. I had made the call.

I'd won my first court battle an hour ago when the judge allowed me to put Eric on the stand. He told the jury who Ellen Colby was, why we'd gone to meet with her. The jury now knew she'd been murdered. I used Eric to authenticate the picture he'd taken of Ellen Colby's chest wound. He'd been just about as angry as Cannon. He sat in the back of the courtroom, brooding. But he knew better than to try to stop me once the freight train of my mind was in motion. Cannon was finally starting to figure that out, too.

"Your Honor," I said. "These are extraordinary circumstances. A material witness for the defense was murdered. Silenced. And I can prove it. The jury needs to understand what happened. There was no reasonable way I could have known things would play out like this. Ellen Colby was willing to come forward and tell her story."

"A story that had absolutely no relevance to the issues in this trial," Rafe said, his voice booming.

"It had everything to do with it. It could explain Ty Chapman's actions on the evening John Lansky died. Agent Cannon has relevant testimony with direct bearing on both the evidence the state has presented as well as what happened to Ms. Colby."

"Ms. Colby's murder was horrific," Judge Hughes said. "But Mr. Johnson is right. There is no proof at this point that her death had anything to do with Mr. Chapman's case."

"Yes, there is," I said, my temper getting the best of me. I had grace points with Judge Hughes based on past appearances in his courtroom. I knew I'd just used a few of them up.

"Careful, Counselor," the judge warned me.

"Your Honor," I said. "This is a first-degree murder trial. The stakes could not be higher for the defendant. He must have the right to pursue a rigorous defense. Agent Cannon's testimony is critical to that and the events that have transpired in the last forty-eight hours were beyond our control and reasonable knowledge. We couldn't have predicted this. But here we are. If the police had been more thorough ... If they'd more closely examined the evidence they had right in front of them ..."

"All right," the judge said. "But you need to understand you are on a very short leash, Ms. Leary. Agent Cannon may testify, but only to a very limited degree."

"Thank you!" I said.

Johnson protested, but it was over. Cannon was taking the stand.

"I hope you know what you're doing," Ty muttered beside me. I took another gamble and told him very little about what my ultimate plans with Cannon were.

A few minutes later, the judge called the jury in. I called Lee Cannon to the stand.

Tight leash. I thought. I could get this in a dozen questions or less.

"Agent Cannon," I said. "Can you please inform the jury what you do for a living?"

"I'm a special agent with the Federal Bureau of Investigations out of the Chicago Field Office."

"In that capacity," I said, "what types of cases do you work?"

"I've been involved with counterterrorism and organized crime for the majority of my career."

"And how long is that?"

"Fifteen years," he said.

"Agent Cannon," I said. "I'd like to direct your attention to Defense Exhibit number twenty-one." As I'd already admitted it with Eric's testimony, I displayed the picture of the vee-shaped wound on Ellen Colby's chest on the screen.

"Agent Cannon," I said. "Have you ever seen a wound like that before?"

"Yes," he said, tight-jawed.

"Where?"

"Your Honor," Rafe rose. "Same objection as to relevance."

"Overruled," Hughes said. At this point, Johnson knew he'd lose, but he had to preserve the record for appeal if it ever came to that.

"I'll repeat the question," I said. "Where have you seen a wound like that?"

"It's a calling card for a particular organized crime syndicate based out of Detroit. Most closely associated with the Orlov family. We believe they have ties to the Russian mob."

"You've had occasion to investigate this syndicate?"

"I have," he said. "About eight years ago, I was involved in the investigation of the murder of an arms dealer working for a rival gang. The victim had an identical wound on his chest. Two years ago in Philadelphia, a bag man for a different crime family was found in a drainage ditch. He also had a wound cut into his skin like that. Just above the heart. And five years ago, we had an undercover agent who had infiltrated the Orlov gang go missing. He was later found buried in a shallow grave outside with a carving just like that in his chest. Sergei Orlov was convicted of the crime and turned state's evidence. Last year, he was found murdered in his cell with the same carving on his chest."

"Do you know what it means?" I asked.

"I do," he said. "It's the letter vee. We believe it means vengeance. In all of these cases I've described, the victims were either getting ready to testify against the Orlov gang, or had in some way encroached on the territory of the Orlov gang. It's a message. A brand. Once you have it, you're considered a marked man ... person. They own you. So the rest of the world knows how far the Orlovs can reach."

"Are the victims always killed?"

"No," Lee said, his voice going cold. "Sometimes victims are left alive with the brand in order to humiliate them. We own you. That type of thing."

Ty Chapman stiffened. He curled his fists. This was the thing I hadn't told him about. We'd only discussed Cannon's testimony as it related to Ellen Colby herself.

"Agent Cannon," I said. "Do you know how this vee mark is made?"

"I do," he said. "Years ago, I had an informant who worked for the Orlov family. He wore a ring. Fairly large, with a dome-shaped design on the front. The dome opened and there was a vee-shaped blade inside. Sharp as a razor. They'd use it to press it into a victim's skin."

"Agent Cannon," I said. "Would you recognize this ring if you saw it again?"

"Yes. It's not something you forget."

"I see. Agent Cannon, I'd like to direct your attention to State's Exhibit forty-nine. Do you recognize it?"

I displayed the photograph of the ring found on the ground near John Lansky's body. The same photograph I'd shown Cannon back in my office. His scowl returned.

"I do," he said. "It's identical to the ring my informant wore. It's an Orlov ring."

I saw a few members of the jury recoil. It was too easy to imagine it being done to poor Ellen Colby.

"Agent Cannon," I said. "In your investigations dealing with the Orlov crime gang, did you ever come across the name John Lansky?"

"Not during my previous investigations, no," he said.

"Since?"

"Not until you contacted me and briefed me on the details of this case."

"Agent Cannon, what is John Lansky's affiliation with the Orlov family, if you know?"

"I can't say for certain," he said. "But at your request, I looked more deeply into his background. John Lansky was incarcerated in Jackson State Prison seven years ago. At that time, he spent a year as a cellmate to a man named Serge Boris."

"And who is Serge Boris?"

"He is a known affiliate of the Orlov family. He's a hitman for them. He was, still is, serving time for the murder of Anton Zelensky, a rival gang member."

"A year," I said. "You're saying it's come to your attention that John Lansky was cellmates with an Orlov family hitman for a year?"

"Yes."

"Thank you, Agent Cannon," I said. "I have no other questions."

Johnson sprang up. "Agent Cannon, you're not involved in the investigation of the murder of John Lansky, are you?"

"No, sir."

"And you haven't been asked to consult on the investigation of the Ellen Colby murder either, have you? Officially."

"Not as of yet, no. That's going to change as soon as I leave this courtroom."

"You have no direct knowledge that Ellen Colby or John Lansky or anyone else from the Orlov family had anything to do with the events of this trial, do you?"

"I don't, no."

"In fact, you'd never even heard of Ellen Colby before today, had you?"

"No."

"Or John Lansky, for that matter."

"Well, I knew about Lansky from Ms. Leary," he said.

"She told you," Johnson said.

"Yes, sir."

"Isn't it true you can't connect a single fact of this case to anything you've ever worked on, can you?"

"Not yet," he answered. "But as I've testified, there are similarities to ..."

"Not yet," Rafe repeated. "Only what Ms. Leary has coached you on."

"Objection," I said.

"Withdrawn," Johnson said, though he'd made as much of a point as he could.

"I'm through with this witness," Johnson said.

With no redirect from me, Lee Cannon left the stand and we broke for lunch.

Lee practically bolted for me. "Outside," he said. "In the hallway. Now."

I got equally angry stares from both my client and Eric. At least in Chapman's case, I could rely on the deputies to keep him in check.

"What are you doing?" Eric and Lee demanded in unison once we'd found a relatively private space down the hall.

"Eric," I said. "I need you to trust me for a little bit. And I need you to let me talk to Lee alone."

"What? No way. You're kicking a hornet's nest. The Orlov family? You saw what they did to Ellen Colby, if that's what this is. I'm not leaving your side."

Lee flapped his hands, gesturing the same exasperation with me. I'd already gotten this lecture from him when he first showed up.

"Eric, please," I said. "Five minutes. Then I'll come find you."

He and Cannon exchanged a look. "You better talk some sense into her, Cannon."

"What makes you think she listens to me any more than she listens to you?"

"Enough!" I said. "Both of you. Eric, I need a minute."

I grabbed Lee by the arm and half dragged him further down the hallway. Eric finally relented, but I knew he wouldn't be far.

"Cass," Lee started.

"I keep my promises," I said.

"You sure you know what you're doing?" he asked.

"You could have said no to me. If you were that worried about protecting me from what I'm about to do, you could have just not showed up. You could have told me to screw off. You didn't. You're here. Which means what you want, you want badly enough to let me jump off this particular cliff."

I pulled out the flip phone I'd been carrying. Down the hall, I saw a few reporters starting to gather. Just as I'd hoped. They'd probably posted their stories about today's testimony already.

"You're insane," Cannon said. "You really do have some kind of death wish. You should have let me get you into protective custody years ago."

"You never could have kept me safe," I said. "That's something I've always had to do on my own."

With that, I dialed the number of the other person who'd made the same promises as Lee Cannon. He'd been just as powerless to keep them.

"Killian," I said when he answered. Lee Cannon's eyes got big, then hardened. "It's me. How far away are you now?" It was our second conversation. I'd made the first earlier once I had Lee in place, but before he took the stand. By now, I knew Killian would know about Lee's testimony.

"What are you doing, Cass?" Killian said, his tone as angry as Lee Cannon's eyes.

"You've been following the trial, I take it," I said. "How much longer until you get here? I think I've made a terrible mistake."

He was already on his way. Of course he was. But probably for the last time. I just prayed this would all be worth what this might cost me.

Chapter 33

He came. I knew he would. I also knew that in calling him here like this, it would likely be the last time I could ever count on Killian Thorne to drop everything for me.

I waited in the parking lot of the Sweet Delights, my favorite local bakery and coffee shop. Killian pulled up exactly twenty minutes after my second call. I was due back in court any minute.

I stood in the shade against the brick wall on the north side of the building. Killian pulled into a spot, slid a pair of sunglasses up his nose, then came out to meet me.

His cocksure swagger. His smile. He peered at me over the top of his mirrored sunglasses and came to me.

"You're all right, a rúnsearc?" he said.

"Don't." My voice was tight. My whole body felt coiled to strike. In another minute, he would too.

"What is it?" he asked. "What have you done?"

"It's time for the truth," I said. "All of it. You've been lying to me for weeks. Months. It stops today. Right now. I know you know I put Lee Cannon on the stand this morning. I'd bet my practice you know exactly what he said."

His shoulders fell. "What is it you want from me?"

"Not here," I said. "You're going to tell the truth where it will actually do some good, Killian."

I looked past him, giving a slow nod. Four men came out of the two cars parked just across the street. Killian turned, sensing the trouble he'd ignored. He'd been too focused on me. It's what I'd counted on.

"What?"

I took a folded piece of paper out of my pocket and handed it to him. Jaw dropped, Killian took it.

"A subpoena? Cass, you can't ..."

"Killian," I said. "That's a court order. Those two deputies are here to make sure you follow it."

"It's for today," he said, looking back at me.

"It's for right now," I said. "I'm putting you on the stand in the Tyler Chapman trial, too."

Eric and Lee Cannon crossed the street along with the deputies. Both of them held anger in their eyes. They knew. Killian wasn't the only one who had been holding back the truth. I hated myself for it. For that and a lot of things.

"You can't do this, Cass," Killian said. "You're my lawyer."

"She's nothing to you now," Eric said.

Hatred flashed in Killian's eyes as he stared at Eric. The two of them had gone toe-to-toe so many times before. The deputies were here as much to keep them from trying to rip each other's throats out as they were to drag Killian to the witness stand if need be.

"Cass," Lee said through gritted teeth. He reached for me, pulling me out of the group, away from Killian and Eric as they decided whether to kill each other.

"Do you understand what you're doing?"

"The only thing I have left," I said.

"You should have just told me the truth. You should have leveled with me that you knew how to get a hold of him this whole time."

"And you knew I was lying," I said. "This is my part of the bargain. I told you if you took the stand and answered my questions, I'd owe you. Well, here he is. After Killian testifies, you do what you need to do."

Another gamble. Lee didn't have enough to bring any sort of indictment against Killian. Whatever he was working on, it hadn't ripened.

Killian broke away from Eric. The two deputies closed in.

"You take another step toward me," Killian said. "I'll rip your damn arms off."

"I'd like to see you try," Eric said.

"Enough," I said. "You're testifying, Killian. I've kept the judge waiting long enough."

"What are you doing?"

"My job," I said. "Defending my client."

"Attorney-client privilege still attaches between you and me," he growled.

"Come on," I said. "We'll talk on the way."

I signaled to the two deputies. Eric moved in as well, only too eager to lay hands on Killian if it came to it.

Angry though he was, Killian knew he couldn't win against all three of them. Lee shook his head, but fell in line too.

"It'll be quick," I said to Killian as he finally started to walk with me back toward the courthouse. "Five or six questions. And I promise you I won't ask you anything that would compromise you in any way."

"Just being here compromises me," he said under his breath so the others wouldn't hear.

"Well," I said. "I suppose you should have thought of that long before you started lying to me."

We crossed the street and entered the courthouse through a side entrance. With Killian at my side, the rest of my angry entourage followed us up the stairs.

Tori waited outside the courtroom. Her shoulders sagged with relief when she saw us.

"Thank God," she said. "Hughes was about to hold you in contempt."

I steeled myself for whatever berating I'd get from Judge Hughes. I was ready for Rafe Johnson's objections as well. Two minutes later, Killian sat in the gallery as I argued for the chance to put him on the stand.

Ty Chapman sat red-faced at the table.

"Your Honor," I said. "Mr. Thorne has relevant testimony to offer specific to the evidence found on John Lansky and the defendant. As I've told him, I only have a handful of questions to ask. I promise you, their import will be clear pretty quickly."

"They better," Judge Hughes said. My heart lifted as he granted my motion to put Killian on the stand.

Then, with his fists clenched and his eyes blazing, Killian Thorne walked up to the witness box.

"You can't do this," Ty muttered to me. "I didn't authorize this."

"You authorized me to fight for your future. You gave me one directive: keep you from spending the rest of your life behind bars. Now if you'll just sit quietly and do what I say, you might have a chance to walk out of here a free man."

"Ms. Leary?" the judge said.

"Sorry," I said. I rose and stepped up to the lectern. Killian identified himself to the jury. I took a breath. I had no notes. No certainty as to what Killian might say. But I knew down to my bones, I was right about everything else.

"Mr. Thorne," I said. "Are you familiar with the Orlov crime family?"

"What?"

I repeated the question. He glared at me.

"Your Honor," I said. "Will you please instruct the witness to answer?"

"He's your witness, Ms. Leary," the judge said. "Fine. Mr. Thorne, you're under oath and were compelled to sit there by court order. So you better answer."

"Yes," Killian said.

"Mr. Thorne," I said. "Do you have firsthand knowledge of the method in which members of the Orlovs dispatch their enemies?"

"Objection," Rafe said. "This is speculative testimony at best."

"I believe I've asked this witness whether he has firsthand knowledge of the killing methods of the Orlov gang."

Judge Hughes frowned, but overruled Rafe's objection.

"Mr. Thorne?"

Killian's face turned to stone. He knew where I was headed.

"Cass," Ty said. "Stop."

"Mr. Thorne," I said, my voice rising. "Do you or do you not have firsthand knowledge of the Orlovs' calling card?"

"Yes," Killian hissed.

"What happened to you, Mr. Thorne? How did you acquire that firsthand knowledge?"

Killian's eyes narrowed. He looked at me, then looked at the judge.

"Answer the question, Mr. Thorne," Judge Hughes said.

"What happened?" Killian spat. "I got jumped by their thugs. A coward who came at me three on one in a dark alley. It was a very long time ago."

"How long ago?" I asked. If I closed my eyes, I could see it. The pain that carved deep lines in Killian's face as he told me about that night when he nearly died. How I traced the imperfections in his otherwise perfect chest. He flinched at first. Then slowly, over time, he'd let me touch him there.

"I was nineteen," he said. "Maybe twenty. My first trip to Chicago."

"What happened?" I asked.

"I told you," Killian said. "They jumped me. I was getting out of a car. Three men threw a sack over my head. They pulled me into an alley. Beat me within an inch of my life. I woke up in the hospital."

"You almost died, didn't you?" I asked.

"Yes," he answered. "They had to take out my spleen."

"They stabbed you," I said.

"Yes."

"What else did they do, Mr. Thorne?"

He wouldn't answer. He was a statue.

"Mr. Thorne," I said. "What did they do to you?"

"They cut me," he hissed.

"Can you describe the cut?"

Killian closed his eyes. I knew he saw it too.

"A mark," he said. "A vee."

"I'm sorry," I said. "Can you repeat that? Louder? The court reporter needs to be able to hear you."

"A small vee," Killian said. "Just above my heart."

"Mr. Thorne," I asked. "Do you still have that scar? A vee cut into the skin above your heart?"

No answer. Just that deadly glare.

"Mr. Thorne?" Judge Hughes said.

"No," Killian spat.

"No, you don't have that vee scar?" I asked.

"No."

"Why not?"

"Because I wouldn't let them brand me," he said. "I wouldn't give them the satisfaction. So I clawed it out!"

"You clawed it out?" I asked. "By yourself?"

"Yes," he said. Killian held up his right hand. He made a claw with it and mimicked raking it across his own flesh.

"So you still have a scar," I asked.

"You know I do," Killian said, the corners of his mouth lifting in a smirk. I heard a noise behind me. A growl of anger. It was Eric.

"Mr. Thorne," I said. "I need you to show the jury. Let us see your scar."

"Your Honor," Rafe said.

"Your Honor," I interjected. "It is within our rights to explore each and every bit of evidence the prosecution has introduced against my client. If there is an exculpatory interpretation of that evidence, not only is the jury entitled to hear it, they will be mandated to infer that interpretation when they deliberate."

"I'll allow it," Judge Hughes said.

"Mr. Thorne?" I repeated.

Killian rose to his feet. Slowly, he opened the buttons of his dress shirt one by one. Squaring his shoulders, he spread his shirt, revealing the ugly, healed scars over his left pectoral muscles. Some scars were deeper than others. At the center, there was just the faintest, puckered circle where Killian had torn the skin around where the brand had been carved. Webbing out from that, were faint lines. What I now knew were claw marks. So many times I'd traced lines through them myself as he lay sleeping beside me. I'd never known. Maybe I hadn't wanted to. I had never asked him to explain until now.

Gasps escaped from a few members of the jury. The scar was familiar to them. They'd seen it before. I would hammer that home at closing.

"Mr. Thorne," I said as Killian sat down. He left his shirt unbuttoned. "I'd like to direct your attention to a photograph that's been introduced as State's Exhibit forty-nine. Do you recognize what's depicted in that photograph?"

"Yes," Killian said.

"What do you recognize it to be?"

"It's a ring," he said. "Similar to one worn by members of the Orlov family."

"And where have you seen that ring before?"

"It's like the one used on me. The one carved into my skin when they almost killed me."

"I'd like permission to hand this witness State's Exhibit fifty," I said.

With some jockeying, the judge allowed it. I handed Killian a pair of latex gloves. He put them on and I handed him the ring.

"Mr. Thorne," I said. "Can you show the jury how that ring works?"

Killian held it up. He pressed the side of the ring. There was a small click, then the dome on the outside of the ring popped open, revealing the razor-sharp blades of the vee symbol inside. They'd missed it. The sheriffs had missed it. They had never tried to open the ring.

"Thank you," I said as I took the ring back. I walked it in front of the jury so they could see. So they would know. Then I placed it back into the tray near Rafe Johnson's table.

"I have no further questions."

Rafe shook his head as he rose.

"Mr. Johnson?" the judge said.

"Mr. Thorne?" Rafe said. "Do you know the victim in this case, John Lansky?"

"I don't," Killian said.

Rafe gripped the sides of the lectern. Again, he shook his head. "That's it. I'm done. I have no questions for this witness. This is a waste of time."

"No further questions from me," I said. Killian rose, not waiting for the judge to dismiss him. Judge Hughes banged his gavel, yelling at Killian as he charged out of the courtroom.

But he decided the better of having the deputies run after him.

"Ms. Leary?" he said, angry. "Call your next witness."

"Your Honor," I said. "At this time, the defense rests."

"Get me the hell out of here," Ty whispered beside me. "Now!"

Chapter 34

IN THE HALLWAY, three keyed-up men seemed ready to rip my head off. I got to take my pick.

"You," I said to Killian. "Inside, now."

I pointed to the open doorway to the court library. There was currently nobody inside.

"Cass," Eric said, surprising me that he was still verbal.

"Not yet," I said. I didn't wait for him to further react. I just grabbed Killian by the shirtsleeve and shoved him through the doorway. Slamming it behind him, I turned on him.

"You have no idea what you've done," he said.

"You lied to me," I said. "You've been lying to me ever since you showed up on my doorstep. You knew. Dammit, Killian. You knew. John Lansky was sent here to find you and kill you. Tyler Chapman got caught up in it somehow. That's why he won't talk. Because of those claw marks on his chest. He's afraid if he talks, someone will try to finish what Lansky started. Either they'll go after Beth. Or him. He's protecting her."

Killian's stony silence confirmed everything I needed.

"You knew," I whispered. "You've had the means to help that man. To help me. All you had to do was be honest. It was you John Lansky was trying to find. That's why you've been trying to hide. And it wasn't a coincidence you showing up at my house last fall a week after Lansky's killing. You put me at risk."

"I've never met John Lansky," Killian said.

"Bullshit," I said. "Are you going to stand there and say I've got it wrong? He was cellmates with a known member of the Orlovs. Cannon confirmed it."

"You have no idea how much you've complicated things," Killian said. "Things would have been fine if you'd let me stay out of sight. You knew I'd come the second you called. You used our relationship to further your own ends."

"Our relationship? What's that, exactly? You show up when you feel like it. When it suits you. When it's going to cause me the most trouble."

He smiled. "It's not my fault your new man can't handle a little competition. Maybe he's got something to fear."

"Shut up," I said. "Just stop it."

"What do you want from me?"

"The truth!" I yelled. "That's all I ever wanted from you. No more lies. No more chess games. No more riddles. Every time you've tried to keep something from me, it has cost me."

"I've protected you," he spat.

"The only person I've ever needed protection from is you! You don't get to claim you're some hero of mine by swooping in to save me from the danger you created, Killian. God. Everyone's been telling me that. Eric's been telling me that. I've been too thick to listen. Because of our relationship. You leverage it when it suits you."

"So do you!" he said. "When you needed to find your sister. When you needed me to save your boyfriend. And now, when you're about to lose a murder case."

My head pounded. It was too much. It was all just too much.

"Cass?" Eric called from the other side of the door.

"Go," I said to Killian. "Just go."

"It's not that simple," he said. "You've exposed me. How long do you think it will take before it hits the internet that you made me testify?"

"You'll land on your feet," I said. "You always do. No matter whose head you drop a house on."

Eric opened the door. "Cass," he said. "You need to get back into the courtroom. Johnson's ready to deliver his closing argument. He's telling the judge he isn't putting on a rebuttal case."

"What?"

"It was for nothing," Killian said. "This has all been for nothing, Cass."

"I think you need to get out of my sight," Eric snapped at him. "If I ever see you so much as look at her ..."

"You'll what?" Killian roared. He crossed the distance from me to Eric in two long strides. They were nose to nose.

"Stop!" I yelled. They'd raised their voices enough to draw attention from other people in the hallway.

"Enough." Lee Cannon stepped between Eric and Killian. It was perhaps the bravest or most dangerous move he'd made in his whole career.

"I'm taking you out of here," Lee said to Killian.

"I'd like to see you try," Killian said.

"I'm offering you my help, idiot," Lee said. "You've been trying to lay low? I know a safe house."

"You think that'll keep me safer?" Killian said. "Once word gets out I've trotted off with the FBI?"

"No one will know," Lee said. "I'll make sure of it."

"Killian, go with him," I said. "For now."

He looked down the hallway. There were people everywhere.

"Give me a few minutes," Eric said. "I'll get the deputies to clear the hallway and the service elevator. No one will see you leave. Plus, they're all more interested in what's happening inside the courtroom."

"Cass?" Tori said. Breathless, she came running down the hall. "Judge Hughes is calling for you. Rafe's ready to go. The jury is already seated."

I nodded. "You got this?" I said to Eric, then to Lee.

They both gave me terse nods. I purposely didn't look at Killian. For one thing, I was afraid I'd lose control completely and rip his face off.

With Tori at my heels, I headed back into the courtroom. Beth Chapman sat quietly weeping on a back bench. Her belly churned and rolled as the tiny life inside of it seemed to grow restless like the rest of us. Ty wouldn't look at me as I sat beside him. He stared straight ahead and simply muttered, "I sure hope you know what you're doing."

So did I. With that, Rafe stepped up to the lectern and prepared to address the jury one last time.

Chapter 35

"MEMBERS OF THE JURY," he said. "You've heard a lot of sensational testimony. I'll be frank, a lot of it shocked even me. And I'm not, by nature, easily surprised. But I was this time. Not because I heard a single viable defense to Ty Chapman's actions. Or a reasonable explanation to why he brutalized and killed John Lansky. And let's be clear. He did that. Don't let a single word of Cass Leary's incredible attempt at misdirection sway you from those facts.

"Tyler Chapman killed John Lansky. He crushed in his skull with a rock. He kept beating him, even after Lansky was already dead. He left nothing of his face but a bloodied pulp. His blood, his DNA was found at the crime scene. He was positively identified as being the last person with John Lansky. He was seen walking with Lansky into the very woods where Lansky was killed. And he was seen running from those same woods. Cut. Bruised. Bloodied.

"There is no doubt Chapman is the one who committed this horrible crime. Zero. It's not even close to reasonable doubt. There's zero doubt. Think about that."

Rafe paused. He shook his head and let out a bitter laugh. "I'm sorry, ladies and gentlemen. You'll have to forgive me because I am truly at a loss. This case has shown me things I never thought I'd see at trial. The brutality of the crime, first of all. I told you, it's the worst I've ever seen. I pray I'll never see anything else like it in my career. I pray none of you ever see anything like it again. But the thing is, it's your duty to make sure it doesn't. It's your duty to serve justice for John Lansky.

"The defense wants you to believe some incredible story about who John Lansky is. That he's connected to some nebulous mobster family. None of which were brought forth to testify. No names. No faces. Not a shred of a real connection to this case. None.

"But fine. Let's ride the fantasy train right along with Cass Leary for a moment. Even if John Lansky were the devil himself, it doesn't matter. He was murdered. We don't take the law into our own hands. Not in a civilized society. If you do that. If you punish John Lansky for some made-up past, well then, God help us all.

"So Cass Leary told a good story. It was shocking. Riveting actually. It would make a good movie. Only this is real life. A real courtroom. And your task is to determine whether Tyler Chapman committed the crimes charged. Whether the evidence supports his guilt beyond a reasonable doubt. That's the keyword here. Reasonable.

"We don't know exactly what happened out in those woods. We never will. But the thing is, we know enough. More than enough. Ty Chapman is guilty. Nobody else. Lansky didn't deserve his fate. And for that, Tyler Chapman must be held accountable. That's all I have to say. Thank you for your time."

Shaking his head. Rafe Johnson went back to his table.

"Ms. Leary?" Judge Hughes said.

My blood zinged with adrenaline. Had I done enough? Was Rafe right? If I were a member of that jury, what would I think? As I rose and took my place at the lectern, I had no earthly clue.

"Thank you," I started. "This can't have been an easy week for any of you. The circumstances of this case *were* brutal. Mr. Johnson is right about that. He's also right that your task is to determine whether he, Mr. Johnson, has presented enough evidence for you to find Tyler Chapman guilty of murder.

"Murder," I said. "First-degree murder requires premeditation. Planning. Later, the judge will instruct you as to what that planning entails. What level of premeditation is required? It's a high burden. As it should be.

"Guilt is what you must determine. Only guilt. Not innocence. You are not charged with the task of finding Mr. Chapman innocent. You must only ask yourselves whether the state has proven their case. Guilt. Beyond a reasonable doubt.

"Mr. Johnson spent so much of his time ... all of his time, really, in his remarks trying to convince you to disregard what you now know about John Lansky. What you now know about Tyler Chapman?

"It's reasonable, ladies and gentlemen, to conclude that John Lansky wasn't who he said he was. He wasn't who he pretended to be to the people of this town. What he was was a trained killer. He went to prison for assaulting another man. That's a fact. He became well acquainted with a member of the Orlovs while serving time for that assault. Spent almost a year in a cell with him. That's a fact. Near his body, with his DNA on it, was a ring worn by members of the Orlov gang. It was John Lansky's ring, members of the jury. That's a fact. But not just any member. An assassin. A hitman. That also is a fact.

"So no," I said. "We don't know exactly what happened in those woods. But we don't have to. It was written on Tyler Chapman's very flesh."

I went to my laptop and pulled up the booking photo of Ty Chapman's naked chest. The raw, angry claw marks right above his heart.

"These wounds," I said. "They were made with anger. In desperation. Mr. Johnson wants you to believe they were made by someone fighting for his life. Well, they were. But not by John Lansky. You heard the medical examiner's testimony. The detective's. John Lansky had no skin beneath his fingernails. Because he isn't the one who wounded Ty Chapman in this way. I put it to you. Ty Chapman did this to himself. He did it so he could claw away at the brand John Lansky tried to carve into his skin, just like Killian Thorne did when he was nineteen years old. The brand that would mark him for death by the Orlov family. Ask yourselves. These claw marks would bleed. And yet, Melissa and Brian Boyd only saw a very small amount of blood on Mr. Chapman's *white* tee shirt. Why? Because at the time they saw him, Chapman only had a small wound there. Only the vee carving made by John Lansky's ring. Ty Chapman clawed his own skin off *after* the Boyds saw him. After John Lansky pressed the blades of his ring into Tyler Chapman's skin. When he tried to kill him."

I held up Lansky's ring and snapped open the dome covering so the jury could see the razor-sharp vee at its center.

"Just like Killian Thorne did," I said. "You saw his scars. They're the same. Tyler Chapman did the same thing Killian Thorne did when he survived an attempted murder by a member of the Orlov gang. He clawed the mark out. He would not allow himself to be branded. He fought for his life.

"Tyler Chapman fought for his life that night. He was confronted by a trained killer. We'll never know what transpired between the two of them. But we don't have to. We know enough. This was no premeditated murder. By the legal definitions you are bound to apply, this was no murder at all. The prosecution hasn't proven it. They haven't answered the questions they must.

"Tyler Chapman is not guilty. The prosecution has fallen short of their job. It's dissatisfying, not knowing what really happened out there. I'm the first to admit that. Maybe Rafe Johnson jumped the gun. Maybe he should have waited. Asked more questions. Demanded the police conduct a more thorough investigation into who John Lansky really was. But he didn't. So you have to deliberate using the facts he did present. Woefully inadequate though they are. That's your job. Just because someone else didn't do theirs doesn't mean you have to fix it for them.

"So, ladies and gentlemen, you have no choice. We ... have no choice. The state has not met its burden of proof. They have not proven that Tyler Chapman is guilty of murder beyond a reasonable doubt. As such, I ask you, I implore you to do the only thing you can. Deliver a not guilty verdict. Thank you."

I went back to my seat. Rafe Johnson had almost turned purple. He barely waited for Judge Hughes to give him permission before he delivered his short rebuttal in a blistering tone.

"Fantasy," he shouted. "That's all you've been given by the defense. Fantasy. And frankly, I'm surprised this court allowed it. Don't be fooled. You have a guilty man in front of you. I pray you do the right thing."

Then he sat. Beside me, Ty still refused to look at me. But this time, I saw the hint of a smile light his eyes.

Chapter 36

THEY HAD MOMENTS. Seconds, really. The judge delivered jury instructions and sent the panel of men and women off to decide Ty Chapman's fate. One of the deputies took pity on the very pregnant Beth Chapman and let her go to her husband. She collapsed into his arms.

"It's over," he whispered, kissing the top of her head. I found that a strange thing for him to say. From where I sat, this thing was only just beginning.

"Thank you," he said to me, holding Beth up.

"It's not too late," I said. "You can still tell me the truth, Ty."

He turned his attention back to his wife. "It's going to be okay now," he said. She whispered something to him. I suddenly felt like an intruder. I quietly gathered my things and stuffed them back into my messenger bag. Tori went to get my car out of the lot. I knew I'd find at least Eric waiting for me back at my office. Killian had finally left with Agent Cannon. A blessing. I didn't think I could face either one of them right now.

"I've pulled your car around to the side entrance," Tori texted me as I found a spot in the back of the courtroom. "Coast is clear here."

I texted back a quick THX. Behind me, Beth and Ty communicated in that shorthand husbands and wives often have, their foreheads pressed against each other's.

"Time to go, Chapman," the deputy said, breaking them up. Beth hugged Ty again, holding him in a death grip.

"I'll take care of her," I assured Ty. He gave me an odd smile.

"Beth," I said. "Tori's outside with my car. We can drive you home."

Beth shook her head as she finally broke away from Ty. The deputies placed cuffs on him. He winked at Beth as they led him out of the courtroom.

"Come on," I said to Beth, putting an arm around her. She stiffened. I let go. "Let Tori and me take you home."

"I have my car," she said. "I'm all right. How long do you think it will take them?"

We walked out into the hallway together, choosing the stairs over the elevator. Beth held her stomach with one hand, the railing with the other.

"I honestly don't know, Beth," I said. "I don't expect we'll hear anything today. It could take days. It could take weeks. Though I predict this will be a shorter deliberation."

"They could find him not guilty?"

"They could," I said.

We'd reached the landing. I led Beth to the service exit. Tori had pulled my car right up to the curb. Again, Beth declined to go with us.

"Your car is clear on the other side of the lot, Beth," I said. "At least let us take you to it."

She shook her head. "I like to walk. I'm fine. I need air. Just call me when you know anything."

We said our goodbyes. I slipped into the passenger seat. We watched Beth waddle around the corner.

"Is she going to be okay?" Tori asked.

"She's numb, still," I said. "I think she understood today might be the last time she'll get to hug her husband or be with him outside of prison walls."

"You really think none of it matters?" Tori said as she started the quick drive back to the office.

"I don't know," I said. "Rafe made a lot of good points. He was right. We were lucky Judge Hughes let so much in. If this were a civil trial, Rafe would have a mountain of issues to bring on appeal."

"They feel sorry for him," Tori said. "I could read it on their faces. And they feel sorry for Beth. They believe something else was going on out in those woods, Cass. They're not going to come back with first degree."

"Then I've done all I can do," I said. "That's the only thing Ty Chapman has ever said to me of substance. He doesn't want to spend the rest of his life in prison. But even without a first-degree conviction, he's looking at a mandatory twenty years."

"If they convict," Tori said, smiling. She pulled into the parking lot. This late in the day, Miranda had already gone home. So had Jeanie. There were no other cars in the lot. I expected to see Eric. Perhaps he needed time to cool off.

Weary, Tori and I walked up to the conference room together. She'd already boxed up the trial prep mess. The room looked clean again, ready for the next case that would take over my life.

"You shouldn't stay here tonight," Tori said. She leaned against the door jamb, her silhouette making her growing belly more prominent.

"Neither should you," I said. "Is Matty coming to pick you up?" She came in with Miranda this morning. Matty made up some excuse about wanting to get her tires rotated. In reality, Vangie and my sister-in-law Kate were planning to surprise her with an early baby shower gift. We'd gone in on the fanciest car seat on the market. They were installing it as we spoke.

"Eventually," she said. "He just called. He's running a little late on one of his jobs. He'll be here in about an hour."

She yawned again. I looked at her. Really looked at her. Besides the swell to her abdomen, Tori's arms and legs looked very thin. Her face gaunt. She had dark circles beneath her eyes.

"I'm sorry," I said. "I don't know what I was thinking. You need to go home. Just take my car."

"You're really going to stay the night?" she asked. "Cass, you can't hide out forever. You can't avoid Eric."

I smiled. She knew me well. "I'm fine. If he really wants to duke it out about Killian, he'll figure out where to find me. He hasn't called or texted. So, best guess, he's off licking his wounds for a while."

"He's a good man," Tori said. There was no judgment in her tone, but I could read her face.

"I know," I said. "Believe me."

"We're all just worried about you," Tori said. "There's a lot you've been keeping to yourself."

"I'm sorry," I said. "I really am."

"You could have told me about Killian. You could have told someone."

"I know. Tori, I know I have a lot to answer for. And I will. I promise. Just ... not tonight. Seriously. Just head on home. We'll all come at this with fresh heads next week. In fact, take the whole week off. Let my brother pamper you. You deserve it. You're heading into your third trimester."

"I'll see you tomorrow," she said. "I'll have Matty drive your car back to your place. The girls should have my surprise installed in my car by then." She winked at me.

"Ugh," I said. "You didn't hear it from me. And you better act surprised."

"I will," she laughed. "Just like I'll act surprised at the shower Kate's throwing me next week. And call him! Don't wait for Eric to call you."

Man. I'd have to warn my brother. This woman missed nothing. I gave Tori a dutiful salute as she turned and headed down the stairs.

I felt like I'd been hit by a Mack truck. She was right. I should call Eric. I should ... do so many things. But just then, I just wanted to sleep. I headed back into my office, pulled out the sofa bed, kicked off my shoes and let sweet oblivion take me.

Chapter 37

Dappled light through the slatted blinds woke me. A door closed somewhere downstairs, disorienting me as I tried to remember where I was.

Not home. Not my bed. The rails of the bed frame poked my side through the thin mattress of my office sofa bed.

"Cass?" Eric's voice called up. Shaking the fog from my head, I rose. My teeth felt fuzzy. It was too light. Too late.

Breathless, Eric came into the room. His face fell for a moment, seeing me. Relieved.

"There you are," he said. He hesitated. Taking a halting step before coming fully in.

"Hey," I said, smiling.

"You can't hide out forever, kid." His smile didn't quite reach his eyes. I'd hurt him. Withheld the truth from him. And yet, he was here.

"I'm sorry," I said. "I should have called you. I should have ..."

Eric sat on the bed beside me. He reached for me, cupping my face in his hands.

"Eric?"

"I know," he said.

"You're mad at me," I said. "You probably want to kill me."

He raised a brow. He didn't object.

"What time is it?"

"A little after ten," he said.

I sat bolt upright. Padding the surrounding space, I searched for my phone.

"Where is everybody? Jeanie and Miranda ..."

"It's Saturday," he said. "They have lives."

I ran a hand over my face. "Right. Lord. It wasn't that late when I crashed. I've been asleep for fourteen hours."

"Good. Not good that you're here."

"I'm sorry. About everything, Eric."

"You gonna tell me you realize you should have told me about Thorne? That you knew where he was? That you'd been talking to him?"

I drew my knees up, considering his question. "No, actually. Eric, I couldn't tell you any of that. Despite everything else he is, Killian is still more or less a client."

Eric made a noise low in his throat. He sounded like a ticked-off grizzly bear.

"Cannon thinks you've put him in danger," Eric said.

"Where is he?"

"Thorne? Don't know. Don't care. Cannon said he dropped him off at a motel. When he came back this morning, Thorne had checked out."

"Eric, I have to find him. You and I both know why John Lansky was sent here now. There's a contract out on Killian's head."

"All the more reason for you to stay far away from him," Eric said. "Killian Thorne can take care of himself. He's proven time and again that's the only thing he's truly good for. No matter who he leaves in his wake."

"You really are mad at me," I said. "I get it. I deserve that at least."

"I'm not mad at you," Eric said. "I was. Last night. All yesterday. I don't know what it is about that guy. What kind of hold he has over you? But every time he's involved, you do crazy things, Cass. Cannon was ready to try figuring out how to bring you up on obstruction charges yesterday."

"For what?"

"He's calmed down," Eric said.

"You know what's going on now as much as I do. You know what had to have happened out in those woods? Ty Chapman is innocent … for all intents and purposes anyway. He was in the wrong place at the wrong time with the wrong guy. And now he's willing to take the fall for it."

"In the end, that's his choice," Eric said.

"It's his life! And Beth's life. His unborn child."

"It's his choice, Cass," Eric said. "Everyone's made their choices in this case. You included."

"I did my job," I said.

Eric nodded. I didn't like the stony look on his face.

"Eric."

He shook his head. "I should get going. Leave you to ... whatever it is you need to do. I just wanted to check in on you."

"Don't," I said.

"Don't what?"

"Don't leave. Don't be mad at me. Just ... don't."

"Cass," he said. "I'm trying. I've been trying. But I can't keep having this same go-around with you. These last few weeks ... months ... one thing's been made crystal clear to me. Killian Thorne is never going to fully be out of your life. Which means he won't be out of my life either if we keep going. For a long time, I could make peace with that. I could look at it and convince myself it was no different from me having Wendy in my life. We came into this having lived full lives."

"Killian isn't like Wendy," I said.

"No," Eric said. "He's so much worse. Because the longer you stay associated with him, the more it will cost you. He's going to destroy you. And the worst part is, you know it. But you let him in anyway."

"Are you dumping me?" I asked.

Pain rippled through his face. "I don't ... No."

"Wow," I said. "That's clear as a bell."

"No." He almost shouted it. "No, okay? I'm not dumping you. I love you. I'm in love with you. But I won't sit by and watch that guy keep hurting you."

"I didn't choose this case," I said. "It chose me. And I swear, I had no idea it would end up here."

"I know," Eric said. "That's the hell of it. I know."

My phone started to buzz. I followed the sound. The thing had fallen into the gap between the metal bed frame and the arm of the couch. I slid my hand in the space and carefully pulled it out.

It seemed the entire population of Delphi had tried to call or text me over the past twelve hours. I had four missed calls from Matty. Half a dozen texts from Joe. A call from Lee Cannon, probably to tell me about Killian going AWOL. Eric was right though; the man could look after himself. It was the rest of us I needed to worry about.

"I'm sorry. I really and truly am."

"And I said I know. But Cass, at a certain point, you're going to have to stop apologizing after the fact, and work on communicating with me first."

He rose. Below us, there was a sharp knock on the front door.

"Good Lord," I said. "Did the entire town burn down while I was sleeping?"

I ran my fingers through my hair, trying to tame the tangles. My clothes were rumpled. I smoothed them as best as I could. Breathing into my own hand, my nose wrinkled. I needed a toothbrush.

Eric at least held a hand out for me, helping extract me from the dip in the center of the mattress. We walked downstairs together as the knocking became more persistent.

I looked at my phone. Both Matty and Joe had repeatedly texted for me to call them.

"What's going on?" I asked. It was then I saw the car parked in front of the office. A marked state trooper's car.

"Eric?" I asked as he opened the front door. I recognized Trooper Craig Winters. He worked in the traffic division.

My phone rang. It was Matty. Instinct took over. I slowly brought the phone up to my ear.

"Cass?" my brother said, his voice pained. Panicked. I didn't say anything. I couldn't. Sick dread filled me as Eric asked Winters what was going on.

"A car registered to Ms. Leary was involved in an accident late last night," Winters said.

"Cass," Matty said on the phone. "I need you. Where have you been?"

Eric and Winters spoke, their voices so low I couldn't make out the words. Or didn't want to. As my brother cried on the phone, I let it fall to the floor.

Eric turned to me. "Cass," he said, his voice sounding as if it were under water. "God. Cass. It's Tori. Winters says there was an accident."

Chapter 38

By the time I got there, Vangie and Joe were already in the waiting room. Four empty coffee cups sat on the table beside them. Joe looked up. His eyes puffy and red, my heart sank down to the floor.

"It's bad, Cass," Joe said. "About as bad as it gets."

"Where is she?" I asked. "Was Matty with her?"

Vangie shook her head. "We tried to call you."

"We've been trying to call you," Joe said, accusation in his tone.

"I turned my phone off," I said. "I just finished a jury trial, Joe. I crashed. I'm sorry. What happened?"

"Still trying to figure that out," Joe said. "Matty got in late from a job he was doing in Detroit. Tori's car was in the garage so he thought she was sleeping upstairs."

"She had my car," I said. "Vangie and Kate had hers yesterday, remember? I told Tori to just drive herself home in mine. I slept at the office."

"Matty said it was maybe two or three in the morning. He headed upstairs to crawl into bed with her but Tori wasn't there."

That's when the texts and missed phone calls to me had started. I felt sick. Guilt washed over me.

Behind me, Eric walked up. He'd been on the phone with the state police trying to piece together what had happened.

"She flipped the car," Eric said. "Lost control of it on that curve on Halstead Road."

"They should do something about that," Vangie said.

"That does Tori good how?" Joe snapped. He was worried. My sister put a hand on his knee, trying to settle him.

"A truck driver found her," Eric continued. "He'd been driving behind her. He said there was another car headed in the opposite direction. It crossed the centerline right in front of Tori. He thinks she was trying to swerve to avoid it, and lost control. Went off the road and flipped. She landed upside down in the ditch. They had to cut her out."

"God," I said, sinking into a chair.

"It's lucky that truck driver saw the whole thing," Vangie said. "They're saying if she'd been any later getting to the hospital, she'd already be dead."

"Already?" It seemed like such an odd choice of words.

Just then, my younger brother walked around the hall, looking like death himself. His shoulders sagged when he saw me. Rising, I steeled myself. He'd be angry with me. Blame me. I blamed myself. I should have driven Tori home. I shouldn't have let her leave by herself.

But there was nothing but grief in my brother's eyes. When I held out my arms, he came into them, burying his head into my shoulder. He sobbed. I pushed back, holding up nearly the full weight of him.

After a minute, Vangie took over. Matty went from my arms to hers.

"What are they saying now?" Joe asked.

Somehow, slowly, Matty came back into himself.

"They're trying to control the swelling in her brain. That's the thing they're worried most about. She's out of surgery. They had to drill what they called burr holes. They took out a piece of her skull so the pressure in her brain wouldn't kill her."

"God," Vangie said, putting a hand over her mouth.

"She's got a broken femur. They'll have to go in and set it. Her collarbone shattered where it hit the steering wheel. Her left lung collapsed but they got that re-inflated. They just don't know. They don't know anything. Not until she wakes up. If she ever wakes up."

"Matty," I said. "I'm so sorry. I'm so, so sorry."

He shook his head. "She's alive."

"What about the baby?" Joe asked. Lord.

Matty let out a strangled cry. "He's alive. So far, he's alive. They said at some point, they might have to make a decision though. The strain on Tori's body might be too much. They said I'd have to choose."

"They said at some point," I said. "So we're not there yet. Is that right?"

Matty nodded. "Yeah. That's exactly what they said. Doctor said at some point soon we'd have a decision to make. He's too small though, Cass."

"Him," I quietly repeated. My brother had a son. Tori had shared her secret weeks ago. But this was the first I'd ever got to share the news with Matty.

"Tori wanted to keep it our secret," Matty said. "For a little while longer, anyway. We found out about a month ago at her ultrasound."

"She's only twenty-seven weeks," Vangie said. "Does the doctor think he'll be okay if they take him?"

Matty shook his head. But it wasn't a no. It was more defeated than confusion.

"He said so many things. Something about lung development. Odds. I just can't think about it right now."

"That's right," Joe said. "One thing at a time. What's the plan for the next twenty-four hours?"

"They're just trying to keep her stable. Monitor her IBC? No, that's not it."

"ICP," Eric said. "Intracranial pressure." It occurred to me then, he'd been here before. With his late wife Wendy. She'd been in a car accident years ago. It had left her in an irreversible coma. God. Not again. Not Tori.

"Right," Matty said, pointing to him. "Trying to keep her brain swelling under control."

"Is she in any pain?" Vangie asked.

"I don't know," Matty said. "She's not responding to me. She only fluttered her eyelids a little but the nurse thinks that was just a reflex. I just don't know."

"It's okay," I said. "We're here, okay. We're here. She's alive. We'll make sure she gets the best care. We'll take it an hour at a time. A second at a time. Okay? Is there anything you need right now?"

Matty buried his face in his hands. As much as I believed what I'd said to him, a thousand worries raced through my own head. How would Matty handle all this? What if Tori died? What if she lived but had brain damage? What if his son died? What if he lived but had serious complications? Matty would want to drink. Of course he would. I wanted to.

I said none of those things, but Eric seemed to know what I was thinking. He read something in my face or in my posture. He put a steadying hand at the small of my back. He drew in a slow breath, reminding me to do the same.

One thing at a time. There would be time to worry and deal with all of the things that might come. For now, I knew my brother just needed all of us around him.

I squeezed Matty's knee and rose. "I'll be right back," I said.

I didn't know where I was going. I just knew I needed to walk. A few minutes later, I found myself in the tiny church chapel. I'd been here only once before on the night my mother died. That day, I prayed, begging God not to take her from us. I knelt in the nearest pew and said the same words again. All those years ago, my prayers had gone unanswered. Now. Today. I knew in my heart it would break my brother if they went unanswered again.

Chapter 39

THREE DAYS LATER, and we all existed in a sort of suspended animation. We took shifts at the hospital with Matty. For the first thirty-six hours, he refused to sleep. Refused to leave Tori's bedside. Finally, his body wore out and he agreed to catch a few hours at a time in the family lounge. He slept in a cubicle in a reclining chair, surrounded by other family members praying hard for those they loved.

Vangie did the morning shift. Joe came in for a couple of hours after lunch. His wife Katie stayed through dinner. Then I came. At ten o'clock every night, Jeanie would come to spell me, staying sometimes until two or three in the morning. Then we would start all over again.

Tori looked like a wax figure. Her hands were so cold as I rubbed them, massaging her palms, her feet. Her badly swollen face was mostly covered in bandages. Her body sunk into itself. The large mound of her stomach to me looked shrunken too. Every cell she had fought both for her own life and that of my nephew's.

The decision would have to come soon. Anyone could see it. There was just no way Tori could survive like this. If she were to survive at all, she needed her strength. The baby would take too much.

Twenty-seven weeks, five days, twenty hours. That's how long the life had grown inside of her. The doctor said each day she was able to carry the baby gave him a slightly better chance to survive outside of her. Only the chance he did have was grim. I could see from the nurses' expressions, the doctor's, they would tell my brother soon. Tori or the baby. The love of his life, or his son. If either had a chance to live at all.

On the morning of the fourth day, I practically staggered into the office. Things were quiet. I'd managed to get continuances on everything Tori had in court over the next few weeks. I couldn't let myself think longer than that. Jeanie was covering most of them.

She'd lost an alarming amount of weight herself over the last couple of days. I worried about her too. Her cancer had been in remission for years, but I truly felt a lot of that depended on her staying healthy. On not spreading herself too thin. She was seventy-five years old.

"You look terrible," Jeanie said as I walked into her office.

"Yeah? I was about to say the same thing to you," I said lightly. I plopped down onto one of her leather couches, putting my tired feet up on the coffee table. She reached into her desk drawer and pulled out two glasses and a bottle of bourbon she kept. She poured us each a shot and came to join me.

"It's not even lunchtime, Jeanie," I said.

"Your point?" She handed me my glass. I took it.

"That kid's gonna make it," Jeanie said. "You all worry too much."

"Which kid?" I asked. I didn't sip my bourbon. I knocked it back. I thought about having Jeanie pour me another one. But if I went down that road, I wouldn't be ready when someone needed me.

The front door opened. Eric walked in looking as terrible as Jeanie and I felt.

"Any word?"

"Nothing," I said. "Matty's meeting with the doctors later today. I'd like to be there for it."

"You got a second to talk?" he asked. His tone sounded too official. Jeanie set the liquor bottle down. Eric raised a curious brow, but didn't judge.

"Be at Miranda's desk," Jeanie said. "Take all the time you need. I'm headed to court later on one of Tori's scheduling conferences."

"Thanks," I said to Jeanie.

Eric sat in the spot she'd just vacated.

"What is it?" I asked. "Eric, I swear. I can't handle another bit of bad news."

It was then I noticed his badge clipped to his belt. I'd lost track of my days. Was it Tuesday? Wednesday? He was still on duty.

"I sat in on the interview with that trucker who witnessed Tori's accident," he said. "Cass, he thinks it was deliberate."

I shook my head, trying to let his words sink in. "What are you talking about? Tori was fine. More than fine. She wouldn't purposely run herself off the road, Eric."

"No," Eric said. "That's not what I'm saying. The guy says the other driver didn't swerve. Right when Tori rounded the corner, he turned his brights on, not off. Right in Tori's line of sight. The trucker said he wasn't swerving when he crossed the center line. He said it looked like the driver drove into Tori's path on purpose. He said he stayed in her lane for a few hundred yards."

"I don't understand. Like he was playing chicken?"

"Something like that. Trucker said he only went back into his lane after Tori went off the road. And he did something else. He slowed down. He looked. Almost came to a stop. Then he just calmly drove away."

"He saw all of this," I said. "This trucker. In the dark."

"Yeah," Eric said. "That was my issue too. But he's stuck to his story. I know Detective Shultz from the state police pretty well. He's a good interviewer. He gave this guy multiple chances to change his story. He stuck to it."

"Did he get a license plate? A description?"

"That's the thing," Eric said. "The car didn't have a license plate. It was unmarked. When he passed the trucker coming the other way, he seemed calm. Unfazed. Trucker said it gave him the chills. He rolled up on Tori's car right after that and tried to help her. Called 911."

"I don't ... what are we supposed to do with that?"

"I don't want you driving alone anywhere for a while," he said. "I don't want you *going* anywhere alone for a while."

"You think I'm in danger?" My brain felt trapped in frozen molasses. Later, I'd realize I was in denial. I was trying to land on any explanation other than the one Eric was offering.

"Cass," he said. "Tori left your office. In your car. She's blonde like you. She was wearing her hair in a ponytail like you were that day. She had a suit on. Like you did."

"No," I whispered. "No. Eric?" I rose to my feet. Shaking. It was an accident. It had to be an accident.

I couldn't think. Couldn't hear. Couldn't breathe. Then Miranda's clear voice cut through as she opened the door and called my name.

"Cass," she said. "The court just called. The jury's back. There's a verdict in the Chapman case."

Chapter 40

I HAD a moment alone with Ty before they brought the jury in. My mind still reeled from what Eric had told me.

My car. Tori had been deliberately driven off the road in my car. She looked enough like me from a distance; especially in the dark with the glare of headlights, someone could mistake her for me. She'd been driving away from my office, on a road I would have taken myself had I been heading home.

My car. My fault.

"Cass?" Ty said. I shook my head to clear the fog.

"When the judge comes in," I said, going on autopilot, "he'll call in the jury. He'll ask you to stand. The temptation to speak. To react. It will be strong. It can be excruciating waiting for the formality to play out. The bailiff will hand him the verdict form. He'll read it. Then he'll hand it back so the clerk can read the verdict into the record. They'll have to deliver a verdict for every count written in the charging document. First-degree murder all the way to voluntary manslaughter."

"I know what's going to happen," Ty said. "I know what to do."

"Do you?" I said, trying to control my anger. "We didn't have to be here."

Ty did what he always did. He turned to stone. For the first time since I met him, it would work to his advantage.

"Cass?" Jeanie walked into the courtroom. We were still waiting for all the players. Rafe Johnson was on his way. Jeanie took the task of getting Beth Chapman. That would have been Tori's job. Part of me still expected to see her rushing through the courtroom doors, face flushed, excited about the outcome as much as she was nervous.

Jeanie, however, didn't look nervous. She looked grave. My heart flipped.

"Stay here," I said to Ty.

"Where else am I gonna go?" he joked. The two deputies assigned to his transport stood like gargoyles behind him.

I left the table and went to Jeanie's side. She put a hand on my elbow and guided me into the hallway.

"Don't,' I said, feeling my mental grip slipping. "Don't say it."

"It's not about Tori," she said. "No change there. Matty's going to meet with the doctors in an hour."

"I'll head there right after this then," I said. "What is it?"

"I can't find Beth Chapman."

"What?"

"She's not answering her phone. I drove over to the house and she's not there. Her car's in the garage. I could see it through the window. But she's not there."

"That makes no sense," I said. "I just talked to her last night. She knew this was going to come down at any time. She knows she's supposed to keep her phone on her at all times."

"Well," Jeanie said. "Then she's not answering on purpose. Or she can't."

"Did you check with the neighbors?" I asked. "Bridget Moran is stepping in to act as her birth coach. She's due in two weeks. Maybe she went into labor early."

"Thought of that," Jeanie said. "Bridget hasn't heard from her. They go for a walk around the neighborhood every morning at eight. Beth didn't show. She's not answering Bridget's calls or texts, either."

"All rise!" the bailiff said. The judge was taking the bench.

"Check the hospital," I said. "Maybe things started moving fast."

"Next on my list," Jeanie said. "But then, why wouldn't she have called Bridget?"

There was no time to try to figure it out. Judge Hughes stepped out, adjusted his robe, and sat. I rushed back over to the table and stood beside Ty.

"What's going on?" he whispered.

"Beth's not here yet," I said, deciding not to let on there was anything else for him to worry about. "I'm not sure if I'll be able to get the judge to give her a few more minutes."

"No," Ty said. "I don't want that. Maybe it's better if she isn't here for this part. She'll be too emotional either way. Let her stay home. Her being here won't change any of this now."

He was right. But I couldn't shake the feeling that there was something else terribly wrong out there.

The judge instructed the jury to be brought in. The jury room door opened and the members filed in one by one. I watched their faces, even as I knew the futility of it. Conventional wisdom said, if any of them looked at Ty, it meant they'd found him not guilty. If they avoided his gaze, the news was bad.

From the corner of my eye, I saw Ted Moran. He looked paler than usual. He was also the only supporter Ty had today with Beth AWOL.

No matter what, I needed to speak to him when this was all over.

"Members of the jury," Judge Hughes said. "I understand you've reached a verdict?"

"We have," the foreman said. He was a retired schoolteacher. One of the most attentive members of the jury throughout the trial. That had been Tori's observation, at least. Again, I felt a twinge of dread thinking about her and the meeting my brother faced.

The foreman handed the verdict form to the bailiff. Stone-faced, the judge read it. He furrowed his brow, but his displeasure could mean anything. He handed the form back to the clerk.

"You may read it into the record," the judge said.

Ty went rigid beside me. On instinct, I reached for him, putting a steadying hand on his back.

The clerk cleared her throat. She'd been fighting a cold all week, I knew. It took two tries before she found her voice as she leaned into the microphone.

"We, the jury in the above-entitled action, on count one of the complaint, being murdered in the first degree pursuant to Michigan Compiled Laws Section 750.316, find the defendant, Tyler Chapman, not guilty."

A whoosh went through me. Had I heard her right? First-degree murder. Not guilty. There was no time to fully feel. The clerk kept reading.

"In the above-entitled action, on count two of the complaint, pursuant to Michigan Compiled Laws section 750.317, on the charge of murder in the second degree, we, the jury, find the defendant, Tyler Chapman, not guilty."

Beside me, I felt the whoosh go through Ty. His rigid posture loosened. He leaned forward, bracing his hands flat on the table.

"On count three of the complaint," the clerk continued. "Pursuant to Michigan Compiled Laws section 750.321, on the charge of voluntary manslaughter, we, the jury, find the defendant, Tyler Chapman ... guilty as charged."

Ty let out a breath. I held mine.

On the other side of the room, Rafe Johnson dropped his head and shook it. When he straightened, he stared hard at the jury.

The clerk finished the remaining procedural readings, but I couldn't hear any of them.

Not guilty of first-degree murder. Not guilty of second-degree murder. Guilty of voluntary manslaughter. It meant the jury believed Ty had intentionally killed John Lansky, but that he hadn't acted with either premeditation or in the heat of the moment. It was the least serious offense he could have been convicted of.

"Your Honor," Rafe said. "I would like to poll the jury."

The judge complied. One by one, each member of the jury affirmed that the verdict read was their just conclusion. They were unanimous.

"Thank you," Judge Hughes said. "I commend you for your service. You're free to go. I should advise you that this case has garnered some media attention and you might be approached to speak to the press. At this time, it is your own personal choice whether you choose to do so or not. But as a precaution, I'd ask all of you to wait to leave the building until I can arrange for the deputies to show you out."

Once they filed out, the judge turned his attention back to us. "Mr. Chapman, you've been found guilty of voluntary manslaughter. I'm going to set sentencing in this matter for one week from today. Are there any other matters we need to address before adjourning?"

"I'd like a few minutes to confer with my client before he's remanded back into custody," I said.

"Jury room is empty now," the judge said. "I'll let you arrange that with the deputies. That is all. We're adjourned."

He banged the gavel. Behind me, the spectators started to leave, their hushed tones rising to full voices.

"We only have a few minutes," I said to Ty.

The deputies helped clear a path so Ty and I could disappear into the adjoining jury room.

When I turned to look at him, Ty was smiling. He looked like a different person.

"Thank you," he said.

"Thank me?" I said. "Ty, do you realize what just happened? They believed me. The jury believes that John Lansky was a trained killer. They believe you were probably just defending yourself. It means I could have gotten an acquittal if you'd been willing to help me help you."

"How long can he send me to prison for voluntary manslaughter?" Ty asked.

The man exasperated me. How could he be so damn calm?

"The maximum sentence is fifteen years," I said.

"Fifteen," he said. "Our daughter will just be starting high school. I'll get to be there for that."

"Fifteen is the maximum," I said. "You have no prior record. You were honorably discharged from the Marines. You served in Afghanistan. You volunteer your time at the Veterans Center. All of those things will weigh very heavily in your favor. I can't guarantee it, but I don't see Judge Hughes sentencing you to more than five or six years. And you likely won't serve all of that. With overcrowding, and good behavior on your part, Ty, you'll probably be out in three or four."

He smiled. "Three or four years? Really?"

"Yes," I said. "Really."

"She won't remember," Ty said. "My daughter won't remember me ever being in jail."

"Probably not," I said. "But I should have been able to get you acquitted, Ty. With a little more time, I could have proved once and for all who John Lansky was. You should have told me the truth about what happened out there. What he tried to do to you."

"She won't remember me ever having been in prison," Ty said. "I'll get to be her father. It'll be hard at first. She won't know me. But we can start over."

"Ty," I said. "We need to get a hold of Beth. She's not answering her phone and she's not at the house. I've got my law partner looking for her. As soon as I can, I can make arrangements for her to come see you. It might be a few days though. In all likelihood, you won't see her again until the day of your sentencing."

"I should go back now," Ty said. Maybe he was just in shock. Hell, I was. But he seemed not at all concerned about Beth's whereabouts.

"Thank you, Cass," Ty said. "Beth was right about you. She told me I just needed to listen to her. That she knew what she was doing. I should know better than to doubt that woman. She's incredible. Don't worry about her. Beth can do anything."

The deputies knocked on the door. "Time to go, Chapman," one of them said.

He rose. He was beaming as the deputies came back in and put him in cuffs.

"Three to four years?" he said to me.

"We'll talk again soon," I said. "Rafe Johnson will submit a written sentencing recommendation. We'll get to respond. I'll come see you to discuss it in a couple of days."

He nodded, but didn't seem fully aware of what I was saying. There were tears in Ty Chapman's eyes as the deputies led him away.

Chapter 41

"SHE CAN'T JUST BE GONE," I said. Lee Cannon sat across from me, one leg casually draped over the other as he watched me pace behind my desk. He'd come back to town to gather more information about Lansky.

"The woman is days away from her due date. The day after tomorrow, her husband is being sentenced for manslaughter. She's been by his side since day one. She's the reason I took this case in the first place."

"Cass," he said. "I understand ..."

"You don't understand," I said. "I feel like I'm shouting into the wind."

"Am I the wind in this scenario?" he asked.

"Well, yes."

Eric walked in. He and Lee exchanged a glance that made me want to murder both of them. They were handling me.

"Anything?" I asked Eric.

He shook his head and took the seat beside Lee. "No signs of foul play at the house. I don't have probable cause to get a warrant."

"She wouldn't just leave," I said. "You don't know Beth Chapman like I do. She has been singularly focused on Ty's trial. She wouldn't bail on him now."

"Cass," Eric said. "Maybe you don't know Beth as much as you think you do. The trial is over. Ty's gotten as much of a victory as he can get. You won."

"I didn't win," I said. "My client is going to prison."

"He's essentially getting a slap on the wrist after bludgeoning a man to death," Lee said. "I'd say you're a damn miracle worker."

"You don't know Ty Chapman at all," Eric said. "Nobody does. Who knows what was really going on in that marriage? Maybe Beth figured she'd done her part. Stuck by his side. Now that it's over, she wants a fresh start."

"Lee," I said. "What if she's been kidnapped? What if the people John Lansky worked for are trying to make sure she doesn't cause any further trouble for them? What if they're trying to do to her what they did to Ellen Colby?"

"What trouble has she caused for them?" Lee said. "She hasn't gone to the press. She didn't testify at trial."

"What about Ellen Colby? Has there been any progress on her case?"

Lee looked grim. "We're working with the Wayne County sheriffs. Unofficially, anyway. We're still letting the locals take the lead."

"It was a hit!" I said. "How is that not within your purview?"

"It's not my call," he said. "Believe me. I made my case. The powers that be are confident in their decision to let the locals handle it for now."

"And how are they handling it? By letting it go cold?"

"Cass," Eric said. "I think you're just going to have to take the win on this. You did your job for Chapman. Until there's a concrete reason to think something bad happened to his wife, I think it's safe to assume she's exactly where she wants to be. As far as Ellen Colby is concerned, the woman was involved with some shady people."

"Are you two going to sit there and try to convince me her death wasn't connected to the Lansky murder?"

"Cass," Lee said. "I think we're trying to convince you there's no good outcome for you if you pick at this. Best-case scenario, Ellen's death was connected. These guys? The Orlovs? You've shaken the tree enough. You don't want to cross their path."

"You're both scared," I said, cutting him off.

"Yes!" Eric said. "Because you're probably right. Lansky. Chapman. Ellen Colby. Hell, even Killian Thorne. There's a trail of bodies and violence for anyone who tangles with the Orlovs. You did your job for Chapman. Let it go. Let Wayne County worry about Ellen Colby. It's not your case. It's not my case. If we've learned anything, there will be plenty of murders for us to solve in due time. We don't need to go kicking hornets' nests."

"I just don't accept that," I said. "And I cannot believe the two of you do. Ellen Colby is dead because of me. Because I was going to make her testify. Now Beth Chapman is missing."

"I'm sorry," Lee said. "The Bureau's position has been made clear to me. They're not touching it."

"Are you okay with that? Can you really sit there and tell me this isn't eating at you too?"

"I've learned to pick my battles. So should you. I'm sorry, Cass. I really am. But it's out of my hands. I came down here as a favor to you. If there's more I can do or tell you, I'll let you know. For now? I'm needed back in Chicago. Just ... live your life. Like we said. Take the win."

He rose. There was an awkward moment where Lee debated whether to extend his hand to shake mine. He cleared his throat and turned to Eric. The two of them shared a glance, then Lee showed himself out.

I sat down hard in my desk chair.

"Cass," Eric said.

"Don't." I cut him off, raising a hand.

We sat in silence for a moment. Eric stared at me. I wouldn't meet his eyes.

"Cass," he finally said again, his tone firm. "Let this go."

"I don't think I can," I said. "What if Beth Chapman doesn't show up? Ty's sentencing is the day after tomorrow. She could be anywhere. What if she's dead, Eric?"

"I've been a detective for a long time. Call it intuition, gut instinct, whatever. But I don't think she is. I think it's what we were saying. The woman stood by her man for the jury. Now she wants peace somewhere else. She wants to have her baby away from all of this. Can you blame her?"

"Then why didn't she just tell me that? I would have understood. Eric, I'm scared to death that Beth Chapman is lying in an alley somewhere with a vee carved into her stomach."

"For what purpose?" Eric asked. "What possible reason could the Orlovs have for risking that?"

"To send a message," I said. "Beth's husband killed one of theirs, so they kill her. V for vengeance."

"Sure," Eric said. "Only it would probably be a whole lot easier if they just took care of Ty himself in prison. Going after a pregnant woman who hasn't posed any kind of a threat doesn't make a lot of sense. It may seem like an odd thing to say, but there's a code for these people. They have their own kind of honor. Killing Beth like that would be bad form."

He made sense. I knew it. And yet I still couldn't accept it.

"You said yourself," Eric said. "Ty wasn't upset when you told him Beth was gone. Has it occurred to you that the two of them planned this all along? If it were me, I think I'd want my pregnant wife as far away from all of this as possible. I'd want that for you, Cass. I did want that for you. When Wendy died, it killed me that you were tangled up in it. It was my mess. Not yours."

"Eric," I said. "That's the whole point. What happens to you, happens to me. There was no way I was ever going to let you face all of that alone. Something is wrong. Very wrong."

"So what if you're right," Eric said. "Exactly what can you do about it? I think that's what this is really about. You're looking for ways to control something that's uncontrollable. It's about Tori as much as anything else. And that's the other reason why you need to leave the rest of this alone. We still don't know what happened that night on the road. If there's even a sliver of a chance that was someone coming after you, I'd rather you not give them any more reasons."

"I can't accept that," I said. "If Tori's accident was my fault ..."

"It wasn't," he said. "You didn't do anything wrong."

"Where are you on finding the driver of the other car? The one that the trucker saw?"

Eric's face changed. I knew that look. There was something he didn't want to tell me.

"What?"

He took a breath. "The trucker has changed his story. Now he's saying maybe that other car didn't cross the center line in front of Tori. It was dark. He thinks he was too far away to be sure."

"He's lying," I said. "Or someone got to him. Eric ..."

"I know," he said. "I don't like it either. But it's been over a week since the accident. Ty's trial is over. We've swept your house and office for bugs. I've had patrolmen watching your house and here. There's been no suspicious activity. We'll keep watching. I plan on staying glued to your side for a while. For as long as you'll let me. But again, my gut instinct is telling me the threat has passed."

"Well, that's great news for Tori," I said, sarcasm dripping from my voice.

Eric let out a sigh. "How is she today?"

"Same," I said. "She still hasn't woken up. They've scheduled a C-section for Thursday."

"How's Matty holding up?"

"He's been so strong," I said. "He doesn't leave Tori's side."

"What about you?" Eric came to me.

"I don't know," I said, and it was one of the most honest things I'd said. "I don't know what to do for him."

"Just be there," Eric said. "And let me help."

I met his eyes. I realized that was exactly what Eric had been doing for me this whole time. I squeezed his hand and wished it could be enough.

Chapter 42

WEDNESDAY MORNING. Nine a.m. I stood beside Tyler Chapman in a courtroom for the very last time. Behind us, Chris Dvorak, Ted Moran, his wife Bridget, and a dozen or so other local veterans lined the gallery.

No one had shown up for John Lansky. Not the people who'd sung his praises all over the lake until now. Not when the news broke about Lansky's possible connection to one of the most dangerous factions of the Russian mob.

No one wanted to believe it. Everyone was scared. In various internet circles, Ty Chapman was hailed as a hero. He'd taken care of a problem no one knew we had.

"Mr. Johnson," Judge Hughes said. "The court is advised of your sentencing recommendation. Is there anything else you'd like to add before I make my ruling?"

"Your Honor," Rafe said. "I'd just like to remind the court of the heinous nature of this crime. I've made my position quite clear during trial. It is the state's firm belief that issues were allowed to be brought in at trial that never should have been.

But the jury has rendered its verdict and I'm aware I'm bound by that. That being said, if there were ever a case where justice required the maximum sentence allowed by law to be handed down ... well ... frankly, this is it. I won't reiterate the legal points I've made in my brief in support. But the state, in the interests of justice, respectfully requests that the court sentence Mr. Chapman to the maximum sentence of fifteen years."

"Ms. Leary?" Judge Hughes said.

"I too see no reason to take up the court's time rehashing points made in my written response. However, Mr. Chapman should benefit from a multitude of mitigating factors. He has no previous criminal record. He has acquitted himself honorably both in this court and in his life before the tragic events of this case. He is a highly decorated Marine who served his country in one of our longest wars. His support here today should make that abundantly clear. Mr. Chapman is a family man. Someone who has spent his life serving and contributing to society in a meaningful way. The jury weighed the evidence. Despite the nature of what happened, they were unanimously convinced that the facts presented by the state did not rise to the level of murder. As such, we ask that the court show mercy and leniency in this case. There has been no proof that Mr. Chapman is a danger to society."

Rafe Johnson scoffed beside me. He was already beginning to pack up his things. An act that did not go unnoticed by the judge.

"I'm ready to make my ruling," the judge said. "I'll make this short and sweet. Mr. Chapman, I don't know what happened out there behind the Harmon Arms. What could have precipitated your actions in killing John Lansky? I have serious questions about both your role in it and what Mr. Lansky's purpose was in our town. Whatever it was, you saw fit to take the law into your own hands. If he was a threat, there were any number of other ways to address it. You could have called the police. We, all of us, are bound by a system of laws. We cannot permit citizens, even one as highly decorated as you are, to pursue the route of a vigilante. Had this been a bench trial, you should know, you'd be facing sentencing for at least second-degree murder. But you're not.

"Mr. Johnson is right. The brutality of this crime is unparalleled. I don't know what was in your heart, son. Your soul. I pray you've found peace. I pray whatever demons compelled you to carry out that killing have been quelled.

"The simple fact is, despite what happened out there, I have to respect the jury's wisdom on this. They were the true trier of fact. Their verdict signals to me that they want this court to take into account what brought John Lansky to my town. In light of that, and as your lawyer pointed out, the exemplary life you've led up to that horrible night, I'm sentencing you to seven years in prison. You'll be remanded to state prison as soon as you can be processed."

Judge Hughes took a breath as though he had far more to say. Instead, he merely shook his head and banged his gavel.

Johnson didn't wait a second longer. He stormed out of the courtroom. There'd be a bank of reporters out there somewhere wanting a quote. They'd look for me too. I would have just a few more moments with Ty before they took him back to begin his processing out to a state penitentiary. I'd arranged to use the jury room with Ty one last time.

He practically bounced on his feet as he followed me in. The deputies gave me fifteen minutes. I didn't expect to use more than five.

"Thank you," Ty said. "Do you think I'll really do seven years?"

"No," I said. "As we discussed the other day, you'll likely be out in as little as half that. Probably on a tether for the remainder though. It's possible the state will appeal the sentencing ruling. They can't appeal the conviction itself though."

Nodding, Ty got a far-off look.

"You haven't asked me," I said, taking a seat.

"Asked you what?" he said. Ty stayed on his feet. He was too keyed up to settle.

"About Beth," I said. "Ty, I still don't know where she is. It's past her due date."

"They can't come after me anymore, can they?" he asked.

"What? Who?"

"The prosecutor," he said. "They can't charge me with anything else. I didn't testify. I didn't perjure myself. The law says I can't be charged with any other crimes in connection with what happened that night. Correct?"

"Correct," I said.

"He had his shot," Ty said. "Rafe Johnson. No matter what else might come out, this is over."

"Over?" I said. "You're going to prison. A witness was killed. Ellen Colby was going to take the stand in your defense. She was murdered. Branded with a vee, just like you were. Weren't you? That's what happened? What I told the jury in closing was the truth. You were in the wrong place at the wrong time and cornered by an assassin of the Russian mob. You're right, Ty. It's over. So why don't you tell me the truth? All of it. The cops, the prosecution, they can't come after you for this anymore."

Ty stopped moving. In fact, he went quite still. He tilted his head slightly as he stared at me.

"You're going to prison," I said. "But you could have avoided it if you'd been honest with me from the beginning. So be honest with me now. You were protecting Beth that night, weren't you? Lansky came after her like he came after Ellen Colby. If you've been trying to prove to the Orlovs or somebody else, don't you think you've done it? What possible harm could there be to you now for telling me, your lawyer, the truth?"

He kept my eyes as he sat in the chair across from me.

"Ty," I said. "My associate was run off the road. She's in critical condition, fighting for her life. We don't know for sure, but there's at least a chance what happened to her wasn't an accident. I think whoever tried to hurt her was really after me. And Beth? You don't seem at all concerned about where she might be. This may be over for you, but it's not over for me. It's not over for the people I care about. So tell me. Tell me everything. Who are you protecting?"

"You really don't know?" he asked.

Rage unspooled within me. For Tori. For Ellen Colby. I slammed my palms on the table.

"Tell me!"

Ty didn't so much as flinch.

He took a breath. For a moment, I think he was contemplating calling for the deputy. I couldn't have stopped him. He could have simply got up, walked out of the room, and there was nothing I could do. My job was finished. I'd delivered everything he asked of me.

"I didn't want it this way," Ty said. "That's the first thing you need to know. I didn't want a lawyer. Didn't want a trial. None of it. But Beth? She's always two steps ahead of me. She can turn things around in her head, see all the facets. She's so good at reading people too. Figures out what drives them. What they really want. But you wouldn't know it. You don't see it coming."

"Was she there that night, Ty?" I asked. "The Boyds didn't see her. They only saw you."

"The Boyds," he said. "They don't know how close they came to dying that night. I asked him. Begged him to make them go away. He wouldn't do it. Told me I had to remember my place."

My head spun. Ty was talking in circles.

"Ty," I said. "Who were you protecting? Was it Killian? You saw the scar on his chest. You sat there in trial when he testified. You're good. You've got a face like granite. I don't think the jury picked up on it, but I did. There was no one more shocked than you when I put him on the stand. Ty, I know what it's like to get caught in Killian Thorne's wake. It's my fault. He wouldn't have even been in Delphi if it weren't for me. I think John Lansky was looking for him. Too many people know that Killian and I have a past. That he still cares about me. I'm sorry about that. For how it impacted you."

"That's what she said too," Ty said. "She said if it was you, we could control it all."

"Beth?"

"You asked me," Ty said, leaning forward. "You wanted to know who I was protecting."

"Yes," I said.

Ty smiled. "You."

The word echoed through me. Ty stayed very still, waiting for me to absorb it.

"You, Cass," he said, finally leaning back. "It was always you."

I felt hollowed out. Empty. The answer had been right in front of me. Too close to me.

"You didn't think he'd ever stop looking out for you, did you? Thorne?"

"He sent you here," I said, my throat running dry. "Killian sent you here to Delphi. Ted Moran said you moved in a little over four years ago. It was right after I came back, wasn't it? Right after I left Chicago." God. I'd asked Killian all the wrong questions. He swore to me he didn't know John Lansky. But I'd never asked him if he knew Tyler Chapman.

"Two weeks or so," Ty said.

"You've been watching me," I said. "Living here. Becoming a part of the community."

"You were a job," he said. "I was never supposed to cross your path. Nor was Beth. Watch. Wait. Those were our orders."

"A trained killer," I whispered, recalling Chris Dvorak's testimony. "My God. You work for Killian. This whole time."

"Watch, wait, report," Ty said.

"Then, Lansky showed up," I said. The last piece of it slammed into place.

"Lansky started doing odd jobs for people around the lake," I said, horrified. "For my sister! You're saying ... Lansky was never here for Killian Thorne. He was here for me?!"

Ty merely flipped one hand over by way of affirmation.

"How? What happened?"

"He got very close," Ty said. "That never should have happened. The night of the 10th, I drove by your office on my way home from work. Like I always did. You were leaving by five thirty every night that week. When I passed by, I saw a car parked on the opposite street. I recognized it. I'd seen it around the lake."

"At my sister's?" I said.

"Yes, Cass. I called it in. Asked for instructions. We decided it would be best if I followed Lansky for a while. See where he went."

"The Harmon Arms," I said. "You paid him a visit. For me."

"I'm good at my job, Cass," Ty said. "But he made me. When I came to the door, he was ready for me. I didn't take him out to the woods, Cass. He took me."

"He was going to kill you," I said, existing outside myself. "I got that part right. He was going to kill you. He branded you to send a message to Killian."

"He slipped," Ty said, hatred filling his voice. "The ground was wet. He slipped. So I picked up a rock."

"So you obliterated him that night. Sent your own message. Tore the brand from your chest. Just like Killian did all those years ago. You took his wallet. His gun. Your gun. You thought you got rid of it all. But the Boyds. You couldn't finish cleaning up because they already saw you."

Horror filled me. I truly understood how close Brian and Melissa Boyd had come to losing their lives that night too.

"You're safe," Ty said. "I did my job. And I'm no rat. Killian knows that now. So do the Orlovs."

"That's your deal? You do your time. Keep quiet. You stay protected on the inside. Then when you get out, you write your own ticket?"

He smiled.

"You said it was Beth's idea. Hiring me."

"I tried to stop her," Ty said. "Beth figured it was the best way to make sure Killian kept his promise to us. Even though it was my screw-up. I never should have been seen. John Lansky should have just disappeared. I failed in that."

"He was worried you were going to tell me everything. My God. This whole thing has been a test. Another one of his chess games. Killian let it go on because if you'd have confessed all of this to me earlier, he knew I'd confront him about it. You used me to prove to him you could keep your mouth shut."

"He could have put a stop to it," Ty said. "Beth banked on the fact he wouldn't. She said once it was set in motion, he'd stay close, but he wouldn't interfere. Because Beth was right. You're the best, Cass. Nobody could have done what you did in that courtroom. She was right about everything. Killian owed me. I kept you safe. And you kept me from spending the rest of my life in prison. I screwed up. It got messy with Lansky. The Boyds saw me. That was my fault. Killian could have had me killed. But he didn't. Now you can tell him. Tell him I did my job. I've kept quiet. I'll stay quiet. Do my time. As long as he keeps delivering his promise. As long as Beth stays safe."

"He got her out," I said. "That's why you haven't been concerned about Beth. You know Killian's set her up somewhere safe. That's what you've earned by staying quiet. You'll be safe. Beth will be safe. What about Ellen Colby?"

"I'm sorry about her," Ty said. "But I didn't ask you to go looking into John Lansky's past. I didn't even know she existed."

"She looked like Beth," I said.

Ty shrugged. "A lot of people look like Beth. As far as I know, Lansky never even laid eyes on Beth."

Nothing. All for nothing. All because of me.

There was a knock on the door. Our time was up. My heart pounded outside of my chest. He used me. Ty. Beth. Killian. All of them.

Now, he and Beth were safe. John Lansky was dead. But I knew there were more men like him out there. Tori and Matty were paying the price.

"You tell him," Ty said, rising. "You tell him I did my job, Cass. Because you did yours. But you have to be careful."

"Tori," I said. "Was this the Orlovs? Were they trying to finish the job Lansky was sent here to do?"

"I don't know," he said. "That's the truth. I just know that I'm not out there to do my job anymore. I don't know who is. You should be careful."

The deputies led him out, leaving me alone in the empty jury room. When the door slammed behind him, it felt like thunder.

Chapter 43

I KNEW where I would find him. My last secret. My last lie.

He told me once it reminded him of the Garrettson Beach in County Cork. The expanse of Lake Michigan looked just enough like the Celtic Sea. And yet he loved that this was still Michigan. Still the place I called home.

In another time. The ending to another story that I would never write. We would end up here in Helene. Retire here. Be married here. Even then, a million years ago now, I knew it was a false promise. From a man who didn't really exist.

I'd lied to everyone. Joe. Eric. Jeanie. I'd said it was a new client I was going to see. I'd be back by morning. After today, I would never lie to any of them again.

Most people blew right past the hidden drive winding through the woods. At the end of it, the house opened up, jutting out on its own peninsula, a cliff face with the water churning below.

Killian said we could restore the house someday if I wanted. The foundation was crumbling.

Two fresh tire tracks led to the garage. I parked in the paved circle. He still kept a spare key hidden beneath a loose brick near the front door.

I didn't knock. He had cameras installed all the way out to the main road. He would have had plenty of time to disappear. But I knew he wouldn't.

Killian was waiting for me in the kitchen. Sitting at a large granite island with copper pots hanging overhead. He'd already poured himself a shot of whiskey. He held the bottle poised over a second glass.

"Don't bother," I said. "I want a clear head when I drive back home."

"Congratulations," he said. "You won your case."

"My case?" I said. "What exactly did I win?"

"I'm sure Mr. Chapman is very grateful, a rúnsearc," Killian said.

"Don't," I said. "Don't ever call me that again. It's the thing you say right before you're about to lie to me."

Killian's face fell. His hands were steady as he poured more whiskey into his glass. "Something tells me this is going to be a two-shot conversation."

"Not enough booze in that whole bottle," I said. "I don't need conversation. I can't believe anything you tell me anymore."

He put the bottle down. "All right. You're here. You're angry."

"I'm angry," I said.

"It's over," I said. "Ty Chapman will go to prison. He'll be out in probably three years. He'll wear an ankle monitor, but something tells me whoever his lawyer is at that point will be able to get him transferred to wherever he wants to live."

"His lawyer at that point?" Killian said, sipping his drink. "It won't be you?"

"Why did you come to Delphi?" I said. "The truth. All of it. This is it, Killian. Your one chance to salvage any shred of trust we ever had."

"Feels like you already think you have the answers."

"You've been watching me for years. In Delphi. On some level, I always knew it. I even accepted it to an extent. Maybe even took a strange sort of comfort in it. You'd swoop in when I needed you. Like some sick bat signal. For me. For Eric even. But it was always a lie."

"I've kept you safe," Killian said.

"You mean Ty Chapman kept me safe."

He hesitated as he raised his glass to his lips. Then, he downed the rest of his drink and poured himself another shot.

"I thought I had it figured out at the end of the trial," I said. "You just happened to show up on my doorstep. I thought Lansky was in town looking for you. But he was there to watch me, wasn't he? Cannon said you were making moves that were ruffling feathers with your rivals. With the Orlovs. This was their way of trying to keep you in line. They sent Lansky to start following me. But you were a step ahead. You sent Chapman here first. For four years he's been watching me."

"You want me to apologize for that?" Killian spat.

"Again, you want me to thank you for protecting me from the danger you create. I'm never going to be safe, am I? Not me. Not my family. Tori's in the hospital. She may not survive. They're going to deliver her baby tomorrow at twenty-nine weeks. The odds aren't great, Killian. And it should have been me. This will never end. I can't have it. I can't live with this. You've made it so I can never go home."

He hissed through his teeth as he took another shot of whiskey.

"You showed up on my doorstep that morning, the same day Beth Chapman went to my office. The money she paid me with. It's what you gave her to stay quiet, isn't it? Only she outmaneuvered you. She got to me first."

"She's a formidable woman," Killian admitted. "It was a genius move. I wanted to wring her neck for it. She said she knew I'd let her husband swing for making the mistake of getting caught. For leaving witnesses."

"She convinced you her way was better. Ty gets to prove his loyalty by keeping quiet. You get to keep closer tabs on the case because I was involved."

"Like I said," Killian said. "A formidable woman."

"Not formidable enough to keep Ellen Colby safe. Or Tori. This thing has been unraveling, Killian. It's out of your control, isn't it? The Orlovs want you dead. Lansky couldn't get it done. But there will be others. There will always be others. And I'm involved now, you son of a bitch. I'm out there. My family is out there. Exposed. Collateral damage to a war they never signed up for."

"No!" he shouted. "It won't be that way. I've taken care of it. I can't tell you more than that. Soon enough, you'll see how. You'll understand."

"How?" I said, backing away. "How will you ever be able to put this genie back in the bottle? All you've proven is how much I still matter to you. I defended a man on your payroll. The Orlovs think I'm still working for you. They tried to kill me and hurt Tori instead."

"I don't know that, Cass," he said.

"The trucker who found her said another vehicle tried to run her off the road. That it was deliberate. Now all of a sudden, he's changed his story. They got to him. Or you did."

I said the last bit as a throwaway, but the flicker in Killian's eyes told me I'd hit on it. "My God. You engaged in witness tampering? Obstruction?"

"A show of faith," I said.

"So whoever did that to Tori will get away with it. I can't let that stand, Killian."

"You have to," he said. "You have to trust me that I have a plan to take care of this. To take care of you. You just have to be patient."

"Stop."

"I have a plan," he said.

"I don't want to be part of any of your plans."

He pulled out his phone. Swiping up, he pulled up a picture and slid the phone across the table to me.

I was afraid to look. When I did, I saw a picture of Beth Chapman sitting in a rocking chair, smiling. She looked tired, but beautiful. In her arms, she held a tiny pink bundle with tufts of red hair poking out from a crocheted blanket.

"She's safe, Cass," Killian said. "I deliver on my promises. Safe. Healthy. Rich. She had her little girl last week. Six pounds, nine ounces. They live near a beach. Another small, quiet town. In three years, when he gets out, Ty will know how to find her. They'll have everything I ever promised them."

I slid the phone back to him. "This is a happy ending to you?"

"It's what they signed up for. And it's their reward. Yours is coming. You'll see. It's already set in motion."

"What?" I said. "What's the price, Killian? What deal did you have to make? What part of your soul did you have to sell? If there's anything left."

His expression went cold. "It's already happened. Soon enough, you'll know, Cass. And you'll know it's final. You're safe. I swear it on my mother's soul."

"I don't ... I can't ... No more. We're finished. I'm out."

"Yes," Killian said. "You're out."

"No more special phone numbers. No more secrets. No contact at all, Killian. Clean break. Forever. I have to start over. I thought I was. I thought coming back to Delphi was the answer. But all I've done is hurt the people who love me. All I've done is bring this ... evil ... right to them."

"Go home, Cass."

"I can't," I said. "That's the whole point. It follows me."

"It won't. Not ever again. I swear it. It's done. You have to trust me."

"Goodbye," I said to Killian. He didn't try to follow me. He just poured another shot, raised his glass, and toasted me as I walked out the door.

I turned my back. I couldn't hear another word from him. I walked out the front door, trying very hard to not look back. I kept my back straight as I slipped behind the wheel of my car and drove away from Killian Thorne for the very last time.

My phone buzzed. It was Joe.

"Tomorrow morning. Don't forget," he texted. "Tori's C-Section is set for 10:00."

I let out a breath and texted him back. "I'll be there."

I could barely think straight as I drove the four hours back to Delphi. Everything I said to Killian I meant. If I was the thing bringing danger to my family, then I couldn't stay. I'd have to start over somewhere far away.

The west coast maybe. Or even Canada. I could take the bulk of the Chapman retainer and live on it for a little while. Maybe.

Killian's words thrummed through me. He said he'd set something in motion to keep us all safe. A platitude maybe. Something he'd promised me before. I wanted to believe him, but I couldn't think of a single thing Killian Thorne could give to the likes of the Russian mob that would appease them.

When it happens, he'd said, I would know. But how?

As I pulled into my driveway, Agent Lee Cannon stepped out of his car. He'd been waiting. The grim expression on his face told me something bad had happened.

God, I thought. No more.

Chapter 44

Eric was already inside the house waiting. He rose when he saw Cannon walking in behind me.

"Glad you're here," Lee said. "This concerns you too."

"Where have you been?" Eric asked, virtually ignoring Agent Cannon.

I stood between the two of them. A rock and a hard place. I could make something up. Tell them I just needed to go for a drive. Clear my head. That was all true. But I'd had enough of lies.

"I went to see him," I said.

"Thorne?" they said in unison.

There was little else I could tell them. Not about Killian's empty promises. Not about the last twenty-four hours and everything Ty Chapman had revealed. He was still my client, after all. He knew it. His confession was timed to perfection. He had the benefit of double jeopardy for the murder of John

Lansky. He had the benefit of attorney-client privilege. I could say nothing. Ever.

"I suppose it's a waste of time me asking you where he is, Cass," Lee said.

"He owns a house at the northwest tip of the lower peninsula. A little town called Helene. He bought it a long time ago. Because of me. I can give you the address if you want. But it won't matter, he'll be long gone."

"You're right," Lee said. "It doesn't matter. Because I know exactly where Killian Thorne is headed."

"Are you okay?" Eric asked. Still, the two of them acted as though the other wasn't there.

"I will be," I said. "I need to get to the hospital. Tori's C-section is tomorrow morning. Matty needs me."

"Let's talk first," Lee said. "Something's happened. The news will hit the media any minute now. But I thought you should hear it face to face."

I was tired. Bone-weary. I sank to the couch next to where Eric stood.

"Do you have news about Tori's accident?" I asked.

"Not directly," Lee said. "But ... yes."

Eric sat beside me. I could feel his whole body stiffen. He was like a cobra ready to strike.

"I've heard from a confidential informant of mine," Lee said. "The one I have that's fairly well placed within the Orlov family. I've reached out to him a few times during the last few months but … this person had gone to ground. I thought they were dead, to be honest. Got made."

"They're not going to stop, are they?" Eric said. "Tori was just the beginning. A mistake."

"Maybe," Cannon said. "The Orlovs aren't taking direct responsibility for that accident. Or for Lansky for that matter. But they're not denying anything either."

"They'll never stop coming," Eric said again. "What are you going to do about that, Cannon?"

"That's what I'm here to tell you," Lee said. "Their beef was with Killian Thorne. They tried to force him out. Somebody told them Thorne was talking to us, trying to bring heat to the Orlovs so he could move in on their territory. I can tell you that wasn't true. But someone from his organization *was* talking to us."

I held my breath. I knew the answer to that question. Years ago, Killian's brother Liam accused me of being a snitch. It was all a smoke screen. I barely made it out of that law firm with my life. And all along, Liam had been the one selling information to law enforcement in an attempt to topple his own brother. I kept that secret, along with so many others. I used it to bargain for my and my family's life.

I said nothing. I stared hard at Lee Cannon. Did he already know?

"Liam Thorne's body washed up near the Navy Pier yesterday," Lee said.

The air went out of my lungs. Killian's words burned through me. *I've taken care of it. Soon enough you'll see how.*

"He's dead," I whispered.

"The Orlovs took out Liam Thorne?" Eric said. "Cannon, you're going to have a mob war on your hands."

"No," I said. "You won't."

Cannon met my eyes. The truth passed between us. Beside me, Eric straightened.

"My God," Eric said. "It was Killian. He offered up his own brother as a sacrifice, didn't he? A peace offering. So they'd know the rules applied to him too. If you turn, no matter who you are, you pay the price."

"Lee," I said. "Have you seen the body?"

"It was a positive ID," he said. "There's no doubt. It was Liam. He's dead, Cass."

There was a time I'd known Liam Thorne almost as well as I did Killian. He'd been my boss. The senior partner who had first approached me and offered me a job straight out of law school. He'd given me the proverbial brass ring. A way to escape my small town and do something so much bigger. I knew then it was too good to be true. If only I'd listened to my gut back then.

If only.

"But you saw him," I said. "He wasn't … branded."

"No," Lee said. "He had some broken bones. When the news comes out, they'll say it was likely an accidental drowning. He took his yacht out alone in bad weather. They found the Crowne of Thorne drifting. No one else on board."

He never went out alone. Liam Thorne never drove that boat. He hired someone for that.

Almost five years ago now, I'd been on the deck of that boat with zip ties around my wrists. Liam had stood beside me, giving the order to have me thrown overboard.

So many things Killian had said to me over the years replayed in my mind. So many promises. He would keep me safe. He would make sure his brother never got near me again. There would come a day he would make Liam pay for what he'd done. It seemed Killian had found a way to settle all of his debts at once.

"Thank you, Lee," I said. "For telling me. You're right. That's not something I would have liked hearing on the news."

"Of course," he said. "I'd appreciate it if you didn't talk about it. Didn't tell anyone I was here. I'm breaching protocol in about a dozen ways."

"We understand," Eric said. "This won't go any further."

"Is there anything I need to do?" I asked.

Lee and Eric exchanged a look. "No," Cannon said. "Just … live your life, Cass. Go be with your brother. I'll say a prayer for that baby. And for Tori."

"Thank you," I said. Eric rose and walked Cannon to the door. I could hear the two of them murmuring. Cop talk, for sure. They were also worried about me.

Liam, I thought. He'd been a monster to me in the last few years. But one that I'd tamed. The last time I saw him, I came to him with proof that he'd been selling secrets to the Feds to try and weaken Killian. I thought I'd be able to keep my family safe because of it. And I had. From him. Now I had to trust that his death would keep us all safe once more. Could I?

"Cass?" Eric said as he came back into the living room. "You okay?"

"I don't have a clue," I said.

"He did this for you, didn't he? Thorne?"

"Do you think it will work?" I asked.

"Cannon does," Eric said. "I think we can trust him."

"Yeah," I said. "Me too."

"Killian sent a message to the Orlovs. A sacrificial offering. Strengthened his position. I gotta be honest. I didn't think he had the guts to do something so bold. I thought he'd protect that weasel of a brother until he died."

"I don't know how to feel," I said. "That's the truth. Liam was bigger than life to me for so long. Now he's just ... gone."

"Were they close?" Eric asked.

"Yes," I said without hesitation. "They were very close. It's twisted, I know. They were each other's biggest rivals. They hated each other as much as they loved each other. But they went through so much back in Belfast. They came here and built an empire. I think there was a time they both felt there was nobody else they could truly trust except each other."

"And Liam still thought that was true," Eric said.

"That's how Killian got to him," I whispered. I tried to imagine it. I knew as much as Killian felt he had no choice, or that Liam sealed his own fate, this act could break him. He would be stronger, yes. But Killian had just crossed a line he could never come back from. It would make him more dangerous than ever.

"You really think Killian did this himself? Carried out the hit?"

I met Eric's eyes. Though I couldn't bring myself to say the words, he knew me well enough to understand. Yes. Killian would have had to have done this by himself. Liam would never have let anyone else get that close to him.

"I'm sorry," Eric said. "I know you were close to these people."

"These people nearly destroyed my life," I said.

Eric's cell phone rang. He pulled it out of his pocket. As he read the caller ID, he frowned.

"I'm sorry," he said. "It's work. I've got to head in."

"It's okay," I said. "I wouldn't mind some time alone. The next twenty-four hours might get rough."

"I'll meet you at the hospital later," he said.

I thanked him. We said our goodbyes. After Eric left, I walked outside to the edge of the shore and stared out at the water.

Chapter 45

WHEN THE NEWS finally broke about Liam Thorne's death, I was a world away. My sister Vangie had fallen asleep with her head on my shoulder as we sat in the family waiting room at Windham Hospital.

It was ten a.m. We had been here since four in the morning.

Jeanie walked in bearing a tray of fresh coffee. I'd drunk so much of it, I felt certain my kidneys would float away. Behind her, Eric walked in with a stiff pink box filled with donuts and pastries from the European bakery down the street.

I loved them both for that and a thousand other things.

"Any word?" Jeanie asked.

"They went in an hour ago," I said. "The OB nurse is a friend of Vangie's. She said she'd come out as soon as she could."

"How was he this morning?" Eric asked.

"Good," I said. Vangie stirred. For a moment, she was three years old again. She'd fallen asleep like that so many times when she was little. I'd take her out to the car and let her sleep on me when our father came home drunk and brought chaos to the house.

She didn't remember most of that. To her, it had been an adventure. I would let her sit in the driver's seat and play with the steering wheel while I held the keys in my pocket.

"It's okay, Vang," I said. "No word yet."

Vangie smelled the coffee. Her eyes lit up and she reached for a cup.

A television played in the corner of the waiting room. Liam's face appeared on screen. It was an old picture. One taken from the law firm website. He was handsome. Smiling. Resembling his younger brother enough to send a jolt through me. The crawl across the bottom of the screen declared he'd been found dead, washed up at the Navy Pier, just like Lee Cannon told us. Joe got up. He'd dozed off himself in a corner chair. He reached up and switched off the television.

A short, red-headed nurse rounded the corner, pulling off her paper mask. I couldn't read her face. Vangie rose beside me. My legs turned to water.

"Procedure's done," she said. "Doctor's just closing up. Tori's stable. She tolerated everything really well. Very little blood loss. No complications. Her neurologist is heading down to oversee her transfer back to the ICU."

"The baby," I said, rising to stand beside my sister. She was already in tears. Joe came to my other side. His hand found mine. The three of us linked our arms, forming a solid wall of support. There was only one person missing.

"Small," the nurse said. Her name was Renee Piel. She and Vangie had graduated high school together. "Just over a pound. They had some trouble getting his heart going. It was touch and go there for a minute, but I think you've got a fighter on your hands. Your brother's going to stay with him."

Vangie let out a choked sound.

"He's alive," I said. "My nephew. He's alive."

"Matty's asking for you," Renee said to me. "I think he wants another set of ears."

I handed my purse to Jeanie. There was no power on earth that would have stopped me from charging down that hallway and finding my little brother.

When I did, it was my heart that had trouble going. Renee led me to the window of the neonatal ICU. I saw my brother wearing a yellow surgical gown with matching booties. His face was covered with a mask. His brown hair tucked under a blue surgical cap. He leaned over the tiny isolette containing his even tinier son.

His son. My nephew.

"You can gown up in here," Renee said, showing me to a set of lockers. "There's a hand washing station right inside the door. Mask. Booties. Hat. They won't let you stay for very long."

"Thank you," I said, surprised I could even find the words.

A few minutes later, I was at my brother's side. I expected him to fall apart. He didn't. Instead, I felt his quiet strength as he laid a hand on his son's incubator.

"His name is Sean," he whispered. "Sean? This is your Aunt Cass, the one I told you about."

The lump in my throat turned into an ostrich egg. I rubbed Matty's back. "It's perfect," I said. "After Tori's father."

"Sean Matthew Leary," Matty said. "Just Irish enough too."

"Oh Matty," I said. "Look at him! He's beautiful."

He was. Sean had birdlike arms and legs. So little. He had a tuft of blond hair. He lay on his side with so many tubes and wires. But as I watched the steady rise and fall of his chest, I said a prayer to St. Jude. One I hadn't realized I still knew the words to.

"I love him already, Cass," Matty said.

"I know. Me too."

"They're worried about so many things," he said. "Eleven weeks early. His lungs. His brain."

"Shh," I said. "He's made it this far. And now he's got all of us."

A doctor walked into the room. Matty went rigid.

"No," he said. "Don't. She's not ..."

"Mr. Leary?" the man said. "It's all right. It's Ms. Stockton. She's asking for you."

It took a moment for both of us to process the words.

"Tori," I said. "He means Tori. She's awake?"

The doctor nodded. "Asking is a polite word. She woke up swearing."

I covered my mouth with a gloved hand and laughed.

"Go," I said to Matty. "Go! I'll stay right here. Sean and I will be just fine."

Matty nearly tripped over himself following the doctor out. When they left, I turned back to Sean.

The slow, rhythmic hum of the machines keeping him alive began to soothe me. I don't know how long I sat there. Hours. I knew I would stay forever if that's what it took.

"Welcome to the world, little guy," I said. "Sorry it was such a rough entry. It'll get better. It might not seem like that at first, but you've got a whole army of people ready to love on you. Sorry about that. Just remember though, I'm your favorite auntie. I mean, your Uncle Joe and Aunt Katie will seem cool. Your Aunt Vangie, well, she'll probably buy you all the candy. But I've got a lake. And dogs."

There was a hand on my shoulder. I looked up to see Eric's gray eyes above a blue mask.

"Hey, there," I said.

"Vangie's waiting outside to spell you."

I smiled. "She sent you in here to pull me out?"

"Something like that."

"Look at him," I said. Eric found a stool and pulled it next to mine. "His name is Sean. I was just telling him about the lake."

"I heard," Eric said. "Hey there, little man. Nice to meet you."

"He might not make it," I said, knowing Eric was the only one I would ever voice it to.

"He might not," he said.

"They're saying the odds are pretty bleak."

"Oh," Eric said. "I don't know. He's a Leary. You guys tend to be pretty hard to get rid of."

We sat together. Eric and me. "You should eat something," he finally said. "I'll take you out to dinner."

Eric was quiet and strong at my side. Tears filled my eyes as I leaned back and found his shoulder.

"I love you, you know," I said.

I felt him go stiff. He didn't answer.

"Did you doubt it?"

He took a breath. "No. But ..."

"No buts," I said.

"Cass," he said. "We don't have to talk about this now."

"Yes," I said. "We do. It should be here. Right here."

"Fine," he said. "I love you. I always will. But I can't live with him between us. I can't live my life waiting for the next time he crashes back into it and turns your world upside down."

"Neither can I," I said, turning to him. "I choose you. If you need me to say it, there it is. I choose you, Eric. I choose Delphi. This life. This messy, unpredictable, imperfect life. I choose this little guy. For as long as he's here. I choose Matty, Joe, and Vangie. All of it."

Like every other time in my life, it was like he had a sixth sense. My phone buzzed as a text came through. I pulled it out and looked down.

"I told you, it's done," it read. "This will never touch you again, a rúnsearc. The house is yours. I signed over and recorded the deed this morning. Keep it. Sell it. Do something good with it. KT."

The house in Helene. My God. In this market, it would likely fetch millions. Blood money, perhaps. But enough to secure little Sean's future. If only he could win his fight to have one. I took a breath. I had no space in my brain to think about that now. I showed the text to Eric.

"I choose you," I whispered. I clicked the number on the text and blocked it.

Then we were no longer alone. Vangie walked quietly in. Behind her, Joe waited in the doorway.

"Tori's asking for you," Vangie said to me. "She's in and out. But she's asking for you."

Eric and I gave up our stools for Joe and Vangie. I turned back to baby Sean again, whispering near his head. "Remember what we talked about, kiddo. And don't worry about a thing. I've got your back."

Eric took my hand as Vangie and Joe walked all the way in to sit with Sean, the newest of us. I knew Eric was right; we were all Learys, through and through. And we were damn hard to get rid of.

DON'T MISS DEAD LAW, the next book in the Cass Leary Legal Thriller Series! Cass's latest client finds an unexpected windfall in her ailing grandmother's papers. But this newfound money may be more curse than blessing when Cass

digs deeper into the source of the funds. https://www.
robinjamesbooks.com/dl

CLICK TO LEARN
MORE

DID YOU KNOW?

All of Robin's books are also available in Audiobook format.
Click here to find your favorite! https://www.
robinjamesbooks.com/foraudio

Newsletter Sign Up

Sign up to get notified about Robin James's latest book releases, discounts, and author news. You'll also get *Crown of Thorne* an exclusive FREE bonus prologue to the Cass Leary Legal Thriller Series just for joining. Find out what really made Cass leave Killian Thorne and Chicago behind.

Click to Sign Up

http://www.robinjamesbooks.com/newsletter/

About the Author

Robin James is an attorney and former law professor. She's worked on a wide range of civil, criminal and family law cases in her twenty-five year legal career. She also spent over a decade as supervising attorney for a Michigan legal clinic assisting thousands of people who could not otherwise afford access to justice.

Robin now lives on a lake in southern Michigan with her husband, two children, and one lazy dog. Her favorite, pure Michigan writing spot is stretched out on the back of a pontoon watching the faster boats go by.

Sign up for Robin James's Legal Thriller Newsletter to get all the latest updates on her new releases and get a free bonus scene from Burden of Truth featuring Cass Leary's last day in Chicago. http://www.robinjamesbooks.com/newsletter/

Also By Robin James

Cass Leary Legal Thriller Series

Burden of Truth

Silent Witness

Devil's Bargain

Stolen Justice

Blood Evidence

Imminent Harm

First Degree

Mercy Kill

Guilty Acts

Cold Evidence

Dead Law

With more to come...

Mara Brent Legal Thriller Series

Time of Justice

Price of Justice

Hand of Justice

Mark of Justice

Path of Justice

Vow of Justice

With more to come...

Audiobooks by Robin James

Cass Leary Series

Burden of Truth

Silent Witness

Devil's Bargain

Stolen Justice

Blood Evidence

Imminent Harm

First Degree

Mercy Kill

Guilty Acts

Cold Evidence

Mara Brent Series

Time of Justice

Price of Justice

Hand of Justice

Mark of Justice

Path of Justice

Made in United States
Orlando, FL
29 July 2022

20282334R00214